MAPS, ARTIFACTS,

and other

ARCANE MAGIC

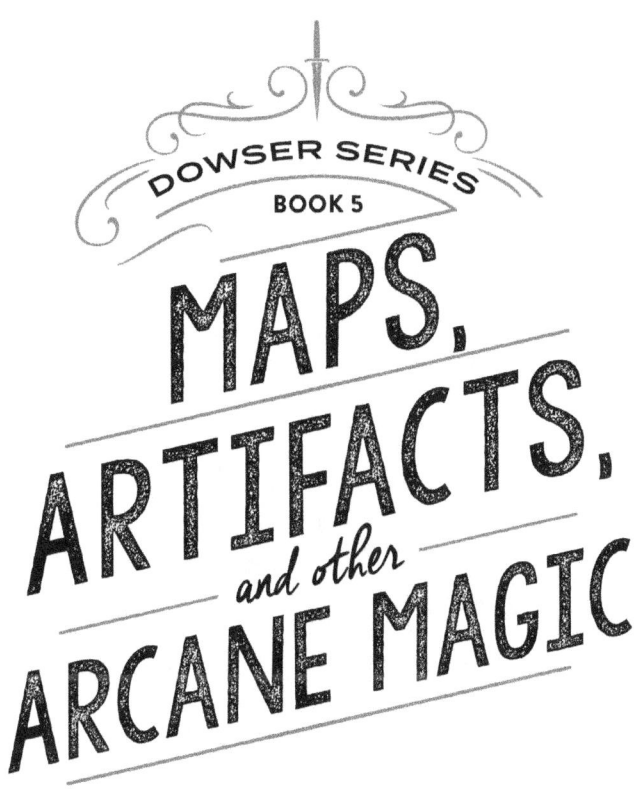

DOWSER SERIES

BOOK 5

MAPS, ARTIFACTS, and other ARCANE MAGIC

MEGHAN CIANA DOIDGE

Author's Note:

Maps, Artifacts, and Other Arcane Magic is the fifth book in the Dowser series. The Oracle series is also set in the same universe as the Dowser series.

While it is not necessary to read both series, the ideal reading order is as follows:

Cupcakes, Trinkets, and Other Deadly Magic (Dowser 1)
Trinkets, Treasures, and Other Bloody Magic (Dowser 2)
Treasures, Demons, and Other Black Magic (Dowser 3)
I See Me (Oracle 1)*
Shadows, Maps, and Other Ancient Magic (Dowser 4)
Maps, Artifacts, and Other Arcane Magic (Dowser 5)

Other books in both the Oracle and Dowser series to follow.

* I See Me (Oracle 1) contains spoilers for Dowser 1, 2, and 3.

For Michael
I'd cross through the darkest of shadows
just to be by your side.

One treasure down, two to go ...

Three months ago, I nearly lost my best friend while retrieving the first instrument of assassination. I also inadvertently released a rival who was definitely unhinged, way more powerful than me, and obsessed with harnessing the deadly power of the artifacts I'd been tasked by the guardian dragons to collect.

Add a sexy sentinel and a nearly immortal vampire to the mix, and what could possibly go wrong?

Knowing my luck, I was about to find out.

Chapter One

Something bit me in the ass.

I shrieked like a toddler deprived of her ice cream cone, whirled around with my jade knife poised to gut the offender, and found myself staring at yet another endless wall of musty old books.

This wasn't the first time I'd been ambushed in the nexus library — the books were damn ornery — but it had been getting worse since I'd admitted to myself that I was lost.

Yes, I — a dowser of some skill — was lost in a library full of magic. I could taste, but not pinpoint, the spiced magic of the dragonskin map that I'd left at the table I was camped out at doing research today. I just couldn't seem to follow that taste back through the shelves and the random stacks of books.

Tomes, not books. That was the proper word to use when the book was leather-bound and handwritten in foreign, dead, or runed languages.

The problem — according to Branson — was that the librarian hadn't been seen in a few centuries. So, organization had crumbled into disarray verging on chaos. Though I had an inkling that the sword master was joking or exaggerating, because there weren't so many dragons in the world that one could go missing for centuries and have no one looking for him.

I sighed and craned my neck in the opposite direction, seeing only an endless row of dusty, haphazardly piled books. I had purposefully made sure I could see the library entrance from my table so that I wouldn't get lost. Except now I couldn't find the entrance or the table.

Something shifted in my peripheral vision and I spun to jab my knife at it.

Nothing was there.

"We'll see who has the last laugh if I get my hands on you," I said. "I'm an alchemist, you know!"

Right. Now I was declaring my magical prowess to a bookshelf. It was childish, but I had a lingering suspicion that the books were only disrespectful because I wasn't a full-blooded dragon.

Dragon prejudice permeated the nexus, and I was the only half-witch walking the halls ... or, at least, currently trying to walk the aisles of the library.

I felt as if I'd been trapped in this damn room since September. And maybe I had. Time moved oddly in the nexus — sometimes incredibly slowly, and what would feel like hours of training turned out to only be thirty minutes when I returned to the bakery. And sometimes — say, if there were any guardians around — minutes turned into hours when I walked back through a portal. My study sessions in the library were usually pretty bang-on in real-world time, though.

And I remembered Christmas, so I couldn't have been stuck here since autumn. It only felt like that because I was getting nothing accomplished but moving the dust around and being a plaything for the books.

Actually, I had accomplished one thing. My outfit rocked. I was wearing the black cashmere and silk sweater dress that my mother, Scarlett, had given me for Christmas. Today I'd paired the midthigh-length sweater with thick black tights and my wine-colored Bondgirl Fluevog boots — a gift from Gran. The sturdy but still stylish boots dressed down the outfit, but I wasn't stupid enough to wear heels anywhere near the nexus anymore, even on my nontraining days.

I'd left my blond curls loose and reapplied my rosy lip gloss frequently to compensate for the lack of heels.

Yeah, I was hoping to run into Warner.

Warner ... sigh.

The sentinel was off hell-knows-where with my father Yazi, the warrior of the guardians. Or maybe he was with Pulou the treasure keeper, while I was stuck in this damn musty library researching ancient maps, dragon lineage, and eternal-life sorcerer sects.

There were more of the latter than you'd think.

I hadn't had any luck figuring out anything about the kid I'd released from the statue in the fortress. The only record I'd managed to dig up from the sixteenth century appeared to have every dragon accounted for — most of them still alive. It wasn't exactly a long list. Dragons had an exceedingly low birth rate.

Though, I seriously hoped Warner enjoyed 'training sessions,' because I was —

"Are you mooning over the sentinel?" a young man asked from above my head.

I looked up.

Drake, my fourteen-year-old training companion, was perched like a watchful gargoyle on the top of the bookshelf to my right. The gold-leaf cathedral ceiling soared dozens of feet above him. If you'd asked me two minutes ago, I would have told you that the bookshelves in this section were a lot taller than the sixteen-or-so feet they currently appeared to be. Also, that they were empty of fledgling guardians whose magic tasted of honey-roasted salted almonds and steamed milk.

"No," I snapped, though I certainly had been bemoaning the lack of progression in Warner's wooing of me — the sentinel's words. We hadn't made it anywhere nearer to my bed. My father apparently had a plethora of duties that he suddenly needed Warner to assume. Though who had been fulfilling those tasks for the four hundred and fifty years Warner had been in stasis, I didn't know.

"It's my birthday in nineteen days," Drake declared. I could always rely on the fledgling guardian to change the subject.

"I know. You told me yesterday." I peered at the books directly in front of me, as if I were exactly where I intended to be and not lost at all.

"Nope," Drake countered as he stepped off the shelf and landed soundlessly beside me. "I told you it was my birthday in twenty days yesterday."

I laughed. Drake grinned at me. His dark bangs had fallen across his forehead and almost covered his almond-shaped eyes. I was always surprised how quickly he grew. He was a couple of inches over my five feet nine inches now, and wearing a loose green printed T-shirt over his leather training pants.

I'd never actually laid eyes on this particular T-shirt, with its sketch of what appeared to be a pile of mushed raspberries and a banana. But its design aesthetic was definitely familiar — and not even remotely appropriate for a fourteen-year-old. "Where did you get that shirt?"

"It's an early birthday gift from Kandy."

"When did you see Kandy?"

Drake's grin widened. He had a secret, and he was never, ever going to let it slip. He was utterly loyal — and completely annoying that way.

"The shirt is obscene," I said with a sniff. "You shouldn't be wearing it. You're fourteen, for Christ's sake."

"The sentinel likes it. I'm not sure what the son of the Christian god has to do with it. And I'm nineteen days away from being fifteen years old."

"Warner is not your stylist."

"Hmmm, what is this stylist?" Drake asked, like a predator who'd just discovered there was bigger game to be hunted. "And where do I find one?"

"You drive me crazy."

"You love me." The fledgling guardian's smile remained, but his tone turned serious. "You'd do anything for me."

"Yes, I would."

"As I would for you."

I nodded, not sure what to say in the wake of the fledgling's heartfelt declaration.

"Pack is important. Loyalty makes us stronger. We are dragons of the same generation. We must have each other's backs."

"Anytime and always," I said, completely serious now. And completely willing to be deadly serious, if necessary. Though he was only almost fifteen, the fledgling guardian was one of my BFFs. It wasn't a long list. If I didn't count family, an inventory would take only three fingers. And I wasn't putting Warner anywhere near the friend category, not until I knew he was more than that as well.

Drake nodded and his grin returned in fuller force than before.

I didn't bother pointing out the obvious flaw in his rationale because I was enjoying the warm fuzzy feeling his declaration evoked. The fledgling had obviously been hanging out with Kandy. But I wasn't a full-blooded dragon. Drake wielded more power at almost fifteen than I would ever wield in my entire life. And I wasn't bothering to include the massive increase in his magical capacity that would come when he assumed the guardian mantle from his mentor, Chi Wen the far seer.

"I thought you were researching maps?" Drake was peering at the shelves of books behind me.

"Sure."

"Then you're in the wrong section, warrior's daughter." Drake sounded far too gleeful at this discovery. "Are you lost ... again?"

So, yeah. I had a habit of getting lost in the nexus. The magic bombarded me here, melding into similar tastes and dulling my senses.

"I was just stretching my legs."

Drake chortled at my lie and I couldn't help but laugh with him.

"You look very feminine."

"Thank you."

"But you should belt the knife underneath the dress." The fledgling guardian was referring to my jade knife, which I wore on my right hip and which was invisible to most gazes, courtesy of a sheath spelled by my Gran. Dragons, however, could see through such magic ... or maybe it was more that magic actually attracted their attention.

"The fabric is too thin. It ruins the line of the dress."

Drake nodded sagely, an affectation he'd picked up from the far seer.

"Shall we discuss the weather now?" I asked with a grin. Drake was practicing his human-world conversation skills in preparation for taking over some of Chi Wen's territorial duties.

The fledgling frowned. "There is no weather in the nexus," he said mournfully.

I instantly felt terrible. Drake didn't have the same freedom of movement I did, though I hadn't spent much time outside in the last three months either. But then, I was content simply watching the seasonal deluge in Vancouver from the cozy comfort of my bakery.

"Cupcakes?" Drake asked hopefully, as if he could read my mind. He couldn't, though. Not yet. But I was fairly certain that was one of the gifts he would inherit when he assumed the mantle of the far seer in a hundred years or so.

"At my table," I answered. "If we're lucky ... they could have been pilfered by now."

Drake set off down the aisle and I followed, rather pleased that I hadn't needed to admit I was lost.

We turned the corner of the bookshelf just as a book made an attempt for my head. I ducked. Drake — reacting to my movement — spun and snatched the offending tome out of the air.

I tamped down on the string of blistering swear words poised on my tongue. Drake had already picked up too many bad habits from me. His guardian, Suanmi the fire breather, had only allowed him to start training with me again last month.

Drake frowned at the brown leather-bound book, then flipped through its handwritten, deckle-edged thick pages. Satisfied, he tossed the book to me.

I grabbed it, even as it attempted to make an escape.

"The treasure keeper's journal?" Drake asked as he zigzagged through the next few stacks of books.

I flipped open the book as I followed the fledgling back to my research prison — err ... table. The smooth leather of the lower back cover and spine were blackened, as were the last dozen or so pages. As Drake had worked out in seconds based on the span of the dated entries, the journal had been kept by the former treasure keeper. The English was old-fashioned, stilted, and written by a cramped hand, but still readable. Pulou had said that his mentor's journals had all been destroyed in a fire — hence the singed back cover — but this one was obviously an exception. Not surprising, given the way it seemed capable of flight — or a directed and malicious launching capacity at least.

"Could this book have been following me?"

Drake shrugged and then picked up his pace. I was fairly certain he'd spied the box of cupcakes on the table I'd claimed for my piles of fruitless research.

The random pieces of furniture strewn about the nexus library had obviously been gathered from different eras. I'd unearthed the utilitarian vintage wooden table exactly where it still stood swathed in parchment, and surrounded by the stacks of books I'd gathered over the last three months. The curve-footed table could have been a Restoration Hardware reproduction, but I was pretty sure it was actually a rectangular dining table from the Ming dynasty. I'd found a black-leather-quilted, dark-wood-framed chair that I was pretty sure was Victorian in an aisle between the nearby bookshelves. It had carved tassels coming out of the mouths of fish on either side of the back frame, and the arm supports were carvings of a woman's face and chest. Though it was the carved Vs on the front corners of the seat that were the dead giveaway.

Yep, I was so bored I was studying the furniture.

I could clearly taste the magic of the tattooed map that I'd spread out in the center of the table. A tattoo that had once resided on the back of the former treasure keeper, who had also apparently written the feisty journal I was barely managing to keep a hold on.

Drake reverently lifted the lid of the bakery box I'd propped up on three hand-drawn atlases. He gazed inside it as if he were uncovering an ancient relic.

"Do all guardians write journals?" I asked him.

"I don't know," Drake answered. "I don't think Suanmi or Chi Wen do." Then, his eyes full of epic sadness, he whispered, "Only three cupcakes remain."

"Eat slowly."

"Yes!" he declared, his mood instantly shifting. "I will savor as you've been teaching me."

The final seventy-five or so pages of the journal were blank, including the ones with the singed edges. I'd have to double-check the dates, but I was fairly certain the entries stopped at least fifty years before the Pulou I knew had ascended in the late sixteenth century. Though the spine and back cover of the journal were burned, the leather wasn't flaking off. The page groups — signatures, I think I was supposed to call them — were hand sewn.

"Tell me the tale of this cupcake," Drake demanded as he dramatically held a newer creation of mine aloft.

I glanced up from the last handwritten page of the journal. "That's a *Vixen in a Cup*. Chocolate gingerbread cake with a salted caramel icing."

"*Vixen in a Cup*," Drake whispered as he carefully peeled the paper off the cupcake. Earlier this year, I'd tried to do away with cupcake holders by using silicone cups to bake. But they were fiddly — the moist, delicate cake broke more often than not — and my customers had rebelled at the breaking of tradition. At least the paper cups I used were compostable.

The final line of the journal read: *Shailaja has broken with the guardians. She has broken with me.*

"Who is Shay-la-ja?" I asked Drake, attempting to sound out the foreign name.

The fledgling, who'd stuffed the entire cupcake in his mouth, could only shrug in response.

"Way to savor." I shook my head and returned my attention to the journal. A rune was drawn in the bottom corner of this half-empty page. A rune that looked like a decapitated, legless stick-person. I set the journal down on the stack of books to the right of the map and anchored it there with a tiny pulse of my alchemist magic. I guess I shouldn't be surprised that a journal written by the treasure keeper — who could create magical portals at will — liked to wander.

Or hide. That was an odd thought. Why would a book be hiding? And in a library? That was a little obvious, though I guess there was that hiding-in-plain-sight thing …

The journal rustled its pages as I withdrew my hand, but it stayed put. I didn't want to alter its magic. I just wanted to be able to read it later. The rune looked seriously familiar — as in, I'd watched Warner collect silver pendants decorated with that same rune from the bodies of sacrificed sorcerers three months before. It was in the fortress that had hidden the first instrument of assassination — aka colorful braids that could kill a guardian.

Warner had attributed the decapitated stick-figure rune to a sect of eternal-life seekers. A supposedly extinct sect of sorcerers whose members — through some sort of human sacrifice — might now be living their afterlife as shadow leeches. They'd manifested in that form in the fortress, at least. I hadn't laid eyes on one since, so they might have been vanquished when the fortress collapsed. I dug around the papers and books strewn across the desk. I had one of the rune pendants here somewhere to compare …

"And this?" Drake asked, holding up a *Buzz in a Cup*.

I went into caffeine overload every time I baked that mocha fudge cupcake with mocha buttercream icing, probably from inhaling the Illy espresso powder I preferred to use. "You've had that one before."

"I know, but you like describing them to me. Rituals are important."

"Just eat it," I said. I wasn't fed up with the fledgling, though I'm sure it sounded like it. I was just utterly fed up with trying to figure out how to trigger the second map that Pulou insisted was to be found within the dragonskin tattoo spread on the table before me.

All I saw were blotches of green and blue, and triangles that I was fairly certain were ocean, land, and mountain ranges. A motif of flowers and leaves adorned one side of the map, while a series of interconnected mechanical-looking blocks were tattooed on the other.

The intersected rainbow from which I'd pulled a key — literally — three months ago, which I'd then used to unlock the first map, had disappeared sometime between us collecting the five-colored braids and the next time I'd unrolled the map. The five-colored braids that were also referred to as an 'instrument of assassination.' One of only three ways to kill a guardian dragon. A completely benign-looking weapon that could kill my father, the warrior.

Yeah, I was freaking frustrated to have wasted this much time between collecting the first and second instruments.

"Is that the map?" Drake asked. He paused his cupcake worship to peer over the stack of atlases I'd spent endless days collecting and poring over, carefully comparing each and every hand-drawn page to the tattoo.

A librarian would have been a welcome sight.

"Here." Drake held a crumpled piece of paper toward me.

I took it. It was already sticky from frosting and I hadn't laid a hand on it yet. "What is it?" I asked as I smoothed the paper open on the table.

"From Chi Wen," Drake answered around the last mouthful of his final cupcake, a simple buttercream-frosted lemon cake I'd dubbed *Joy in a Cup*.

Ah, damn.

I might not have opened the note had I known it was from the far seer. Of all the guardian dragons, I feared the ancient Chinese gentleman the most. Even more than Suanmi the fire breather, who thought of me as an abomination that shouldn't be allowed a continued existence.

The far seer had shown me my future — which he often referred to as destiny — twice now. Neither time had been a particularly pleasant experience. It wasn't just the terrible sensation of displacement and disorientation that came with the far seer sharing his visions, or the feeling of having a tiny bit of your soul ripped away. It was also the terrible belief that what lay before me was ultimately unalterable. The idea that even if I chose to not walk the path before me, the events would still come to pass.

I stared down at the charcoal drawing I'd spread on the table. It depicted what appeared to be a centipede. If centipedes were made of riveted metal plates.

"It's from the oracle, Rochelle." Drake picked crumbs out of the now-empty bakery box.

"Double shit," I muttered.

Drake snickered. "Chi Wen said you'd say that."

"Of course he did."

"But it's not a vision. The oracle is not in a seeing state right now."

I had no freaking idea what that meant, except I was seriously glad I wasn't looking at a picture of me dying, or a vision of someone I loved being killed, since that's what Rochelle usually saw and committed to paper in prophetic charcoal. Up to now, I'd avoided seeing her drawings in person, but the gist had been described to me by Audrey, the beta of the West Coast North American Pack.

"What is it, then?" I asked.

"A tattoo," Drake answered. " 'To match yours,' Chi Wen said. Got any chocolate?"

What did the far seer mean by 'Match yours'? I didn't have a tattoo.

I sighed and set the drawing aside to pull a brand new Ritual Chocolate bar out of my new moss-green Peg and Awl satchel. It was a gift from Warner to replace my ruined-by-salt-water one. Unfortunately, two near drownings in the Bahamas were too much for my beloved Matt & Nat satchel. Yeah, the sentinel certainly knew how to woo me ... and, apparently, he had my Etsy password. The satchel had been on my 'things I love' wish list for over a year.

Drake attempted to snatch the 75 percent Madagascar, made-in-Colorado chocolate bar from me, but I danced away from him with a grin.

He laughed. "Shall we wrestle for it?"

"It belongs to me, fledgling." My tone was far more severe than my smile.

Drake backed off in acknowledgement of my ownership. I was learning how things worked in the dragon world. If you were the strongest, you could hold any territory you wished, as long as it had been evenly and equally divided. No one dragon had a greater gift or responsibility than another.

I unwrapped the bar, then broke it in half. It snapped with the clear, crisp sound that accompanied only the finest chocolate.

"Oooo, it has a stamped batch number and everything … zero seventeen, so you know it's going to be great." I was already salivating for my taste as I handed the other half to Drake.

The fledgling perched on a stack of books that shouldn't have been capable of bearing his immense dragon weight. The books barely shifted.

Ah, to be a full-blooded dragon full of grace and wisdom …

A silver dragonfly flitted down over the bookshelves behind the fledgling and landed on his shoulder. It appeared to be an exact replica of a living, breathing bug. But it was constructed out of metal and animated by a magic I couldn't taste within the concentration housed in the library. Its gossamer silver wire wings fluttered, then stilled.

"Err, is that a dragonfly made out of platinum?"

"Silver," Drake answered, every ounce of his attention on the chocolate in my hand as he waited patiently for me to begin the tasting ritual.

"Silver?" The dragonfly flitted away as quickly as it had appeared. "Magic and silver? Those two things don't go together." Silver didn't hold magic the way gold and gems did, so most alchemists didn't even bother working with the metal.

Drake shrugged. "It belongs to Pulou. The treasure keeper has many unusual artifacts in his collection. It's constructed through metallurgy. The chocolate?"

Okay, metallurgy — yet another thing to add to my ever-growing list of all things magical that it would take centuries to research and figure out … if I didn't actually have a limited brain capacity, which I was beginning to suspect I did, along with a terribly short attention span.

I broke a single square of the chocolate — or a skinny rectangle in this case — off my half. I smelled it until the scent filled my nasal cavities and tickled my taste buds. Then I popped it in my mouth and slowly sucked on it.

Drake copied my movements.

We sat in silence as the smooth chocolate — with just the perfect hint of creaminess — softened on my tongue.

"Rich cacao and strong, almost overwhelming citrus notes ..." Drake murmured. "Is this what magic tastes like to you, warrior's daughter?"

I smiled.

Drake nodded, his expression sage and far too old for his face once again. "What a gift that would be, to taste magic like you do."

I laughed as I attempted to carefully fold the remaining chocolate up in its gold foil, managed to mangle it as always, then slipped it back into the box.

Life lessons from a fourteen-year-old. I never seemed to grow wise enough to not need them. The grass was always greener, indeed.

I settled in with the journal after Drake wandered off, but the chronicle was a difficult read. The English was archaic. I would have to ask Warner to look at it.

Though the sentinel wasn't exactly the reading type ... hmmm ...

"What are you smiling about?" Pulou's voice boomed around the library, jolting me out of reminiscing about Warner's and my last make-out session.

With two deliberate and heavy steps, the treasure keeper was looming over my study table. Pulou appeared to be somewhere in his mid-fifties, though he was more like six hundred years old. He was bundled in the floor-length fur coat he always wore, but it was actually a manifestation of his guardian power rather than a fashion misstep. Today, however, he also had runes inked across his forehead.

Well, that was … unusual.

He glared at me as he continued to dwarf my table.

"Umm …" I really wasn't going to confess to lusting after Warner to a guardian who was also sort of my boss.

Pulou placed an ordinary but expensive-looking pen on the table. It appeared to be a slim, gold Cartier. It wasn't.

Uh oh.

I watched the inked runes disappear from Pulou's forehead.

I tried out a chagrined smile.

Pulou's frown deepened.

The pen twitched, and I grabbed it before it started writing runes all over the map and Rochelle's charcoal drawing.

"It was a prank," I said, lamely attempting to explain why I'd given the treasure keeper a pen that wrote — magically and continuously — on any surface. A pen he'd had me collect from its beleaguered owners. "I wasn't even sure it would act up in your … hands …"

Pulou really wasn't pleased with me.

"Honestly," I babbled, "maybe I couldn't even fix it."

"The pen is now under your guardianship, alchemist." Despite the English accent, Pulou currently sounded a lot like the grizzly bear he resembled. "May it help you on your quest."

That sounded more like a curse than a blessing. But I suddenly remembered my manners and slowly rose to offer the treasure keeper a shallow bow. I was usually forgiven my informal behavior — what with being raised in the human world by witches — but even I could hear the reprimand in Pulou's normally jovial tone.

And it wasn't the pen's naughty behavior that had upset him.

He was pissed that I still hadn't unlocked the map and collected the next instrument of assassination.

Well, I'd been trying, damn it.

Pulou's gaze dropped to the journal currently resting on top of the map, pages spread open. He raised an eyebrow at it, then held out his hand toward me.

Obligingly, I picked up the book and dropped it in his hand. As I did so, the charmed pen leaped from my grip and landed on the desk. I slapped my hand down on it before it managed to start writing.

Pulou looked at me pointedly.

"Won't happen again," I muttered, avoiding his gaze.

"I doubt that," he said. Then he began to flip through the journal.

Normally, things weren't so tense in the nexus and among the guardians. True, they were usually saving the world somehow — vanquishing demon incursions or foiling evil plans I wanted to know nothing about. But ever since I'd retrieved the braids, the atmosphere had changed.

I didn't understand what exactly was going on, but three months ago, I was certain that Pulou would have found the pen's antics hilarious.

"I've never seen this," Pulou said as he peered at the book. "Where did you find it?"

"It found me."

"Interesting."

"Sure." Dragons like to read things into every action and call it fate. But I would place money on the journal simply not liking the taste of my half-blood magic.

"May I borrow it for the evening?"

I didn't know what time zone the treasure keeper was referring to, but I really hoped it wasn't evening in Vancouver yet. I had a date. For which I had purposefully worn the sweater dress just in case I was running late.

"It belongs to you more than me, treasure keeper," I said. "Though it might refer to the map, and that would be seriously helpful."

Pulou nodded. "The items in the library are for all dragons, warrior's daughter." His voice was now gentle. "Do not let anyone convince you otherwise."

Yeah, I was working on not being quite so transparent. But ever since I'd collected the braids — and had been capable of touching them with no ill effect — a few guardians who'd previously been friendly now seemed to avoid me.

Namely, Qiuniu and Haoxin, who were the two youngest guardians. Though it wasn't like we'd all gone for coffee and a chat before either. And guardians had crazy schedules, so I might just be reading too much into their extended absence from the nexus.

Conversely, Suanmi seemed a little less frosty toward me. Which, honestly, I didn't know how to take. We usually only crossed paths during training sessions. Maybe the fire breather just enjoyed watching Drake acquaint me with the hard floor ... over and over again.

I nodded and Pulou patted me on the shoulder. I attempted to not stumble under this assault of kindness.

"I see you have discovered the centipede," Pulou said.

For a moment, I had no idea what he was talking about. Then I turned to look at Rochelle's charcoal sketch lying next to the dragonskin map. "Centipede. Right."

Actually, from this vantage point, the mechanical-looking blocks that decorated the edge of the map looked similar to the body of Rochelle's centipede. Except they were jumbled around and not connected.

"The centipede appears in many myths and tales in both human and Adept cultures …" But as he spoke, Pulou lifted his head as if sensing something only he could hear. "I must go. Your father calls. I will return the journal tomorrow and answer any questions you have. The library will yield any book you desire. You just have to … ask nicely."

I snorted. "Yeah, according to you and the sword master." I'd tried 'asking nicely' already. The library was deaf to my requests.

Pulou chuckled, as if the library might be a cute kid I could win over with a couple of oatmeal cookies. Then he turned away.

"Wait," I said, my mind and gaze still mostly on the map and the charcoal sketch. "Who is Shailaja?"

The treasure keeper stopped with his back to me. He slowly turned his head without turning his body, as if he was thinking about not answering — which would be out of character.

"That name's in the journal," I said. "At the very end. Am I pronouncing it correctly?"

Pulou nodded curtly. "My predecessor's daughter."

"It says she broke with the guardians. What does that mean?"

"She is gone. It's terrible to lose a child that way." Pulou gazed down at the leather-bound journal in his hand but didn't continue.

"Okay," I said. And because I really didn't like the tension that was building up between us, I let the subject drop. "I'll focus on centipede myths now. And leave questions about the journal for tomorrow."

Pulou shook off whatever memory was playing in his head. "Yes."

Then he left.

Okay. Obviously this Shailaja chick was bad news … or a bad memory.

I sat back down at the table and pulled Rochelle's sketch closer. The edge of the thick paper was ragged, as if it had been torn from the oracle's sketchbook. Rochelle had many different tattoos, including a sleeve of barbed wire with a bunch of items snagged in the barbs and a sleeve of ivy winding up her arms. I wondered if she'd drawn the centipede with the intention of adding it to the barbed wire or if she had planned to have it tattooed elsewhere, only to have Chi Wen tell her to tear it out of her sketchbook so Drake could deliver it to me.

'To match yours,' Drake had said. But the only tattoo I had was the one on dragonskin … oh, okay.

I folded the blank edge of the slightly nubby paper and tried to line it up alongside the blocks on the map.

Except they didn't line up.

Or did they?

I touched the square at the bottom right corner of the map. The combination of dragon and alchemist magic danced underneath my fingertips, as if trying to be helpful. The square looked similar to — though not exactly like — the one near the middle of Rochelle's charcoal sketch.

Now that I practically had my nose pressed to the tattooed map, the square in the middle didn't look so square. It looked a little like the head of Rochelle's centipede without the antenna.

I removed my fingers from the tattoo. The taste of its magic abated to its normal ever-present levels. I knew the map was capable of changing — morphing into other views, as it had done the closer we were to the fortress in the Bahamas. But I'd had a key then. A key we'd lost in the Atlantic Ocean when the fortress collapsed.

I'd panicked over that loss. But then when the map changed after we'd collected the braids, I assumed I needed to source a second key to unlock it further.

So what if the key was already embedded in the tattoo? Just waiting to be aligned?

I traced my finger around the edges of the square closest to me. Once again, the magic tingled against my skin. If the square was three dimensional — say like a checker piece, except not round — then I could just apply a tiny bit of pressure and slide it ...

The square shifted underneath my fingertips.

I held my breath, glanced at Rochelle's sketch, and pushed the square until it was as aligned to the same-sized one on her drawing as possible. The other squares along the map shifted to accommodate it.

I removed my fingers from the tattoo.

The map reverted to its previous aspect. Obviously, I had to be touching the tattoo to maintain the realignment.

Pressing my fingers to each square, working one at a time and carefully maintaining contact with the tattoo,

I shifted them all until they copied the order depicted in Rochelle's sketch.

Then I waited.

Nothing happened.

"It's not a centipede yet," I murmured. No antennae.

I scanned the blotchy blue and green areas of the tattoo, but didn't see anything that resembled disconnected antennae.

Then I saw two dots next to some leaves on the top left corner of the map. I reached up and coaxed the dots out from underneath the leaves.

Yes, I was somehow moving two-dimensional objects around on a tattoo, as if it were an iPad. I hadn't bothered questioning the ways of magic for a long while. If I did, I'd be constantly overwhelmed and completely dysfunctional in the Adept world.

The dots had lines attached to them once I pulled them out from their hiding spots. I dragged them over and placed them next to the head of the centipede.

Again, nothing happened. The squares were all lined up with each other, but they didn't mimic the flow of Rochelle's sketch. They had no ... life. None of the vitality that Rochelle captured so effortlessly when she drew ... and smudged.

Her lines were smudged and smoothed, blended and shaded.

I ran my fingers over the edges of the antenna and the squares that I'd collected together. I imagined the way a centipede moved. How it would look if it suddenly ran across the dragonskin.

The magic of the tattoo shifted underneath my fingers.

The centipede took form, twining up the side of the map.

Relieved and invigorated, I laughed.

The blue and green swirl of the center of the tattoo blurred, then solidified into a huge landmass along a coast I didn't recognize. A large body of water was landlocked in the middle of the mass of green. Many triangles dotted the entire area. A huge lake surrounded by mountains?

The atlases on either side of the table rose up in the air.

"That can't be good," I muttered. Then I flung my arms around my head as the books dive-bombed me.

I stumbled out of my chair, knocking it backward as the column of books Drake had been perching on tried to knock me off my feet. I smacked them away as I grabbed the map, pen, and Rochelle's sketch, quickly stuffing them in my satchel.

Then the books on the shelves behind me thought slamming against my head and shoulders looked like fun, so they got in on the action.

I ran for the entrance to the library, thankful that I could see it from my table so I wouldn't get lost. As long as it didn't move, of course.

Books of all ages and sizes swirled around me as I ran. I could have cut them down with my knife, but that would have ruined them. I was pretty sure such destruction would be seriously frowned upon.

Running in the eye of a book hurricane, I made it to the exit. I would have cleared the archway without further trouble, except the Persian carpet underneath my feet tripped me.

Yes, I swear it deliberately tripped me.

I tumbled through the archway and slid — face down — across the marble floor. I came to a stop only a few inches from a pair of impossibly handsome caramel-skinned feet.

I groaned internally. Only one male in existence could have feet that beautiful.

I cranked my head to the side and peered up through the tumble of blond curls obscuring my vision.

Qiuniu, the guardian of South America, aka the healer, was peering down at me. The breathtakingly beautiful dragon was wearing nothing but a simple pair of beige linen shorts.

I stopped myself from groaning in appreciation of this display. Even for a girl happily dating a gorgeous, rugged dragon and eagerly hoping to take him to her bed — hopefully tonight — that was a lot of smooth, well-muscled, practically hairless skin.

"The library doesn't react well to the manipulation of magic." The Brazilian healer had no discernible inflection in his Latin lilt, as if I wasn't sprawled prostrate at his feet.

Well, maybe he got that reaction a lot.

"Right. Check," I said, rather than exploding into a rant about no one telling me these things ahead of time. Even public pools had 'Rules of Conduct' signs posted at their entrances.

I gathered my feet underneath me and rose.

Qiuniu didn't help me up.

I straightened my sweater dress and my satchel, then smoothed my hair. Well, as smooth as it got.

The healer watched me, though without any hint of his usual playful flirting. "You appear unharmed."

"I am."

He spun away before the second word was out of my mouth.

I watched him walk away, feeling sad as I did so. It wasn't as if we'd been friends before, but I would have counted Qiuniu among the more supportive of the guardians.

Yeah, the mood in the nexus had changed. And not for the better. To my mind, anyway.

The books hadn't followed me through the archway. A glance back determined that they seemed to be slowly returning to the shelves and stacks. That was a bitch, because I would have liked to get my hands on the atlases I'd set aside, so I could compare them to the landmass the map had shown me. Now I'd have to collect them all again.

I almost stepped back into the library, then reminded myself I had a date and wasn't sure of the time. Coming face to face with guardians tended to speed things up in the outside world, and I'd just had two uncomfortable chats.

So I headed home.

Chapter Two

The nexus might be filled with magic and gilded decor, but I was never more content than when I stepped back through the portal and returned to my bakery, Cake in a Cup.

Of course, it probably helped that I had to cross through a pantry filled with chocolate, vanilla, and other delectable scents to enter the bakery kitchen from the basement.

Tonight the kitchen was already dark, though a quick glance at my cellphone informed me it was only 5:37 P.M. I protected the cellphone in a lead-lined pen case from the magic of the nexus and the portal. That didn't protect it from multiple near drownings though, so this was yet another new iPhone. I'd charged the guardians for the replacement. They could afford it, and could have mentioned the possible water issues on my last assignment.

The bakery kitchen was only lit by the digital clocks on the oven and microwave, but I stopped to admire it for a moment anyway. I pressed my hand to the cold, smooth, stainless steel of my workstation, and allowed the remaining adrenaline in my system to drain away. Getting attacked by books might have seemed amusing from the outside, but it wasn't pleasant in the experience. Though it was the encounter with Qiuniu that really had me on edge.

I could taste Gran's grassy lilac witch magic and my mother's strawberry from the storefront, but I couldn't hear them talking. Unfortunately, that wasn't unusual. Gran and Scarlett — even after everything we'd been through in the last year and a half — weren't ever going to be friends.

Still, I liked the idea of them enjoying a coffee and a cupcake after closing together. Maybe they were sitting underneath my trinkets by the French-paned front windows …

My phone pinged, and I checked it to find a text message from Kandy, who was still healing in Portland. She'd come for a visit at Christmas, and we'd gone skiing up in Whistler. Well, she and Jorgen, her Norwegian friend from London, had skied. I'd gone to the spa, then poked around the town under the guise of shopping. I was eyeing a couple of empty retail locations for a possible bakery. I'd been thinking of expanding, but the rent in Whistler village had put me off. Plus to expand, I'd have to lose Bryn — my part-time baker and full-time employee — from the current store, because she was the only person I trusted to run a new location. Though Whistler would put her closer to her extended family in Squamish, so she was open to the idea.

My phone pinged again, reminding me of the text I still hadn't read. I peered at the incomprehensible series of symbols before I realized that Kandy was now sending me obscene emoticons that I probably didn't want to figure out.

I typed back.

Miss you too.

And hit send.

That would satisfy her. She hated it when I got mushy.

I wandered out into the bakery storefront. The shop was closed and buttoned up already. January was a quiet time for cupcakes, though I'd needed to extend my hours throughout December. Gran and Scarlett were sipping lattes and nibbling on cupcakes at one of the bistro tables by the French-paned front windows.

Scarlett lifted her strawberry blond head and flashed her signature smile as I entered. She was reading a spellbook. I could pick up the hints of witch magic from it even with the bakery display case between us.

I smiled back. It was actually impossible not to smile at Scarlett when she smiled at you. Her witch magic was heavily flavored in charm and charisma. Hence the reason my cupcakes *Charm in a Cup* and *Love in a Cup* were frosted with strawberry buttercream.

Gran swiveled away from her laptop to look over at me. Behind her green-rimmed reading glasses, her indigo eyes were an identical match to mine and Scarlett's, but her gray hair was neatly pulled back into a thick French braid that reached her tailbone.

Eye color was the only physical characteristic I shared with this side of my family. I was taller, bigger, and snarkier than the petite, polite women before me. I might be considered pretty by most, but Gran and Scarlett fell firmly into the 'beautiful' class.

"Hello, my Jade," Scarlett called. "You're back early. I saved you some of Bryn's hot chocolate."

"Perfect." I abruptly changed directions, crossing behind the counter over to the espresso machine. A small warming carafe sat to one side of the machine, where I assumed I'd find the chocolate fix I suddenly needed.

"You look nice," Gran said.

Poor Gran. She held out hope that one day I'd bring Qiuniu into the Godfrey clan. She had a thing for the Brazilian demigod. And honestly, who wouldn't? If you liked your men prettier than you could ever hope to be. And, you know, it didn't freak you out that he was one of the nine guardians of the world and all the magic in it. Thankfully, Gran seemed to like Warner as well.

Yes, I got all that from a fairly neutral comment about my outfit.

"Thanks," I answered. "I have a dinner date … hopefully." Warner didn't exactly wear a watch. Or own a calendar.

"The sentinel looked in about an hour ago," Scarlett said, her smile indicating that she more than approved of Warner as boyfriend material. "Said he'd be back soon. He promised to help Pearl move some furniture."

I laughed. I couldn't imagine Warner doing something so mundane.

"I'm renovating the back bedrooms," Gran said coolly. "Adding an en suite and a walk-in closet."

I lost the smile. She meant Sienna's old room. "Okay," I said as I applied myself to carrying an empty mug and the entire carafe of hot chocolate toward the high round table my mother and grandmother occupied.

Scarlett's face fell and Gran's shoulders stiffened, but they didn't speak. That was also okay. We were all talked out about Sienna.

I placed the full carafe on the table and turned back to snag a third stool. I might bury my feelings about Sienna, but I never kidded myself about chocolate. I was going to drink the entire jug, savoring every last drop. Why deny it? Why make multiple trips to fill my mug?

I slung the strap of my satchel across the stool, intending to sit on it because there was no way I was resting such a pretty new bag on the floor. Gran and Scarlett managed to fill the table they shared without actually occupying the same space. That was a feat, but the distance between them must take so much energy to maintain. I kept my mouth shut about it, though. Scarlett and I might have both been raised by Gran, but we'd had exceedingly different childhoods.

Gran returned to hunting and pecking on the keyboard of a brand new laptop. She was creating some sort of calendar. I could taste the protection spells Scarlett and I had arranged to have placed on the computer as a joint Christmas gift. Gran's magic wore away at technology. The spells buffered that wear, though they wouldn't last. Adhering magic to technology was a super-specialized gift, but Scarlett had discovered that Wisteria the reconstructionist had a good friend and second cousin, Jasmine, who was particularly good with technology. She'd laid the wards for us.

Anyway, it appeared I was interrupting a coven prep meeting. Apparently, the bakery was neutral territory.

"Some nasty spells in that book," I said to Scarlett as I poured myself a mugful of bittersweet hot chocolate made from ganache and steamed two-percent milk. Most places used whole milk, but I found that coated the bite of the chocolate in too much cream for my taste.

"Yes," Gran answered tersely. "We're discussing its … review at the next meeting."

Scarlett brushed the curls off my right shoulder, leaving a trace of her calming magic behind.

I smiled at my mother, then stole her cupcake.

She laughed as I dug into another of my limited-edition creations, *Blitzen in a Cup* — a rich but airy chocolate cake that was heavy on the mocha and iced with eggnog buttercream. I was removing these from the menu next week when I ran out of eggnog, so I was pleased there were a few left over today. I might not be a fan of coffee as a drink, but I never turned it down paired with chocolate.

Someone knocked at the window.

I glanced up into the eyes of a four-year-old child and froze with the cupcake an inch from my mouth.

The preschooler grinned. Her brown eyes were still way too large for her face, but she didn't look quite as starved as she had three months ago while wrestling me for the instrument of assassination in the Bahamas. My right knee — which she'd shattered with a single kick — still ached when it rained. And it rained a ton in Vancouver. A remembered jolt of pain ran through my knee and up my right thigh at the sight of her ... here ... in Vancouver, not buried in the ruins of a fortress at the bottom of the Atlantic Ocean.

I never had been the lucky sort. I didn't even bother to buy lottery tickets anymore.

She'd found normal kid-sized clothes somewhere. If you called a four-year-old wearing only a yellow-print sundress in January normal.

"Jade?" Scarlett prompted.

The kid rapped her knuckles against the French-paned window again. A tremor ran through the glass. Gran let out a low hiss.

Yeah, I'd felt that too.

A child shouldn't be able to rattle the glass of my bakery front windows, because they were protected by wards. Wards primarily constructed by Gran and designed to keep out any Adept I hadn't granted entrance to.

"Do you know that child?" Gran asked.

"She's not a child," I answered. "And yes. Unfortunately. She's the crazy dragon kid from the freaking fortress."

I placed the cupcake down and stepped away from the table toward the front entrance. I kept my body parallel to the windows and my hand on my invisible knife at my hip. "You need to go up to the apartment," I said, speaking to Scarlett and Gran behind me. "When did Warner say he'd be back? Did he go through the portal or out into the city?"

"Don't be silly," Gran said as she closed the screen of her laptop. "We're not leaving you alone with her."

I paused, standing face to face with the child with only the glass of the French-paned front door between us.

Shadows deeper than the night gathered around her, obscuring the lights from the stores across the street, the traffic between, and the pedestrians …

Oh, God. West Fourth Avenue was always filled with people. Nonmagical, vulnerable people.

The Adept weren't supposed to call attention to themselves. There were so few of us, we really didn't need the scrutiny of nonmagicals. Everyone feared what they didn't understand, and with Adepts so severely outnumbered, we didn't need that kind of fear and hate focused on us. We already had different levels of governing bodies — like the witches' Convocation — which laid down laws governing conduct and the use of magic. We had smaller entities like individual covens that enforced these laws. The shapeshifters had their Assembly and their packs for enforcement. The vampires had the Conclave and — as far as I could tell — Kett for enforcement. The sorcerers had their League.

The child glowering at me from the sidewalk was a dragon, and technically her actions were governed by the guardians — arguably the most stringent and moral of all Adepts. But I didn't believe for one second that she cared one bit about exposing us all to the humans on the sidewalk behind her.

"Jade?" Scarlett asked quietly from behind my shoulder. "Are you going to ask her in?"

No one with a drop of magic in them could pass through Gran's wards without an invitation. Normally this wasn't an issue, because Vancouver was considered a magical backwater. Though lately, more Adepts had been checking in at the bakery instead of seeking out Gran — who was the Adept of power here — to ask permission to visit Godfrey witch territory.

"No," I said. I tamped down on my instinct to block Scarlett from the child's fevered gaze. "What do you want, kid?"

The child slowly raised her hand and pointed a tiny finger at my heart.

"You?" Scarlett asked me.

"No. My necklace."

I pulled my knife, but before the blade had even cleared the sheath, the girl slammed a fist into the magic of the ward between us. The runes along the edges of the doorframe lit up with witch magic.

Gran screamed.

The preschooler somehow grabbed the magic of the wards, peeling it away from the door in a manner I wouldn't have thought possible.

Gran stumbled. Scarlett ran back to her.

The kid ripped a chunk of the ward magic from the doorway even as I reached out with my alchemist senses and tried to grab hold of it.

Pain seared through my head and I stumbled — my magic was tied to the wards, along with my grandmother's.

Gran fell.

I pulled on the protection magic stored in my necklace, using it to buffer me from the kid's ongoing demolition of the wards as I turned to see Scarlett gathering Gran into her arms. Blood was gushing from Pearl's nose. She was unconscious.

The kid came through the door before I'd managed to clear my head.

Wood and glass exploded. I shielded my face with my arms as I twisted away from the kick the kid aimed at my knee. She grabbed my elbow, yanking me forward and down in order to head-butt me.

Yeah, first the attempted knee kick, then a head-butt. The kid liked to use the same moves, and why not? They obviously worked. I certainly hadn't figured out how to counter them.

I stumbled back, reeling as I tried to gather the frayed magic around the doorway and knit it back together.

I managed to get a simple magical web woven just before the child decided we were shaken enough for her to press forward. She took a step beyond the doorway. The magic of the ward grabbed hold of her and attempted to eject her. Unfortunately — maybe because Gran was unconscious — the wards weren't quite strong enough to toss her ass into the street.

The kid fought, clawing and snarling as the magic wrapped around her and lifted her off her feet.

I felt Scarlett's magic bloom behind me and hoped she was putting up a protective shield around Gran. But I didn't take my eyes off the dragon child caught in my hastily resurrected bakery wards, and floating about two feet off the ground.

Jesus, what the hell would that look like to passersby?

"Mom, the pedestrians!"

I didn't have to elaborate. Scarlett's strawberry magic shifted to run parallel to the bakery wards. A perimeter cloaking spell of some sort, I guessed. My mother's witch magic wasn't just limited to charm and charisma.

"I asked you what you wanted," I said to the snarling kid. "Use your words, you freaking brat."

It was taking all my focus just to hold the wards around the rabid child. There just wasn't enough power in the wards without Gran bolstering them to keep her at bay for good.

The child quieted and looked at me thoughtfully, an expression far too old for her four-year-old face. She resembled a koala, actually, what with her large brown eyes and wide, flattish face. A nasty, vicious marsupial clinging to the damaged wards of my bakery. Yeah, I was pissed, but I was still attempting to be reasonable. Even after all the destruction she'd waged in the last few seconds, she was still just a kid with a load of screwed-up magic running through her and scrambling her brain. A kid who hadn't even known who her mother was three months ago.

"I came for you, alchemist," she finally said. "And your tasty magic." Her refined English accent was completely at odds with her appearance. She smacked her lips, as she'd done on the altar in the Bahamas after biting me.

"For help?" I asked. "Do you want me to take you to the nexus? Busting through my wards isn't a terribly nice way of asking for help."

The rabid koala grinned that creepy grin that would have haunted my nightmares — you know, if I hadn't already seen much, much worse things.

"I came for you," the kid repeated. "For your tasty magic."

"Listen, that's just creepy —"

Then the child interrupted me in the middle of the etiquette lesson by reaching out and shredding the remaining bakery wards.

Pain ripped through my head, and I lost control of my limbs as my connection to the magic was severed. Even Scarlett cried out from the backlash.

I stumbled, falling to my knees in the broken glass and splintered wood of the door. But I still managed to get my knife between me and the kid.

Except she didn't go for me.

She ran straight for Scarlett and Gran, with her shadow leeches flooding into the bakery after her.

My mother's strawberry magic rolled through the bakery. She erected a barrier between herself and the dragon kid just seconds before the girl slammed against it.

The child shrieked, punching her tiny fists into the blue magic that now whirled around Gran and Scarlett. The reverberation of her frustrated blows brought my mother to her knees as I gained my feet.

I batted away the shadow leeches, who were darting in and around me as well as tasting the magic of my mother's barrier. From this vantage point, I couldn't tell if Gran was breathing or not as Scarlett pulled her mother across her lap, then somehow tucked the barrier she'd thrown up even closer around them, concentrating its magic. I'd never seen my mother look so fierce.

Despite the child and all her smoky, spiced dragon magic filling the bakery, my senses were flooded with strawberry.

"She held that barrier against a greater demon, kid," I said as I stalked toward the child. "Your magic is no match for her."

The girl spun to face me, her hands clenched into tiny fists at her sides. "My shadows will take care of it for me."

She wasn't lying. My mother's shield shifted underneath the shadow leeches attempting to latch onto it. Though she didn't speak or take her eyes off the kid, I could see the effort it took for Scarlett to hold the leeches off. They'd eventually strip my mother's magic, just as they'd stripped all the magic from the fortress where they'd been created.

Maybe even created by the rabid koala standing before me. A crazed baby dragon who barely came up to my waist, and yet had gotten by me and two powerful witches in a matter of moments.

I shuddered at the thought that a dragon could be capable of such terrible blood magic, though it was obvious now that she was in league with the leeches — or even controlling them.

"Well, then," I said. "I guess I'll just have to give you a spanking and vanquish your pets one by one."

I backed this threat up by thrusting my knife into the nearest shadow leech and sending a pulse of my magic into it. The shadow thinned, stretching in all directions away from the blade, then disappeared with a brief, high-pitched whine.

The preschooler barreled into me like a tiny freight train … a tiny train driven by a crazy koala, and capable of hauling thousands of pounds of concrete.

She hit me midwaist. I stood against her assault — but at the last second, I just couldn't bring myself to gut her.

Her momentum spun us back through the tables and stools. We missed crashing through the glass cupcake display case by mere inches.

The kid reached up and latched onto my necklace with both hands. I couldn't get her pinned or contained. She was tiny but crazy strong, and moved as if she had more than four limbs. Completely like a rabid koala. My choice of nickname was becoming even more appropriate — which was unfortunate for me, because I only dubbed her with it to make myself feel in control of the situation.

It also didn't help that the shadow leeches rolled over and around us, so I had to keep them off me at the same time I was wrestling her.

I had no freaking idea how to subdue a freaking dragon.

"Jade!" Scarlett cried out. Then the shield she'd been holding between her, Gran, and the shadow leeches flickered and dimmed.

"Hold on, Mom!" I brought my elbow down on the evil toddler's head. Something nasty snapped in my arm, but the kid's head lolled sideways.

I'd stunned her, though she still clung to my necklace like a tentacled barnacle.

I lunged, carrying the kid with me as I slashed and sliced the shadows around Scarlett's faltering shield. The leeches backed away, pressing up into the corners and edges of the bakery.

Scarlett's shield fell.

"All right, Mom?" I was trying to untangle the crazed koala's fingers from the wedding rings of my necklace, while keeping my knife raised against the shadows at the same time.

The kid began muttering and mumbling. If she was speaking English, I didn't understand the words.

"Mom, can you put the shield back up? I need to cross through the portal and dump this kid on the guardians. But I don't think the shadow leeches will be able to follow. I'm worried —"

The child's head reared up. Her eyes blazed with gold. Then somehow, she began pulling the magic from my necklace like she'd ripped the wards off the front door.

"Mine. Mine. Mine," she cackled.

"Not yours!" I reached out for the magic she was drawing away and tried to anchor it back into the necklace.

I dropped to my knees in an attempt to force the kid to stand on her own two feet. I needed to alleviate some of the weight she was exerting on my neck, which was starting to feel like it might snap in two.

She wrapped her legs around me tighter. For each finger I got unhooked from a wedding ring, she managed to grab onto another.

A gauzy rainbow of magic — pulled from my necklace in our tug of war — wrapped itself around and between our heads and necks. It tasted of … everything. Everything I'd ever collected, every spell I'd defended myself from, every Adept I'd ever known …

I was going to need to hurt her to get her off me.

I called my knife into my right hand.

"Jade," Scarlett whispered. Her voice was soft and sorrowful.

"Jade," the child repeated, as if just figuring out my name. Then she loosed her hand from my necklace and pressed it against my cheek. "You will help me."

She pushed to turn my head toward Scarlett and Gran, who were once again surrounded by shadow leeches. Every inch of the bakery around and above both of them seethed with waiting, eager darkness.

"You will help me," the child repeated. "Or my shadows will take every last drop from your witches."

"I've already vanquished at least three," I said. "I can take the rest ... and you."

The leeches pressed closer to Scarlett. She was sitting back on her heels but still upright. Gran was in her lap, and I could see her chest slowly rising and falling with breath.

"Can you?" the kid asked, sounding interested in the possibility. "Can you guarantee their survival?"

My mother locked her gaze to mine, but I couldn't read anything but defiance from her.

"I've been trying to help you." I ground the words out through my burning anger. She was just a kid. Or, at least, she was trapped in a child's body, her magic dampened and contained. That was enough to make anyone crazy. I didn't go around picking on crazy people ... well, not on people who'd gone crazy through no immediately apparent fault of their own. I had to keep reminding myself of that fact.

"I want the magic of the necklace ... and the knife."

"Absolutely not," I said.

The shadow leeches squeezed against Scarlett and Gran. My mother moaned quietly. I could see the leeches tasting her magic, pulling it from her.

I couldn't just stand around, torn between gutting and perhaps killing a messed-up dragon or watching my family be stripped of their magic and possibly killed in the process.

I reached up for my necklace.

The child cackled and disengaged herself from me.

I lifted the necklace from my head. All the magic surrounding me pressed against my dowser senses as I slung the necklace across the child's outstretched palms.

Her hands were so tiny that she couldn't close them around the thick gold chain.

"I can't give you the knife," I said, lying through my clenched teeth. "It's spelled only to me."

"No matter," the lippy koala purred in her uppity, overly posh accent. "When I'm reborn, I will simply take it." Intent on the necklace, she took a step back from me. The magic I'd spent years collecting in the chain and its wedding rings danced around her head, stretching between us as if it were still tied to me.

"Call off your shadows," I said. I flicked my right wrist, which I still held at my side, to call her attention to my jade knife.

The child lifted her gaze to me, then nodded. The leeches moved a few feet away from Scarlett and Gran, lining themselves along the French-paned windows and blocking out the lights from the busy street beyond.

The child continued to pull the magic from the necklace. I could see it settling on the skin of her face, neck, shoulders, and arms. Years and years of residual, wild, and even malicious magic collected by me and placed in the necklace to create a personal shield. A shield reinforced by my own alchemist powers.

What did a dragon need with alchemist magic?

As the child drained the necklace's reserves, I slowly inched closer to Gran and Scarlett, still on my knees. I could feel Scarlett's magic gathering behind me.

I felt the instant Gran woke.

The preschooler slowly pivoted, continuing to face me as I moved. But she didn't pause in draining the magic from the necklace until she had every last drop of it wrapped around her in a multicolored gossamer body-suit. She raised her arms, holding the necklace aloft.

"Now!" she commanded.

I raised my knife, ready for the shadow leeches to attack.

They didn't.

"Now! Now!" the rabid koala repeated, locking her once more fevered eyes to me.

"Now what?" I snapped.

"Now make the magic mine, alchemist."

"Make it yours? You're a person, not a freaking necklace."

"Now!" the child demanded with a stamp of her foot. The shadow leeches rustled around us.

"Fine," I muttered. "You asked for it."

I reached out with my alchemist powers to pinpoint her dragon magic. Then, pressing against all the magic from the necklace that she'd dressed herself in, I shoved and mashed the two power sources together. God, I hoped she choked on it. No one could take that much magic into themselves without passing out — and maybe never waking up. She was a mortal being, not a car battery.

Let her pass out. Then I'd drag her ass into the nexus and let the guardians deal with the magically induced coma that was the fallout.

Except she didn't falter. Somehow, with my help, she sucked the layer of gossamer magic into herself. Her skin briefly glowed with the golden light I attributed to the portals. Then the lingering taste of the witch and sorcerer and dragon magic that I'd collected in the necklace was gone, nullified by her dragon spiciness.

I could feel Gran crafting some spell behind me, the grass-and-lilac taste of it overriding all the other magic in the bakery.

I readied myself to lunge forward to follow whatever Gran was going to throw. Dragons were naturally resistant to offensive witch magic, but Gran was no ordinary witch.

The child was changing. It was subtle at first, but as she absorbed the magic she siphoned from the necklace, she began to grow. To mature.

As I knelt waiting on Gran, the four-year-old before me transformed into an eight-year-old, then a twelve-year-old. Then, shaking and sweating gold-infused drops of magic with the effort, a sixteen-year-old.

The sundress she was wearing stretched and shortened to more than risqué proportions. A slight sweetness that I couldn't identify began to temper the sootiness of her dragon magic. Her magic was evolving along with her form. Unfortunately, I was pretty sure that more strength and power would come along with that evolution.

The newly transformed teenager dropped her hands to examine her outstretched arms. The necklace fell to the wood-slat floor.

She frowned. "Not enough," she muttered, kicking the necklace away as if it was a piece of trash. She glared at me. "I'll take the knife now."

"Come and take it from me," I said, slowly rising to my feet. I felt Gran and Scarlett do the same behind me.

The teen's eyes flicked to take in all three of us. Then she turned, scanning the room, and for a brief moment I thought she was just going to walk away. Then with a nasty smile, she stepped to the side, reached down, and stirred her hand among broken stools, tables, and glass to retrieve the dragonskin map.

Ah, dammit. It must have fallen out of my satchel.

With a snap of her wrist she unrolled the map and gazed at it. I held my breath, worrying that she was going to tear it to pieces.

"Ah, I thought I recognized you," she murmured, speaking to the map as if it were an actual person. Then she tilted her head toward me. "Let's trade."

"Let's not."

The shadow leeches rippled around us again, which made me realize they were responding to the teen's anger. It was as if they were connected on an emotional level. That was creepy, with an extra serving of creepy on the side.

"No," I said, raising my knife. "You might have caught us unaware the first time. But look around at the magic in this room, crazy koala. You won't make it out of here with your pets if you stand against us now."

I was bluffing, and trying not to freak out about the map she was clenching in her hand. I had no idea what she was capable of with all the magic of the necklace in her, though maybe she'd used all that up with her transformation. I hadn't even known it was possible for a person to absorb magic like that. Even Sienna had needed an innate binding ability, blood, and sacrificial magic to steal and keep the magic of another Adept. But that was different, and attempting to hold all that power had driven my foster sister crazy — bat-shit, blood-frenzied crazy.

Here, the child had charged herself like a freaking battery, then used that power to unlock whatever had held her full dragon form in check. Partially, at least.

The teen raised her chin and straightened her back like a haughty princess. "I … I …" she faltered, as if unable to remember her own name. Then, with a smile full of satisfaction, she remembered. "I, Shailaja, daughter of the treasure keeper, one of the guardian nine, demand your aid."

"Shailaja, eh?" I said mockingly, instantly recognizing the name. "Now where have I read that before …

oh, right. Pulou's journal. Something about you being a bad, bad dragon."

Shailaja curled her lip at me. "I should have known a half-blood wouldn't be powerful enough to fully awaken a dragon. But even talentless and feeble, you are an alchemist, so you must have other objects of power. Or access to objects of power."

"No."

"No?" This answer confused her. Now that she was a teenager, any residual sympathy I'd had for her was long gone. Odd how a sneering teen could do that in a single pouty, demanding second.

"You don't say no to me," Shailaja said. "You don't stand against a true dragon. You don't —"

"Yeah, yeah," I interrupted. "Wrong era, baby koala. We do what we want around here."

The teen lunged for me.

Gran's spell — some wicked blue lightning that imprinted itself on my eyeballs — met Shailaja halfway, hitting her neck-to-torso. She flew off her feet, ending up pinned to the far wall. She hung there, suspended, shrieking and writhing underneath Gran's lightning spell. The shadow leeches swarmed around her as I stalked forward.

I felt Gran stumble behind me, Scarlett's magic rising up to anchor her. The power dancing and streaking around me was exhilarating — all the hair on my body was electrified with it — and I wanted to laugh and twirl around in the intoxicating energy.

Instead, I reached into the seething mass of shadow leeches obscuring my sight of Shailaja and came up empty-handed.

Then the shadow leeches also disappeared.

Gran released the spell. The charged air still danced against my skin as I spun around to scan the bakery.

Shailaja was gone.

Stepping through the ruin of my front door, tables, and chairs, I retrieved the depleted necklace. I looped it around my neck three times and instantly felt more grounded.

Scarlett righted a stool, then helped Gran over to it. Still dowsing for the teen's magic, I jogged into the kitchen, then out into the back alley.

The cool of the evening hit my overly warm face, but I didn't stop to enjoy it or calm down. I needed all the adrenaline I could hold right now.

I ran back through the kitchen and into the storefront. Scarlett was pressing a glass of water into Gran's hands.

I crossed to the front door, ignoring the broken glass and wood as it crunched underneath my feet. I could taste Scarlett's perimeter cloaking spell, so it was still in place around the bakery. But the kid — Shailaja — had stripped the wards.

She'd stripped the bakery wards and attacked my family. She'd attacked and damaged my home and family.

I began to shake — not as the adrenaline drained from my system but as more pumped in. I rode the anger that had been burning in my belly and now flooded my chest, flushing through my neck and face.

She knew the bakery was vulnerable without wards. I had absolutely no doubt that the freaking brat would come back. She wanted something, so she took it.

Not again. Not here. Not with my family.

I laid my jade knife across my left hand, then deliberately and deeply sliced across my palm. I squeezed this hand, heedless of the pain, and allowed drops of my blood to fall at the base of the doorway. Then I pressed the bleeding cut to the sides and top of the doorframe.

"Jade!" Scarlett gasped behind me, completely aghast.

Ignoring my mother's dismay, I stepped from the bakery onto the sidewalk of West Fourth Avenue. As I passed through Scarlett's spell, the evening was suddenly filled with car engines, tires turning on pavement, and people dashing through the light rain to and from the various restaurants and coffee shops across from and around the bakery. I slowly stepped along the outside windows — my shoulder brushing the glass as I passed — and allowed drops of blood to fall from my cut hand all along the footing of the exterior concrete wall.

Then I stepped back inside, sliced my hand a second time to reopen the wound, and traced the entire footprint of the bakery in my blood, including the exterior alley wall.

Scarlett and Gran watched me, utter disbelief etched on their faces.

I didn't stop.

I performed blood magic without giving it more than a second thought. And in front of two members of the Convocation. I was seriously surprised they didn't slap me in chains and press black magic charges against me on the spot.

They were obviously in shock at my audacity, at my seething anger. That was fine by me, because it was better for everyone if they didn't try to stop me until I had the new ward in place.

Or maybe they just weren't sure how to stand against me. Maybe they weren't sure they could stop me if they tried.

I went upstairs and placed drops of my blood all around the edges of my apartment as well. The wards on the second level were undamaged, but if I was going dark, I might as well go all the way, all at once.

I had to slice my palm seven times to finish the job.

I didn't even feel lightheaded. I didn't feel anything at all. Perhaps I was in the thrall of the blood magic I was about to perform. Or maybe I was the one in shock, though my actions felt just and my choices crystal clear.

I could leave my family vulnerable, or I could protect them.

Two options.

Either. Or.

Blood trumped rock, paper, and scissors.

Okay, maybe I was a bit lightheaded.

Chapter Three

Gran and Scarlett were waiting for me in the basement of the bakery.

A witches' circle was inscribed in the dirt. Gran stood at the north edge with the broom she'd used to draw the circle, watching as Scarlett lit the last few candles.

They were going to help me erect the protection spell. A ward based on blood magic. A vein of magic that Gran, at least, had spent decades denouncing and policing via the Convocation.

Emotion tightened my chest and neck, threatening to choke me. I stumbled on the rickety wooden steps that led from the pantry to the basement.

I'd expected condemnation. I'd expected to be disowned. Any respectable witch who performed blood magic or black magic would likely end up excommunicated for the practice.

Of course, this wasn't my first time.

And I really wasn't a witch.

Gran looked up at my stumble, set the broom against the boxes and wooden storage pallets behind her, and reached her hand out to me. "Come," she said. "If it's to be done, it should be done quickly."

Scarlett set a fourth candle at the eastern edge of the circle, then straightened to take Gran's other hand.

I closed the space between us, quickly shucking my boots and tights so I stood barefoot in the packed dirt at the west edge of the circle. I linked hands with my mother and Gran. They'd also removed their shoes. The portal, so well hidden that even Warner hadn't known it was there, thrummed contentedly away on the patched concrete and brick of the east wall.

"Your magic is depleted," I murmured. The taste of strawberry and lilac lingered on the back of my tongue, but not as strongly as usual.

"The weight of the spell won't fall to us," Gran said. "We're here to anchor you."

"So I don't get lost in the blood magic."

"Don't make light of it, Jade," Scarlett said, as chastising as I'd ever heard her.

"It's the only way I know how to secure you quickly," I said. "I'll have to go after her. She has the map."

"We know," Scarlett whispered, sad but supportive at the same time.

"We're here," Gran said. "Now gather the magic before it degrades further. Gather the magic in your blood. Allow it to remain anchored where the drops have fallen. But weave it together, then command it to do your bidding. Scarlett and I will hold the circle."

I closed my eyes and reached out with my dowser senses to find every drop of blood I'd left all around the edges of the bakery and the apartment, inside and out.

Normally I couldn't taste or see my own magic. Wisteria, the reconstructionist, had once told me it was blue-gold in color. But now that it was parted from me, I could feel it. I could feel it waiting for me. Blood heeded blood.

I'd created two other magical objects with blood magic before. One was the sacrificial knife I'd originally created in London one terrible night to free a young necromancer, Mory, from my sister's evil machinations, and which I'd painstakingly reshaped into a more traditional dagger and given to Warner for Christmas. I'd also drained and sealed Sienna's magic — both stolen and natural magic — into the katana my father had given me. I hadn't deliberately used blood magic that night in Tofino. But blood — mine and Sienna's — had coated the sword, and I was fairly certain that was what made that particular act of alchemy possible. Thankfully, that terrible creation was in Pulou's possession now.

I'd also sealed the spells on my jade knife with my own blood, but only after I'd been stabbed with it twice by Sienna. So I didn't consider that a deliberate practice of black magic, though perhaps I was being willfully blind.

I might not be well versed in blood magic, but I did know that every object I created with alchemy — blood based or just energy driven — wanted to return to me. Magic heeded magic.

So even though finding the drops of blood was as easy as closing my eyes, calling the magic in each drop to the forefront, smoothing and connecting it to the drops on either side, then reaching out to stretch those points of magic up and out until they enveloped the entire building was much, much more difficult.

I understood instinctively that if I hadn't held Scarlett's and Gran's hands and breathed in their magic while I channeled the power of my blood, I might have been pulled away myself. I understood how I could have opened my eyes but never really come back to myself. Maybe leaving too much behind in the magic of the blood wards … maybe creating a thirst I could never quench.

I was shaking as I visualized all the woven magic coating the interior and exterior of the bakery and the apartment, coaxing and pulling it to gather at the center of the roof directly above us. I fell to my knees as I drew that gathered magic around and down to the base of the building to meet me in the witches' circle.

Scarlett gasped as the magic filled the circle and danced between our clasped hands and outstretched arms. She and Gran remained standing as I anchored this called magic into the ground beneath us. This would now be the heart center of the wards. The next Adept who wanted to destroy the protection surrounding the bakery and the apartment would have to be here, standing before the portal, to access the core of the magic. And if they'd already gotten this far inside, I imagined we'd already be lying dead or dying at their feet.

"Nothing of magic enters without my permission," I informed the core of the spell dancing in the circle before me. "No thing, spell, or weapon. No Adept. Except we three, and Kandy, Kett, and Warner."

"So much magic," Scarlett murmured.

"And the portal?" Gran asked.

"I don't think I can ward against the portal. I don't think anyone can ward a portal of the treasure keeper's construction, except maybe another guardian. It's a secret, though."

Gran looked pointedly at Scarlett. "Is it a secret?"

Scarlett nodded stiffly. "It is."

"You haven't mentioned it to Yazi?"

"I just said I hadn't."

"I could try …" Utilizing the magic in the circle another time was a tantalizing idea. I'd be happy to do it again. And again.

Gran squeezed my hand. "It's done, Jade. Let it go."

For a moment, I didn't want to. I wanted to watch the magic dance all twinkly blue in the circle before me. I felt powerful and whole here. In control, in command.

"It's done as you asked, Jade," Gran said. "Let it go."

I nodded. But before I fully released it, I channeled some of the protection I'd created into my depleted necklace. Then the magic settled into the ground until only a soft, circular glow remained, hovering a few inches above the dirt. As I watched, that glow slowly faded. And it was done.

I waited for the blood magic to cause an urge toward murder and mayhem to arise in me, but I just felt weary. And more mentally than bodily.

Gran harrumphed, but she seemed pleased enough as she disengaged her hand from mine to begin snuffing out candles.

Scarlett turned my hand over in hers to look at the half-healed cut marring my palm. It appeared that even half-dragons took extra time to heal from multiple cuts in the same spot. Though the severity of the cut might also have something to do with the magic of my jade blade, which was wickedly sharp.

I was seriously glad Shailaja hadn't gotten her hands on my knife. My necklace had been bad enough. Though the crazy dragon seemed slightly more stable in her more mature form than she had as an unhinged pre-schooler, I still didn't want to be the one who'd handed her a deadly weapon.

Scarlett lifted my hand to her mouth and placed a soft kiss on my palm. Her magic brushed against my skin and a healing spell tingled along the edges of my wound.

"Gran needs to sleep," I said. Scarlett's magic — from holding the protection circle against a dragon and shadow leeches — was also depleted.

Scarlett nodded. "I'll take her upstairs. Then I'll come help you clean."

"I'll be fine," I said, not a hundred percent sure I wasn't still in shock. Yeah, I was way too calm for my own good. "Like you said, Warner's on his way."

Scarlett pressed her hand to my cheek and turned toward Gran, who also stepped up to touch me lightly on the shoulder.

"I'm sorry," I said. Tears were suddenly threatening where there hadn't even been a hint of them before. "I couldn't figure out how to contain her without really hurting her."

"She'll be back," Gran said. "And you'll be ready."

"No," Scarlett countered sharply. "You'll call your father. She's a dragon. She's his responsibility."

"Yeah, but the map's mine. She's already gone after an instrument of assassination and gotten a nasty lesson in why dragons can't wield them, so why take the map?"

"The map is a piece of power," Gran said. "She was seeking objects of power."

"But then why come specifically to Jade, Pearl?" Scarlett asked. "I think you're wrong. She needed Jade's alchemist powers. Taking the map was merely leverage."

"Thank you, Scarlett," Gran said frostily. "I was attempting to soothe your distraught daughter."

"Jade is far more resilient than that, mother," Scarlett said.

"Yes, daughter. But it is nice to be babied once in a while."

Scarlett snapped her mouth shut on her mounting indignation. Yeah, Gran did that to us all.

"I have a containment spell for your satchel," Gran said as she hustled ahead of us up the stairs to the pantry. "So nothing accidentally falls out. It was going to be a birthday gift, but I see you need it now. Give me an hour or so."

She disappeared into the pantry. I looked at Scarlett, but she shook her head.

"A little spell isn't going to kill me," Gran snapped from above us. She'd poked her head back through the doorway.

"Bottomless would be nice too," I mused, thinking of all the things I had to cram into my bag these days. Chocolate bars, maps, cellphones, knives, artifacts —

"Not in an hour!" Gran snapped. Then she disappeared into the bakery kitchen.

Scarlett laughed under her breath as she climbed the stairs after her mother.

Geez, I hadn't been asking for a bottomless bag ... just saying it would be nice.

The damage to the bakery storefront was worse than I'd allowed myself to acknowledge. I'd have to close for a few days, maybe even a week, and order a new door ... and new tables ... and new chairs.

Anger washed through me. Fierce, burning anger seared through the steady resolve that had gotten me through the altercation and the building of the blood ward. I was probably looking at thousands of dollars' worth of damage. My heart and soul was in this bakery.

I was shaking again. I needed to stop shaking before I did something extra stupid, so I found a broom, grabbed a garbage can, and started cleaning.

I had to remember to remind Scarlett to remove the cloaking spell from the bakery tonight. And put up a closed sign. Otherwise, I wasn't sure what people would think if they came for cupcakes, then couldn't find the store. I wasn't sure what sort of spell Scarlett had used. I wasn't sure if I should call the police. Should I file a report? Could you even file a vandalism report without any witnesses? But if I didn't file a report, wouldn't that call extra attention to the damage? Customers were going to ask questions.

Oh, God. I was melting down over mundane things so I didn't have to think about a crazy dragon running around with my map.

The second I'd secured the blood ward, I should have walked right through the portal and sought out Pulou.

But I didn't. Even knowing that I should didn't make me move in that direction.

I was just so, so angry.

A dragon had done this. A dragon had been allowed to do this. Pulou knew about the kid who'd been in the fortress. Pulou knew about the shadow leeches. Pulou had spent hours and hours with Warner, dissecting every last thing the sentinel knew about his era and the instruments of assassination.

Pulou hadn't even given a second thought to the kid. He'd answered my questions about the creation of the shadow leeches with urgings to unlock the map and secure the next two instruments. He'd admonished me to focus on the important task at hand and let the guardians handle everything else.

Do your duty, alchemist. Let the smarter, stronger dragons worry about everything else.

The broom handle snapped in my hands. Frustrated, I flicked the broken top piece into the wood-slat floor, where it embedded itself about three inches deep.

A cold wash of adrenaline ran down my spine.

That was stupid. So, so stupid to damage the bakery floor even further, and in a childish rage. Plus, a broken broom wasn't exactly useful.

I took a deep breath and looked out the bakery window. Oddly, the trinkets there were still hanging exactly where I'd strung them, completely undamaged.

A pale, white-blond man was standing on the sidewalk, watching me through the broken door. He could see me despite the cloaking spell.

The anger boiling in my stomach eased, and I almost started crying again with the relief of seeing him. But that wouldn't be the proper way to greet an old friend — a mentor — who I hadn't seen in months.

"Kett," I breathed as I stepped closer to the entrance.

He smiled — a fleeting, cool expression — but didn't approach.

I kicked something that sounded like metal. Momentarily distracted, I reached into the shards of glass and splintered wood that were once the door to pull one of my trinkets out of the debris. Obviously, the ones that had previously hung over the doorway hadn't come through as unscathed as the ones in the windows.

My eyes welled with tears. I looked up, met Kett's gaze, and instantly knew that he was livid despite his earlier smile. Not by his face, which was chiseled out of ice, but by his shoulders. The twist of his shoulders betrayed his ire.

"It's just a trinket," I whispered.

"Is it?" he answered.

I twined the trinket — green sea glass collected from Jericho Beach, a cameo found at a yard sale, and a 1958 Canadian silver dollar strung on a silver chain — around the palm of my left hand. Across the wound that Scarlett had partially healed with a kiss. It wrapped three times, mimicking brass knuckles when I was done. If I closed my hand firmly enough, I would crush it. Mangle it with my dragon-inherited strength.

"Is everyone unharmed?" Kett asked, surprising me that he cared. But then, I called him a friend, didn't I? What friend wouldn't care?

"The bakery took most of the damage." Then I asked, "Won't you come in?" I assumed I needed to invite Kett through the new blood wards, which would explain why he still stood at the far edge of the sidewalk. I thought I'd already made his invite implicit. But then, I'd never constructed a blood ward before.

Or perhaps he just enjoyed standing in the shadow of the streetlight.

He smiled again, though I could still see the anger he held at bay. "You've fortified the wards with your own sweet, sweet blood," he murmured, his eyes glowing red. But in a blink, they cleared back to his typical ice blue, which I could see despite the deepening darkness of the evening. "I don't think I will test my mettle tonight."

His tone held no condemnation. Not a drop. For what was blood magic to a vampire but everyday life?

"I was attacked."

"By a creature stronger than you?"

"I hope not."

Kett nodded. He scanned the edges of the bakery, then looked up to the apartments above. Mine, which overlooked the alley, and Kandy's, which stood empty and awaiting the return of my werewolf best friend.

I stepped through the wards covering the entrance, crossing the sidewalk in two strides to wrap my arms around Kett's neck. Taking without asking all the cool comfort he had to offer.

He stood just shy of six feet, and with my boots back on, I was only an inch or so shorter. I pressed my cheek against his and breathed in his dark peppermint magic. He wrapped his arms around my back to hold me gingerly, as if I might be a precious piece of china.

"You're angry, but not with me," I whispered, aware but not really caring that the street was really too full of people to be making such a display of myself.

"Never at you," Kett replied. He pressed his hand briefly to the back of my head, then dropped his arms.

I took the hint and stepped back so a few inches stood between us. I could still taste his magic from there. Could still steal the calm that came from that cool taste. I'd never found peppermint so soothing, not before I met Kett. The vampire still scared me, but in a we-are-all-capable-of-extreme-darkness sort of way now. We'd shared a life bond for a terribly brief moment. Perhaps that magic still lingered between us. Perhaps waging a war together against a demon horde summoned by my sister — and surviving — was a stronger bond than anything else could ever be.

"Tell me everything," he said.

"The dragon kid came. She demanded my necklace and used its magic to transform into a teenage version of herself. She wanted my knife as well, but I wasn't stupid enough to just hand her a deadly weapon. Then Gran kicked her ass."

Kett's lips curled, minutely and briefly, at my characterization of Gran. He was a fan of Pearl Godfrey's, through and through. I think she scared him just a little.

Apparently, that was what it took to get an ancient vampire's attention.

"The child from the fortress?"

"Yes."

Kett knew about the map, which he'd helped decode, and about the fortress in the Bahamas. He hadn't really met Warner yet — other than during their brief skirmish in Seattle. Somehow, they were never in Vancouver at the same time.

"She took the map." I was loath to admit the last part.

"Interesting."

Again, I could hear the anger underlying the vampire's normally icy tone. "You're pissed."

"Indeed."

"You're going to help me get the map back."

"If you wish."

"Don't play me, vampire."

"Never."

Kett brushed his fingers along my necklace. He was a big fan of it as well. I imagined that was part of his pissiness. "Not completely depleted," he murmured.

"I topped it up when I sealed the wards."

"With Pearl and Scarlett?"

"You can feel that?"

Kett inclined his head. I wasn't sure it was a great idea for the Executioner of the Conclave to know that the Godfrey coven performed blood magic together.

"Will others know?"

"No," Kett replied. "Other Adept will feel a powerful ward, but only those intimate with the smell of your blood will comprehend its construction."

"So you. Kandy?"

"Possibly Desmond. I can only guess that a guardian or Drake could tell as well."

"They don't tend to drop in for cupcakes."

"They will come now."

I nodded but refused to worry about that. Guardians didn't care about things like blood magic as long as someone wasn't wielding it to destroy the world.

Kett slipped his hand into the front pocket of his jeans and pulled out two wedding rings. A matching set of plain gold bands. He held the rings out to me, the metal glimmering with a hint of red where they rested in the palm of his right hand.

"Jesus," I said. "You aren't asking me to marry you, are you?"

Kett smiled, tight-lipped and cool. "For your necklace. I found them and thought you might wish to add their magic to the chain. The timing appears to be auspicious."

"From a pawn shop, right? Not from someone's dead fingers?"

Kett closed his fingers over the rings to hide them — but he couldn't hide the tiny taste of magic I'd picked up.

"Married vampires?" I asked, as casually as possible for someone who desperately wanted the items offered. The rings would go a long way toward healing my most prized possession. Okay, one of my two most prized possessions.

Kett opened his hand and looked at the rings. "Is it so impossible?" he murmured.

"Did you find them in London?"

"I endeavor to make my visits to London as brief as possible."

"So no time for window-shopping."

"No, but Paris provided some distraction."

"French vampires?" My voice squeaked rather unbecomingly with excitement. I ignored his 'distraction' comment. There were only three things that distracted vampires … blood, unique magic, and power plays. All of which were cans of worms best left unopened.

Kett smirked and inclined his head, but said nothing.

"A story would be nice," I whispered as I wrapped my arms around myself. I was chilly, but I also needed to stop myself from simply snatching the gift from him.

Kett looked confused for a moment. Then he nodded and cast his gaze over my head again, up at the building behind me, though he wasn't really looking at it.

"Brethren of mine," he whispered.

I hadn't been expecting a glimpse into his life when I'd asked about the rings. His cool tone was a further balm as I leaned in to lose myself, even if just for this breath, in his history.

"Siblings, if you will. Married before they were turned."

The vampire never shared his past. He seemed perfectly pleased to live fully within the present.

"Companions of mine for a century or so. But …" He looked down at the rings. "Ill fated."

Some terrible sadness was buried in those two words. Something with an utter finality that I didn't want to dig into right now. I couldn't taste a drop of darkness in the pair of wedding rings Kett held.

"I would be honored to accept this gift, Kettil, Executioner of the Conclave."

Kett stiffened. Well, his shoulders tensed at least. "I offer the gift as a friend, Jade Godfrey. No machinations attached."

He might have been teasing, but I didn't totally get it. Granted, I was enamored with the idea of adding the rings to my necklace as quickly as possible. Yes, I was easily distracted by bright shiny things. What else was new?

"Thank you," I said.

Kett tipped the rings into my waiting hand without touching me. The hint of vampire magic tingled in my palm — more of an energy than a flavor. Not enough for me to taste, but more than enough to lift my spirits.

"Everything can be fixed," I said, rolling the rings in my hand and already planning how I would add them to my necklace.

Kett was watching the blood flow through my neck. I hadn't caught him doing that since the first evening we met.

Stupidly, I froze. Completely freezing in front of a predator was a bad idea. It only served to reinforce their idea of you as easy prey.

"What are you doing?" I whispered, suddenly aware there were fewer people around on the sidewalks and streets than before.

Kett didn't answer. But he did reach out to press his fingers lightly to the inside of my left wrist. I was still cupping the rings in that same hand.

"You're not trying to seduce me, are you, Kett?" My voice wasn't as steady as I would have liked it to be.

"What would I do with you, Jade Godfrey, after I caught you?" he murmured, his gaze still on my neck. "I already know that your blood and I don't mix."

"You're basing that assumption on seeing my blood burn demons, on the beach in Tofino. You're not pure demon, and I'm not pure dragon."

Kett dropped his hand and lifted his ice-blue gaze to mine. He was smiling now, amused, with no hint of red in his eyes. So he hadn't been lusting after my blood. "Do you wish for me to seduce you?"

"Okay, asshole. I misunderstood. You don't have to rub it in."

"Don't I?" he asked with a millimeter of raised eyebrow.

I snorted, then glared at him. If he'd been a human male, I would have assumed he was being lewd with that comment.

His smile turned into a grin. "Your magic is intoxicating, and you've been liberal with it tonight."

Ah, yes. If it couldn't be about blood for the vampire, then it was all about magic. I wasn't a hundred percent sure sex was even the same thing for vampires as it was for the rest of us. I was betting it was a combination of sucking and mind games. Pleasant mind games, but feeding nevertheless.

"I have no idea where to start looking for her," I said. I was becoming skilled at thinking about more than one thing at a time. Or maybe I was just obsessed about the map. It wasn't every day that I met my immortal demigod father, then discovered that objects existed with which he could be murdered. Objects I was tasked to collect and return to the safety of the guardians.

Though destroying them would obviously be a better idea. However, Warner was being stonewalled over that particular notion by Pulou.

"She took the map deliberately?" Kett asked.

"Yeah, I think so. Though it might have just been a bargaining chip … to get her hands on my knife."

"Or she wants the next item."

"Maybe she thinks it contains enough power that she can use it to facilitate her transformation further."

"Anything that could kill a guardian would have to be that powerful."

"But I'm not sure she can access that magic, being a dragon. Though I obviously haven't laid hands on the next item myself. And none of this explains what she was doing in the Bahamas in the first place. The statue appeared to be of an adult woman, not a kid."

Kett offered this conundrum his version of a shrug — a slight lift of one shoulder. The motivations of others weren't something that particularly interested the vampire. He was all about end results. I gathered that held true for vamps in general. The 'why' was boring to ancient immortals. Only the final prize was worth their time.

"I just figured out how to read the map," I said. "But I barely got a glance."

"A glance will do," Kett said.

"Oh, yeah?" I asked, smiling at his confidence. "What do you propose to do with a glance? It didn't come with much detail. Just part of a landmass."

"We only need a general location. We have a powerful dowser for the rest."

"We'd still have to get the map out of my head. I doubt I could draw it with any accuracy. We could go to the far seer, but ..."

"That might take months."

"Yeah, and every time he touches me ..." I didn't finish my thought. Kett wasn't the right person to talk about the future with. Time meant little to him. Or it meant everything ... I wasn't totally sure, actually. But it didn't scare him in the least. I'd get no empathy from an immortal being whose very existence thwarted destiny ... twice.

Kett brushed his fingers lightly against the inside of my left wrist again. The cool kiss of his peppermint magic filled my mouth. That was all the comfort he had to give, and I'd take every last taste of it.

"The map," I said, forcing myself to refocus.

"San Francisco."

"Sorry?"

"There is an amplifier in San Francisco who will help me catch a glimpse of the map in your mind."

"Why not just take me to a reader?"

"Someone powerful enough to get through your innate ability to shield your thoughts is not someone to trust."

"That's some big condemnation coming from a vampire."

Kett inclined his head. "An elder of the Conclave," he said with a twist of a smile.

"Oh? A seat at the table, hey?" I wasn't sure if Kett was actually happy about this appointment or not. I know that Scarlett had refused a seat on the witches' Convocation for many years, though that might be more about her turbulent relationship with Gran rather than a concern over being mired in bureaucracy. Maybe Kett had similar concerns about his grandsire and paperwork.

"So I introduce you as 'elder' now? Not executioner?"

"I'm still the latter, but you should never have need to introduce me."

Right, there was that.

"You're going to need to pass through my wards to get to the portal," I said.

Kett showed his utter disgust at the idea of traveling by portal. Again, this was barely a twitch of his upper lip, but to me it screamed in ALL CAPS. Knowing a vampire this well was probably way, way bad for my health, but I was done with worrying about it.

"I'll meet you in San Francisco," he said. "I have the jet." Then he melted off into the shadows between the streetlights.

"Private jet, eh? Nice," I said. The vampire didn't respond.

No other plan or schedule ... just 'meet you in San Francisco.' At least it was a step forward when I didn't even know where else to start. If Shailaja had taken the map because she knew how to read it, then our only chance of stopping her might be beating her to the location of the second instrument of assassination.

"I'll need to change, at least." Though the taste of his magic was dim, I spoke into the air as if he could still hear me.

"I'll text you," he said, his breath cool on the back of my neck. "Bring the dragon."

I wanted to spin around and grab him just to prove that I could, but I didn't want to ruin his game. He liked to play, and I missed that part of my life.

"San Francisco," I muttered as I turned to look back at the bakery windows. "That's new."

Again, the bakery was more trashed than my brain was ready to acknowledge. And here I was, ready to run off and hunt a possibly insane teenage dragon with Kett.

As I watched through the splintered front door, Warner stepped from the kitchen to survey the ruin of the storefront. His face was a storm of emotion. He looked up to see me watching him.

I tried to smile, but I couldn't force the expression to actually manifest.

I was suddenly so cold.

I wrapped my arms around my chest and stepped back into the bakery. The adrenaline was wearing off, but the anger was still simmering in my soul.

Chapter Four

/stepped through my newly constructed wards, never breaking my gaze from Warner as he crossed around the still intact bakery display case. The blood magic clung to me like a comforting cobweb. Yeah, it was probably a bad sign that I found the byproduct of blood magic comforting.

Warner was dressed in dragon training leathers, and his dark blond, newly chopped short hair highlighted his wide brow. Actually, everything about the sentinel was wide — jaw, shoulders, hands — and too big, too manly to be considered beautiful, which was fine by me. Preferred, even. He wore the sacrificial knife I'd created in London openly displayed in a sheath built into his leather pants on the left thigh, though he drew with his right hand.

Normally I'd take a moment to ogle his leather-enhanced, hard-muscled physique, but I shivered instead. The chill that had grabbed me outside still had a hold on me.

Warner ran his dark-green gaze down and across every inch of me as I moved to stand before him, crushing the broken glass still covering the floor of the entrance underneath my boots as I went.

This look — so full of concern, then rage — was not the one I'd anticipated when I'd smoothed on black tights and a cashmere sweater dress this morning.

"You are unharmed," he said.

"Yes."

"Who has done this?" The heat of his question sent a shivered thrill through the cold settling into my bones.

He was angry. Absolutely livid. Smoldering with it. My dragon … ready to inflict his brutal justice on the culprit.

I smiled, an involuntary and inappropriate response. "The kid."

"The child dragon?" The sentinel was the sharpest tool in the bakery, which was completely fine by me. Especially because he didn't seem to find me slow at all.

"She calls herself Shailaja now," I said.

Warner stilled. "Shailaja?" he echoed, though he pronounced it differently. Harsher. More German, his accent breaking through his adopted speech patterns for some reason.

"She's a teenager now," I said, filling the awkward space that had suddenly wedged between us. "She pulled all the magic from my necklace. She was holding the leeches over Scarlett and Gran, and she pretty much forced me to somehow help her absorb it. Or use it to counter whatever was containing her magic."

"A teenager," Warner muttered. I was getting the idea I wasn't the only one in shock now. And something about Warner's shock was putting me on edge … well, further out along the edge I was already perched on.

"She said something about needing more magic, but then Gran kicked her ass."

Warner hadn't taken his gaze from me, but he'd been looking more through me than at me since I'd mentioned the crazed koala's name. Though he did look momentarily impressed by Gran's magical prowess, so he was listening.

"Shailaja was the former treasure keeper's daughter," he finally said.

"I know."

He nodded, not bothering to question where I'd come by this knowledge.

"You knew her, then?" I asked.

"I did," Warner answered. "Guardians do not often have children after they have ascended. The former treasure keeper and my mother had been guardians for at least five or six hundred years before they chose to procreate. In contrast, you are the only child of a guardian in your generation. It was unusual that there were two of us when I was ... younger."

"So you 'knew her' knew her?"

Warner's reaction was awkward and stilted enough that I had to get the big question out of the way, and out of my mind.

"I don't understand the significance of the repetition. We met when I began training at fourteen. She was a few years older."

"You were together?"

"We were no more than ... children of guardians."

"Sounds to me like something to bond over." I narrowed my eyes to let him know I was serious.

"Indeed," he answered. Then he curled his lip in a smirk. "I gather your jealousy indicates that things are not as dire here as they appear."

"I'm not jealous of that crazy ... b ... witch." Warner raised an eyebrow at me, then crossed his arms and settled his hip back against the counter as if he was waiting for some confession.

"You haven't kissed me yet!" I cried. Hell, if I was going to be irrational, I was going to go all the way.

Warner had his arms around me before I'd even spoken the last word. The taste of his black-forest-cake magic — all creamy dark chocolate and sweet cherry — enveloped me as he ran his hands up my arms to grasp my shoulders, then captured my lips with his.

I sighed, opening my mouth to him and pressing my body fully against his. Everything about Warner was broad, and all that broadness made me feel deliciously petite. I loved feeling petite.

"Don't be angry with me," he murmured against my lips. "Shailaja broke with the guardians. That was … unprecedented. And when she disappeared altogether …"

I wrapped my arms around his neck and lightly rubbed my cheek against his rough jaw. "When she disappeared?" I prompted.

"I thought … that the warrior —"

"Yazi? My dad?"

"The former warrior," Warner clarified. "It is the warrior's task to execute any sentence."

I pulled slightly away from Warner so I could see his face. He looked grim. The sentinel never withheld information from me, but some days I wouldn't mind that information coming with a bit of candy coating.

"My father is the executioner of the dragons?"

"If necessary. The sword delivers a clean death. But any sentence that doesn't fall to the warrior becomes the treasure keeper's responsibility."

"Because Pulou keeps more than just treasure." Yep, that was a new tidbit. There was a dragon prison somewhere. I shuddered to think what it contained.

"Yes."

"So the instruments of assassination aren't the only weapons capable of killing a guardian."

"The warrior's sword has never been raised against another guardian. I doubt it's been raised against any dragon more than once in a millennia."

"But you're saying my father is powerful enough to kill guardians."

"No."

"No?"

"I don't know."

"I don't like it when you don't know something."

"I know."

I sighed and pressed my face into the curve of Warner's neck, welcoming his warmth and momentarily blocking my sight of the destruction of my bakery.

He ran his fingers through the curls at the top of my head. Then down my neck and between my shoulder blades to the small of my back. Then up again.

I wanted to stay crushed against him forever, but I couldn't ignore the heavy pit of guilt in my stomach any longer.

"She has the map," I said, hoping my words were completely incomprehensible when muttered against his neck.

Warner's hand stilled. "She took it deliberately?"

"Kett asked the same thing."

"The vampire was here?"

"After. Before you returned."

Warner stayed silent, thinking, and I didn't interrupt or break our embrace. In a minute, we'd have to be moving forward, and I wanted to delay that for every second possible.

"It was unfortunate that the vampire wasn't here for the altercation, or Kandy," Warner said. His tone was distant, as if he was thinking out loud. "I understand that vampires are almost as skilled at tracking as werewolves."

"Not in this case," I said. "She was swarmed by the shadow leeches, then disappeared like she did in the fortress in Hope Town."

"She's in league with the shadow demons, then. I thought … perhaps … that there was a chance that the shadows had simply kidnapped her from the fortress." Warner — for all his assertion of not being romantically involved with Shailaja — sounded pained at this prospect.

I looked up at him. He offered me a fleeting smile. An affectation he'd picked up from me … and Scarlett, smiling through pain. Sometimes I wasn't sure how well I knew Warner, or how much of his persona was constructed through the chameleon nature of his dragon abilities.

"I guess it was silly to think a six-hundred-year-old boyfriend wouldn't come with a past, when every twenty-plus-year-old I know probably has a worse one."

Warner's grin widened. "I'm not six hundred years old," he said, falling readily into the fight I always picked with him. "I'm at most fifty-five … and who are all these twenty-plus-year-olds that you know?" He capped his playful banter with a sexy growl and a possessive squeeze of my hips. "They sound far too young for the warrior's daughter."

I kissed him, again pressing myself against the long length of him, but now being on the edge of rough with the lip lock. God, I adored this man. I adored that he knew when to be serious and when to be playful. I adored that he was possessive, and yet believed that I was more than capable of taking care of myself.

I adored that he liked Kandy, and ... well ... tolerated Kett. Or at least the idea of Kett, because they hadn't exactly spent much time together yet.

I flicked my tongue in and out of his mouth. He groaned so softly that I felt it more than heard it. The involuntary noise turned my limbs to mush. He always seemed so in control, and it was way sexy to hear him otherwise.

"We should probably go after the map," I said, regretfully breaking contact with his lips just enough to speak ... between kisses, of course. "But I can't leave the bakery like this for Bryn to find. She'll call the police."

"Is it your brownie's day off?" Warner asked, still paying more attention to kissing me than anything else.

"Jesus, sixteenth century, you can't go around being rampantly racist anymore," I chided, attempting to remain playful and remember that he grew up in a completely different world. "Bryn is First Nations."

"Brownies are not connected to First Nations ancestry." Warner nuzzled my neck.

We were like freaking chaste teenagers. "God," I groaned. "I'm so tired of acting like I'm sixteen. We get the map back, then we're going straight to bed."

"I'm not sure what acting like you're sixteen has to do with that —"

"Well, I don't know what the hell a brownie is either," I cried, aware that I was being utterly, frustratingly dramatic and over the top again. "Other than a girl who aspires to sell cookies or graduates to sell cookies. You know, Brownie. Like a baby Girl Scout."

He had no idea what I was talking about. I clenched my fists, barely stopping myself from hauling off and punching him in the shoulder.

Warner eyed me. "Your mood is shifting rapidly tonight."

"Don't you dare."

He tilted his head, and now eyed me like the minefield I was. When he spoke, he did so slowly and deliberately. "You're angry, and you keep stuffing that anger away. I certainly don't mind being a distraction, but perhaps you would feel better if we went after the map."

"There goes any chance of being mysterious and compelling," I grumbled. Then I covered my face with my hands, digging my fingertips into my sinus cavities around my eyes in an attempt to relieve my growing headache.

"I find you exceedingly compelling, warrior's daughter."

I peeked through my fingers to find Warner grinning at me. A look that demanded to be kissed off his face.

"Stop grinning at me like that," I growled in mock frustration. "Or we'll never get the map back."

Warner dropped the grin. "We'll get the map back, Jade."

I bobbed my head in unconvinced agreement and stepped back from him to survey the ruin of the bakery. "It's going to take hours to clean this, and I can't even call Gran's handyman until morning. Or at least that would be the polite thing to do."

"Which is why I asked after the brownie I assumed you'd acquired to clean," Warner said, still keeping his tone measured and even for my sake, rather than his own. I got the distinct impression he liked me a little crazy.

"I don't know what a brownie is," I said.

"I wondered why you were washing the bowl of the standing mixer the other day ... Again, I assumed it was the brownie's day off."

"That was two weeks ago," I grumbled. Annoyingly, dragons didn't wear watches or follow any particular calendar. "So brownies clean?"

"Among other things, such as the repairs the door needs."

"And I can just hire one?"

"Well, no. They choose," Warner said. "They set their terms. And you don't pay them, not with money."

"And a brownie is an … elf?"

Warner looked aghast. "Absolutely not!"

Okay. I should have expected that a cleaning elf would be criminally insane. I hadn't even known for sure that elves existed beyond fairy tales and whatnot until he reacted like that.

"What elf do you know?" Warner narrowed his eyes at me. "They're worse than vampires. Have you befriended one? How does it enter this dimension? Does your father know?"

I crossed my arms and narrowed my eyes right back at him. I had no idea what the hell he was talking about, but I was learning to bluff. Dragons liked to appear all knowing — and, unlike certain vampires, they could usually deliver that — so it was better to appear all knowing right back at them.

"The brownie?" I prompted.

Warner huffed, then begrudgingly dropped the topic of elves. "We can make a request when we cross through the nexus. I assume you have a plan that involves telling the treasure keeper about she-who-claims-the-name-Shailaja?"

Right. I'd been hoping to avoid the chat with the treasure keeper, actually.

"So that's how it's going to be?" I asked. "She-who-claims?"

"That is for the best."

"Whatever." I was exhausted already, and was guessing there would be no nap time in my near future. "I need to change."

"You look quite fetching."

And just like that, I was grinning at my dragon like an idiot again. Even though I had only a loose understanding of what 'fetching' meant to Warner, I got the context through his tone.

"It'll be warmer in San Francisco."

"San Francisco?"

"Yeah, we've got a date with a vampire."

"Great. Just … great."

I laughed, and the last of the tension between us dissolved.

I tiptoed upstairs to my apartment in the dark to find my satchel, which Gran had left on the steamer trunk coffee table in the living room. The bag tasted of her lilac-and-grass magic until I looped it over my head so it slung across my body to rest on my left hip. Then it just felt like part of me, similar to my necklace and knife. I wondered if Gran had the time to complete the containment spell she'd promised me before she fell asleep, but I didn't want to wake her to ask. She had taken Scarlett's bed, and my mother was curled up in mine.

After checking the weather app on my phone, I decided that it wasn't too warm in San Francisco for an outfit that Warner obviously liked. So I just added rosy lip gloss to my ensemble, then jogged downstairs to grab some American cash out of the newly repaired safe in the tiny office off the bakery kitchen. I'd learned to always have various currencies and my passport securely zipped in a side pocket of my satchel at all times these days.

Before I locked the safe, I also — rather mournfully — tucked Kett's vampire wedding rings onto the top shelf. I wasn't going to have the time to attach them properly to my necklace until I dealt with my rabid koala problem, and I didn't want to risk losing that rare gift.

I remembered to leave a note for Gran and Scarlett about 'brownies' not just being the chocolate delicious ones you can eat, and to let them know I was heading into the nexus to confront ... err, talk to Pulou.

Warner was waiting for me in the bakery basement. He hadn't bothered flicking on the bare light bulb that hung in the middle of the room. He actually couldn't stand perfectly straight down here. The ceiling was low, only six feet.

He turned to watch me walk down the wooden stairs from the pantry, but his expression was more serious than admiring.

"Your new blood wards are powerful, but they don't block the portal," he said. "It's still open to anyone who knows of its existence."

"Yeah, Gran mentioned that. But I don't think I can ward against the treasure keeper's magic."

Warner touched the concrete and brick wall before him thoughtfully. I waited for him to question my use of blood magic, but he didn't. Dragons might be a judgmental bunch, but magic didn't scare them. Or maybe they just didn't see it in terms of good and evil, as witches did.

"Nor can I," he said, dropping his hand to his side. "But it's a concern."

"You think Shailaja could use it?"

Warner shrugged. "If she is the daughter of the former treasure keeper."

His 'if' hung between us, but I didn't bother to stoke the fight that could potentially lie behind it. If Warner wanted proof of Shailaja's identity, that was his prerogative.

"Only Pulou, you, and I know of this doorway," I said. "I understood it was constructed by the current treasure keeper, not the former."

"Your father doesn't know of it?"

"I don't think so."

"The warrior hasn't visited the bakery?"

"Not while I've been awake. Possibly never." I reached for the magic of the portal and bid it to open. Warner contemplated me, and perhaps the actions of my not-particularly-fatherly father. I didn't expect — or pine for — much parenting from Yazi, who'd only known of my existence for less than two years now. I'd been peachy keen for twenty-three years without a male role model.

"Your hair glows with golden fire in the magic of the portal," Warner murmured. So I wasn't the only one capable of being serious and flirty at the same time.

"The magic of the portal is golden, sixteenth century," I snarked as I stepped by him. "You might want to dig deeper with the wooing."

"Is it?" he murmured behind me.

I walked into the welcoming magic of the portal, reaching my hand back for Warner without turning. He linked his fingers loosely through mine. We didn't need to touch to cross together into the nexus — I barely needed to think about my destination anymore — but I liked reaching out to him. I liked that he always responded in kind.

Chapter Five

The magic of the portal buoyed me as I passed through it. However, I was pretty sure that what was really giving me the energy to walk away from my beloved bakery and pursue the crazy teenage dragon Shailaja was the handful of Inaya chocolate discs from Cacao Barry — a 65 percent blend of intense but balanced cocoa — that I crammed in my mouth as I'd crossed through the pantry.

"Speaking of teenage dragons," I said as Warner and I stepped through the door that connected the nexus to all the North American portals, not just to the bakery. "Watch out for Drake. He's already snuck up on me once today."

"The fledgling takes his training very seriously. But he has yet to sneak up on me." Warner grinned at me teasingly.

I stuck my tongue out at him and his grin widened. I laughed, glancing around the gilded, columned rotunda that was the core of the guardian nexus, aka the transportation station. But with portals, not trains or buses or airplanes. The other eight intricately decorated doors were currently closed. No dragon in sight ... or within reach of my dowser senses.

Though Drake could still sneak up on me, the more time I spent in the nexus, the more I adapted to the overwhelming magic that dwelled here. I'd been wondering for a while now if the nexus was situated on the grid point portal of all grid point portals — the wellspring, perhaps — or whether it was simply that the residual magic from nine demigods left a brain-melting impression.

"You know … speaking of teenagers —"

"No," Warner said, cutting off my foolhardy thought before I fully articulated it. "No to Drake. He doesn't need any more encouragement. And I don't wish to raise the ire of the fire breather."

"She might be thawing. See what I did there? Fire … thawing …"

"No," Warner repeated. "She's beginning to think you're useful. That's not the same."

"I miss Kandy. You're not as fun, Mr. Sentinel."

Warner grinned. "I'm not the same kind of fun."

I laughed but didn't follow his flirty lead. I felt like a good portion of my attention and a hunk of my heart was still pulled back through the closed portal straight into the trashed bakery. "So this … brownie?"

Warner thrust his hand into my satchel and pulled out the half-eaten Ritual Chocolate bar that I'd partially shared with Drake in the library.

"Hey!" I yelled, instantly ready to wrestle him for it. Obviously, Gran's containment spell didn't protect against thieving dragons. Though she hadn't promised that —

Warner tossed the bar over his shoulder like it was a piece of trash. I barely managed to stop myself from gouging his eyes out, and just ended up staring at him as if he'd gone completely bonkers instead.

He winked at me.

The bar disappeared from the pristine white marble floor.

I stifled a scream of frustration over wasted chocolate. "I've seen that cleaning spell before." I gritted the words out between clenched teeth, aware I had my hand resting on the invisible knife at my hip. Chocolate bar stealing wasn't worth a gutting, but throwing away fantastic chocolate might be.

"Mistress Winterbloom?" Warner called. "The warrior's daughter has a request."

I gave him a look. It wasn't a nice one. I was almost certain he was screwing with me. I hadn't quite figured out his sense of humor yet.

A reedy voice spoke from behind me. "Mistress Winterbloom no longer attends the guardians, Warner, sentinel of the instruments of assassination, son of Jiaotu-who-was. She has retired her placement and moved into the beyond."

I flinched. It was rare these days that anyone magical snuck up on me. I slowly pivoted to see a tiny woman with olive skin and massive brown eyes standing behind me. She was holding my half-eaten chocolate bar in hands that looked way too large for her tiny body. She stood about a foot and a half tall and was wearing a tunic similar to the one the far seer preferred, but without the gold stitching.

The brownie — assuming the name wasn't part of whatever elaborate joke Warner might or might not be playing on me — scanned me toe to head, then down again. She clicked her tongue, but I couldn't tell if it was an affectation or disapproval of my outfit.

"I have slept many years," Warner said. He hadn't moved from behind me. "Are you Mistress Winterbloom's daughter or granddaughter?"

The brownie tilted her head to look around me, and I stepped to the side so she had a clear line of sight to Warner.

"Grandniece," she said. Then with a flash of pale pink magic — or maybe pale peach — tasting of lemon verbena, she smoothed the cardboard wrapping of the chocolate bar and tucked the ragged foil neatly back inside. She even repaired the cardboard tab opening that I'd ripped though I was trying to be careful. The restored chocolate bar now looked pristinely new. "Winterblossom. Miss."

"Pleased to meet you, Miss Winterblossom," Warner said. "The warrior's daughter's place of business has been attacked."

The brownie's eyes widened as Warner spoke, until they occupied over half her face. Then they narrowed with anger. "The bakery?" she squeaked fiercely. She curled her too-large hands into fists and placed them at her hips.

"Yes, but —" I said.

She disappeared.

I whirled to look at Warner questioningly.

"Wait," he said. Then he turned toward the other half of the nexus and scanned the closed doors. "Treasure keeper, the sentinel and the alchemist attend you."

His words — or, rather, the magic conveyed by his words — hung suspended in the air for a moment. Then the polished ebony-etched door that led to the territory of Southern Africa — Baxia's domain — clicked open to swallow the summons. I hadn't had any interaction with Baxia, also known as the rain bringer, since I'd first tumbled into the nexus. The fact that I'd been dragging a demon with me hadn't made me many BFFs among the guardians, though I didn't get the sense that Baxia had even spared me a second glance. From Drake, I'd heard that she preferred to walk the soil of her territory rather than the hard marble of the nexus. I hazarded a guess that it was the politics that kept her away. Politics and bickering that I'd only begun to really notice since retrieving the first instrument of assassination.

Miss Winterblossom appeared before me, with a noticeable but muted popping sound announcing her arrival. So apparently, she didn't always sneak up on ignorant Adepts.

"Unbelievable," she spat. "What immoral creature would do such a thing to such an oasis?"

And I instantly and desperately loved her. She'd seen my wounded soul and felt protective of it. I opened my mouth, but she silenced me with an upthrust palm.

"I will make it right," she declared. Then with a flick of her large hands, she unfurled a pink apron with a ruffled edge, emblazoned with the Cake in a Cup logo.

Then she spun, becoming a blur of pink-streaked browns. When she stilled, she was wearing the apron like a sleeveless dress. She smoothed her hands over it. Then with great satisfaction, she tucked my half-eaten chocolate bar in the front pocket, which spanned her chest.

"Thank you, Miss Winterblossom," I said, not really knowing what the hell was going on at all.

"You may call me Blossom," she said. "I like cake in a cup." Then she disappeared.

"Umm," I said, looking at Warner for an explanation.

He grinned. "She comes and goes as she wishes. She doesn't belong to you."

"Of course not."

"You don't pay her, I mean. But you may leave her gifts."

"Like the chocolate bar?"

"I believe she just expressed her preference for cupcakes."

"Right."

"It's a blessing to have a brownie in your household, but they will not tolerate any slight from you ... or an invading force. Their magic is simple but powerful. As you've noted, the family usually passes down the responsibility of a household through generations."

Warner was more confident in my powers of observation than I was. "Okay. And the apron?"

"Claiming her place, Cake in a Cup, and probably your apartment. They are now ... well ... her dominion. Brownies can get a bit possessive with age, but Blossom appears to be younger."

Lovely. "Younger than the sixteenth century, at least," I said. "And the tunic she was wearing? Have I just swiped the far seer's brownie?"

Warner laughed.

"That's not an answer," I grumbled. "Chi Wen scares you just as badly as he scares me."

Warner sobered instantly. "The far seer doesn't scare me. Neither does the future ... except for the parts I'll miss."

The air was suddenly heavy with everything that was still unsaid between Warner and me. With everything that naturally always took time to know about another person, but also with everything I was pretty sure was keeping him out of my bed.

My internal musings — on the barriers between Warner, me, and my bed — slammed up against thoughts of the mission or hunt that we were about to embark on. Then it all clicked into place. The pain of my own stupidity lanced through my heart like a heated needle, wickedly sharp.

"Shailaja has the map," I whispered.

He nodded tersely.

Oh, God. I hadn't thought through the ramifications. Warner was the sentinel of the instruments of assassination. Even Blossom had known.

"Oh, God." The seared pinch of pain in my heart expanded as my mind exploded with the worst of the consequences of losing the map to Shailaja. "I should have ... maybe I could have ... I just let her take it!" I broke out in a light sweat, feeling the beginnings of panic.

"It will be fine."

"You're tied to the map."

"No," Warner said, his voice measured and his phrasing carefully chosen. "I'm tied to the instruments or to an incursion of the location of the instruments."

"That's the same thing!" Now I was shrieking, which wasn't at all sexy, but I couldn't seem to stop. I'd just done one of the stupidest things I'd ever done before. All because I'd been trying to not hurt a kid.

"It's not," Warner said. He brushed his fingertips against my cheek, giving me a taste of his magic.

I closed my eyes against the concern and compassion in his green-blue gaze. "I fucked up."

"I'm tied to the map, yes," Warner said, "because that was the strongest way the former treasure keeper could anchor that part of the sentinel ... sorry, I don't know the proper word in English ... the sentinel's magical installation? Incantation? Invocation?"

"In his own skin."

"Exactly." Warner maintained his soothing tone, reinforcing it by lightly running his fingers along my upper arm.

Goddamn it, I was such a baby.

"We know that the treasure keeper had somehow retrieved the key to the fortress of the braids," Warner said. "So he must —"

"The centipede!" I shouted in his face.

He paused in his babying of me to raise a questioning — maybe even slightly irritated — eyebrow. I liked that a lot better than the babying.

"Sorry, that was abrupt. The key to the second map is already imbedded in the tattoo. The blocks on the side move to form a centipede, and then —"

The door to Southern Africa blew open with a blast of heat and rain that hit us like a hurricane.

I stumbled to keep my footing. Warner just leaned into the onslaught. Had I been questioned about it two seconds before, I would have sworn that weather couldn't travel through the portals or enter into the nexus.

Baxia stepped through the open portal onto the white marble floor. Her otherwise bare feet were adorned with exceedingly cute golden toe rings and ankle bracelets inlaid with various gems. The storm that had pummeled Warner and me whipped back and around the guardian of Southern Africa. This left us exceeding damp and windblown, whereas Baxia's bright African-inspired print maxi dress appeared to be bone-dry. Her ebony skin reminded me of the finest dark chocolate from Madagascar. I tamped down on the pure envy that rose as I stood before the powerful and beautiful guardian.

The rain bringer had come to the nexus.

Pulou stepped through the portal after Baxia, his fur coat showing no evidence of him having just walked through a hurricane. The remaining vortex of water and heat snapped back with the magic of the portal as the door closed behind the guardians.

Warner dropped to one knee and I curtsied deeply. I'd never actually spoken directly to the rain bringer. I understood her guardian gifts had something to do with water, or the control of water. Either way, a guardian who was preceded by a hurricane was definitely someone to bow before.

"Alchemist," Baxia said. Though her accented English was lyrical, my title was spoken with a sharp edge, as if the guardian was unhappy to find me standing before her. "You do not have permission to enter my territory. If something lies between my borders that is deadly to guardians, you will let it sleep."

Pulou shifted his feet uncomfortably. I peeked up through my curls to see Baxia glaring at the treasure keeper.

"Is that understood?" she asked him. Her guardian magic — an intoxicating blend of too-dark-to-ever-be-sweet chocolate, well-ripened papaya, and a hint of tobacco that lingered long on my palate — momentarily rose to cloak her in a golden aura.

Wind stirred, lifting the unruly curls off my face. The storm threatened to return as the question — or, rather, the declaration of war — hung between the two guardians.

Pulou turned his stoic gaze on my still partially bowed head. Then I figured out the question had actually been directed to me … or at least through Pulou to me, but for me to answer.

"I understand, guardian," I said. "I would never walk where I wasn't welcomed."

"The map doesn't lead you to Africa?" Pulou asked, sounding as if maybe he was hoping it did. He was cruising for a bruising, as Gran would say.

Yeah, and guardians were supposed to be peace-keepers. "Not that I know of, treasure keeper," I answered. "We're here to request passage to San Francisco."

"The map leads you to North America?" Pulou asked. "A second time? That is surprising."

"Not the map —"

"No one enters my territory," Baxia repeated. Then she padded away. Magic glinted off her toe rings in a way that made me itch to add them to my necklace. Yeah, my magical magpie tendency was verging on obsessive-hoarder-disorder territory these days. I deliberately looked away from the guardian's flashy feet. I really wasn't interested in turning into Blackwell. The sorcerer was so obsessed with collecting powerful objects and powerful people that he'd allied himself with my blood-frenzied sister and risked the wrath of the West Coast North American Pack — twice. I knew which lines were not to be crossed. At least, I hoped I knew.

Pulou grumbled something that sounded suspiciously like, "Stroppy biddy." Then he turned to me. "You've unlocked the map, alchemist?"

I straightened, looking the treasure keeper directly in the eye and fully prepared to unleash every bit of the tongue-lashing he deserved for allowing Shailaja to run around unchecked.

Pulou eyed me expectantly.

Expectantly ... expecting that I had the ability to unlock the map and the skills to retrieve the instruments that threatened the existence of the dragons ...

Instruments that guardians couldn't even touch.

I snapped my mouth shut.

Pulou frowned. He looked at Warner, then back at me. Waiting.

I twined my fingers through the wedding rings of my necklace. Though it held only a fraction of the magic that it usually did, it grounded me.

"The child has returned," I said.

Pulou tilted his head, listening intently.

"Though she no longer wears the guise of a toddler. She's more of a teenager now ..." I knew I needed to get to the point about the map, but I was trying to figure out a way to ease into it.

"She calls herself Shailaja," Warner interjected.

Pulou looked at him sharply.

"She completely trashed the bakery and held Jade's family at the mercy of her shadow leeches, until the alchemist used the magic of her necklace to unlock the containment spell that held her in child form."

Pulou's expression turned stony, but was filled with disbelief. "Did you know her magic, sentinel?"

"No, guardian. Not while she was in her child form," Warner answered. "And unfortunately, I wasn't there when she attacked the bakery."

Pulou ran a hand through his short-cropped, slightly thinning brown hair. "This is difficult to believe."

Warner stiffened. "You doubt the alchemist?" He sounded ready to beat Pulou to a pulp for some insult that had gone completely over my head.

"No," Pulou answered, turning his gaze on me. "I apologize."

"I wasn't able to contain her," I said.

Pulou waved this statement off as if it was a given, or maybe just inconsequential.

"She took the map."

"Deliberately?"

"Why does everyone keep asking that?"

"It makes a difference, doesn't it?" Warner said, his muted tone informative rather than reprimanding. "With her presence at the fortress, and now tracking you."

"She was interested in my necklace … and my knife."

"In your magic," Warner countered. "To lift a spell that might have better been left in place."

Pulou sighed. "This is why guardians do not procreate easily … except when they're enthralled in a fertility ceremony." He smirked at me.

"My mother had something to do with that."

"A beautiful witch indeed," Pulou said, his voice trailing off as he lapsed into deep thought.

The silence stretched so long that I looked over at Warner to find him staring at me … the kind of staring that was probably completely inappropriate in front of a guardian dragon who was also pretty much my boss.

"You blame me." Pulou spoke so quickly that I flinched, then blushed over being caught staring deeply into my boyfriend's eyes. "For the child."

I shifted awkwardly, not sure how to answer without lying.

"The task I've set for you is dangerous, alchemist. No one would fault you for stepping away."

Well, that was insulting. "Then who else would do it if not me?"

"No one," Warner said quietly. "The warrior and I should track and apprehend the child who claims to be Shailaja, and let the other instruments lie hidden. As they should be."

Pulou eyed Warner, displeased that he was attempting to rehash their ongoing argument over the collection of the instruments of assassination.

"I'm not shirking," I said. Stupidly stubborn — that's me, all day long. "It's my fault she has the map. We get it back, then we can talk about the other stuff later."

"How did the child track you?" Pulou asked.

Err, I didn't actually know.

"Blood," Warner answered for me. "From when she bit you in the fortress."

Pulou narrowed his eyes. "The child of the treasure keeper," he murmured, like he was trying to piece together something.

"She'll come for Jade," Warner said.

"But she'll need another object of power first," I said. "She wanted my knife, but then decided I wasn't powerful enough to unlock a true dragon."

"You have a lead on the location of the second instrument?" Pulou asked. "One that takes you to San Francisco?"

"Yes," I answered. I didn't bother to mention that the 'lead' involved Kett. The guardians' prejudice toward vampires was so fervent that it bordered on genocidal.

"Then we will set a trap," Pulou said. "You and the sentinel will hunt the instrument. Since she believes she needs your assistance, alchemist, the child will most likely hunt you in turn. The warrior and I will follow when most appropriate or most able. Perhaps the far seer has you in his gaze, alchemist. That would be helpful."

Pulou eyed Warner contemplatively. The sentinel's countenance was stormy, to say the least, but that didn't appear to bother the treasure keeper. "It is too bad your mother is no longer with us, Warner Jiaotuson. I've never met a slyer hunter. Her successor is still young … and not an advocate of collecting the instruments."

"I'm not an advocate of Jade being bait," Warner said, completely ignoring the reference to his mother and being far too pissy for his own good.

Pulou stepped forward to clap a hand on Warner's shoulder. The sentinel actually stumbled under this friendly assault.

I attempted to hide my glee over Warner's protectiveness but completely failed.

Pulou smirked at me over Warner's bowed head. "The alchemist will have her way, sentinel. Which, in this instance, also happens to be my way. You will have to be content with the warrior and me at your backs." Pulou removed his hand from Warner's shoulder and looked at me. "I assume your father can track you?"

Err, I wasn't sure about that.

"You share magic," Pulou added. "As the children of guardians usually do."

Yeah, I hadn't missed the obvious link between my knife and my father's sword, either. We could both call our weapons forth with a mere thought, though my knife was carved out of jade and my father's sword was a manifestation of his demigod power. So 'sharing magic' with the warrior of the guardians seemed a bit of an extreme statement.

"Jade's personal magic acts like a natural shield," Warner said. "Especially when she wears the necklace."

"I'm not taking the necklace off," I said.

"Of course not." Pulou drew a nasty-looking dagger with an emerald-encrusted hilt from within his coat, then flicked the blade toward my face so quickly that all I could do was watch helplessly as it blurred by my cheek.

A two-inch lock of my hair fell into Pulou's open palm.

"What the hell!" I cried. "That's my hair. I have to, you know, grow it. Like deliberately."

Pulou laughed, as if I were simply being amusing. His expression suggested he thought I was oh so cute. And maybe I was, but not in this particularly pissed moment.

I crossed my arms and glared at the treasure keeper, then at Warner when he tried to cover his own laughter by coughing.

Jerks. Shag cuts were so 2014.

"So, San Francisco?" Pulou prompted.

Chapter Six

*I*was still grumbling about being shorn as Warner and I crossed back through the First Nations-carved door that led to North America via a portal that Pulou held open for us into San Francisco. We arrived in a posh living room filled with modern and uncomfortable-looking steel and glass furniture, but which looked oddly empty nonetheless. Lacking a personal touch, maybe. Not that I was one to judge ... all the homey touches in my apartment were courtesy of Scarlett.

"He needs the lock of hair to track you," Warner said as he systematically scanned the room.

"Well, I guess it's better than biting me."

The portal snapped shut behind us.

What appeared to be tall windows covered in light-filtering solar shades ran the entire length of the right-hand side of the main room. Highly polished dark gray concrete flooring spanned the living room into the kitchen and through the hallway beyond.

"Whose place is this?" I asked.

We were standing holding hands like school kids, so I couldn't taste a lick of any magic other than Warner's black forest cake, which was currently tickling my palm. All the multitude of possibilities presented by an empty apartment in the middle of a city where no one knew us ran quickly through my head. Maybe the square-edged gray couch didn't look quite as uncomfortable as I'd previously thought.

"Haoxin's, I imagine," Warner said.

"San Francisco is a seat of power for the guardians? Really?"

Warner laughed. "I believe her family is from the area."

"Sorry?" The idea that guardians had family shouldn't have been so surprising, but it was. "Her family? I mean I know that not all dragons live in the nexus."

"Actually, only the nine and Drake reside in the nexus."

"Branson?"

"He has an apartment in Shanghai … as do many of the dragons. Drake's family was from there. His mother was apprenticed to Chi Wen before the fire."

I stared at Warner. Yes, with my mouth hanging open. "Okay, you've been awake for like three months and you know about everyone's family lineage?"

Warner laughed in a slightly stilted way that made me regret the 'awake' part of my comment. "Not much has changed," he said. "I simply figured out the new parts … Haoxin, Qiuniu, Drake, Branson, your father …"

"And Jiaotu."

"Yes."

The dragon who currently carried the mantle of Jiaotu the silver tongued had held the position for only three hundred years or so. He'd inherited it from Warner's mother. He was really kind of a jerk — a friend of Suanmi's — but I kept my mouth shut about that because I assumed Warner and the guardian of Northern Europe had some otherworldly connection that I didn't want to mess around with.

"Do you ... I mean ... This is an odd question to ask my boyfriend. Did you ... do you have a home?"

"It still stands, but I've been staying in the nexus." Warner squeezed my hand, then dropped it. I sensed the Q&A was over, as it should be. We had a map to retrieve — a map that was key to more than just a second instrument of assassination. A map that could possibly be used to summon Warner. Maybe even into a deadly situation.

"Where does it stand?" I asked Warner as he crossed to open the window shades. "Your home?"

"Stockholm, Sweden," Warner answered. "A townhouse in Gamla Stan ... Old Town."

"But your accent ... your natural one ... sounds German."

"My father was German." Warner paced the length of the shades, unable to figure out how to open them.

"He raised you," I said. "Like Gran raised me."

"My mother was the guardian of Northern Europe." His tone was closed off, stiff. Though I thought it might be the shades that were bothering him, not my questions.

I glanced around, spotting a Control4 in-wall touch-screen panel to the right of what I assumed was the front door. I crossed to the panel, rejigging my assessment of the apartment from posh to exceedingly posh. Haoxin certainly knew how to spend money on modern conveniences. I stepped closer to peer at the panel, then started randomly selecting icons.

The first of those controlled the lighting. Flat-mounted pot lights eased on to highlight the modern art hanging over the sandstone fireplace. The painting just looked like a stormy sky to me. But then, I knew nothing about art. In the center of the main room, nine glass pendant lights shaped like teardrops illuminated the glass-and-steel dining table with a blue-tinted glow.

It took a bit more digging to trigger the shades, which rolled up and tucked into the window casings as if they no longer existed.

"Wow," I said. "I guess we're in San Francisco all right."

The apartment was in a high-rise that boasted sweeping views of the bay and what I was fairly certain was the Golden Gate Bridge. The evening below us was awash in bright city lights that faded at the edge of the dark water. If the moon was out, I couldn't see it.

"The human technology is impressive," Warner said as he gazed out at the city. "But Vancouver is more beautiful."

If I were making a pro and con list about dating Warner — not that I was ... at least not on paper — loyalty would definitely fall in the top five of the pro column.

The broad shoulders and great ass I was currently ogling while he surveyed the streets below us would be in that top five as well.

I sighed and fished the lead-lined case that held my cellphone out of my satchel. I was pretty sure I'd already figured out what icon on the control panel triggered the fireplace, and no matter how stiff the sofa looked, I knew I wouldn't mind doing some 'lounging.' Unfortunately, duty was dictating this trip, not my hormones.

I booted up my phone and wandered into the kitchen area, which was so pristinely clean it might never have been used. A brand new iPhone and iPad sat in docks to the far right of a white quartz counter that ran the length of the wall, breaking only for the convection cooktop and the gorgeous — and insanely expensive — Sub-Zero fridge at the far corner. No pretty, terribly useful island. Not a single appliance on the counter. Un-used and unloved.

Happily my phone had started. I was always anticipating a time when the lead box would lose its effectiveness as a barrier against the magic of the nexus and the portals, which had a tendency to fry technol-ogy. "So brownies clean all these places for you guys?" I asked as I applied my thumbs to my phone and texted Kett.

We're here.

"Usually," Warner answered. "Though occa-sionally they will take exception, and it takes years of cajoling to mend the breach."

"Breach?"

"Don't ever offer to pay a brownie and you will be fine. You're respectful and kind. Unprejudiced."

"Oh, yeah? Would you put those traits in my top five?"

"Top five?"

"On the list of reasons to date me."

Warner grinned, the smile transforming his serious 'sentinel' mode into 'sexy dragon stalking across the liv-ing room toward me' mode.

I laughed — a low, husky sound I'd started making when I was around Warner — and leaned back against the kitchen counter to take a moment to enjoy watching him.

Normally, I liked this part of a courtship. The get-ting-to-know-you butterflies, the surreptitious glances, the thumbs rubbing against wrists while holding hands at a movie. But with Warner, I was ready to dive in, to feel his warmth, to truly taste his magic. Still, I had this foreboding shadow at the back of my mind … a 'what if' shadow that I had to constantly brush away to stay in the right now, right here.

Warner closed the space between us, then reached over to smooth one of my curls between his forefinger and middle finger. He stopped halfway down.

No, correction. He was holding the curl that Pulou had shorn. Teasing me with it.

I narrowed my eyes at him.

His grinned widened.

"Are you playing with me, sentinel?" I purred as dangerously as I could. Baking cupcakes most of my days didn't give me much of a hard edge to access.

"Yes."

Ah. The slumbering butterflies deep in my belly woke up.

My phone beeped.

"Goddamn it to freaking hell," I grumbled. I was doing way too much grumbling these days.

Warner laughed as I glanced at my phone. The tilt of my head freed the curl from his grasp, and I tried not to mourn that lost connection.

> *I've been waiting.*

I was surrounded by grumpy old men. Kett ... Pulou ... Hell, I was becoming one of them. I texted back.

It hasn't even been an hour.

> *It's been twenty-eight hours exactly.*

I looked up at Warner, then out the window, where it appeared no later than it had been when we left Vancouver. "Kett says he's been waiting over a day."

Warner shrugged.

"That means she has a crazy head start," I said. "She could have the instrument by now!"

"No." Warner's tone and shoulders were tense as he stepped back to the living room windows. "I would know."

Right. Except ...

"Except she got into the fortress of the braids without waking you last time."

"I've been thinking about that."

"And?"

"Either she can indeed mask her presence from me ... from the guardian magic that binds me to my task, which I think is highly unlikely ..."

"Or?"

"Or it was the magic of the fortress that kept her hidden. Had she managed to retrieve the artifact and remove it from the fortress, it's likely I would have been called to her location."

My phone pinged.

>*Still waiting.*

Great. My boyfriend was laying out possible truths on me while the vampire was getting pissy. I texted back.

Where should we meet you?

"Okay," I said, breathing deeply to moderate my rising panic. "We have time, then."

Warner nodded but didn't answer. I felt like apologizing for losing the map again but kept my mouth shut.

> *Pier 43 1/2 Fisherman's Wharf.*

I googled 'Fisherman's Wharf' and 'Pier 43 1/2' though I thought the second part might be way too obscure to be helpful. I had to wait a beat for my map app to figure out I wasn't in Vancouver anymore. According to the blue dot, we were only blocks away. I texted back to Kett.

Ten minutes.

"Kett sent an address. I texted that we could be there in ten minutes."

Warner nodded, then closed the space between us, brushing his shoulder against mine comfortingly. "We'll find the map, Jade."

"Okay."

"Good. Okay."

My phone pinged again.

>*Bring your dancing shoes.*

We're going dancing?

>*That's what you call it.*

What do you call it?

>*Hunting.*

Then he sent me a red devil emoticon.

"The vampire just sent me an emoticon," I said with utter disbelief.

"I have no idea what that is," Warner said archly as he crossed to the door. He might be okay with Kett for my sake, but he wasn't going to be friendly about it.

Warner deliberately and carefully folded his hand around the door handle, but then waited without opening it. The handle glowed with golden magic that rose to swirl around his hand. Then the door clicked open.

Warner grinned at my questioning look. "In case we want to come back," he said. "You should leave an imprint as well. Human technology might be fun, but magic trumps it every time."

I shook my head. "I wouldn't be so sure about that, sixteenth century. Humans have created some highly destructive weapons in the last seventy-five years alone."

Warner snorted.

I let the subject drop as I crossed to the door. Now that it was open, I could see the inactive runes on the inner doorframe. "Wards on a guardian's apartment. Who would dare enter it?"

"Any who thought a portal might lie inside."

"A portal that would take them to their deaths in the nexus. If they could even figure out how to walk through it in the first place."

Warner shrugged. "I doubt they would die for their stupidity, but I believe we've already established that not all Adepts love dragons. Or wish to be ruled by the guardian nine."

"Like the eternal-life sorcerers."

"Yes. Shadow leeches now, as you call them."

"Yeah, I was still hoping their origin was just a guess."

"A well-reasoned one." Warner stepped into the hall, scanned left, then right, and crossed toward an elevator.

I was a complete Pollyanna when it came to the practicing of black magic. Except, of course, when performing it myself. Imagining Shailaja as a child — or even a teenager — sacrificing sorcerer after sorcerer to move through the traps of the fortress of the braids made me ill. As best I'd figured, she'd summoned some sort of demonic entity through the deaths of the sorcerers ... but to what end? Consume their souls? Their magic at least. And now those entities were tied to the rabid koala. That was their 'eternal life.' I shuddered at the thought.

Pushing all the what-ifs that kept accumulating without definitive answers out of my head, I pressed my hand to the door handle, keying the lock to my magic. While I waited, I glanced down the hall to see Warner examining what I assumed was the stairwell door, based on the glowing red exit sign above it.

The only other door in the corridor was the un-numbered one across from me. The entire floor appeared to contain only two penthouse apartments. Again, posh.

"Alarmed," Warner said, dismissing the stairs.

"How would you know, sixteenth century?" I teased.

He laughed. "The sign was pretty clear about using it only in case of emergencies."

I laughed, tugging the apartment door closed behind me to follow Warner into the elevator.

Then we stepped out into the night to dance … or to hunt with a vampire.

San Francisco was a lot like Vancouver, only way bigger. The similarities — as far as I could see quickly and at night — included green parkland between the city and the water, a big bridge spanning a body of water to connect residential areas, and wharves and warehouses — some converted, some not — on the waterfront. San Francisco's streets were laced with tram tracks, while Vancouver had trolley bus lines zigzagging above its major streets.

I was, however, exceedingly disappointed to discover that the Ghirardelli Chocolate Factory was no longer in operation. The massive red brick building that occupied an entire city block was now called Ghirardelli Square, and housed a bunch of retail shops that hawked way more than chocolate.

Though if we were still here tomorrow, I was so dropping by the chocolate marketplace and denting my credit card. Thankfully, portal magic didn't melt artisan chocolate. Of course, getting it by the dragons unplundered would be a feat.

Warner and I hustled by the square with its taunting, massive steel signage screaming GHIRARDELLI over my head. You know, as if the entire building contained nothing but vats upon vats of chocolate … Okay, obviously I was having a hard time letting that dream scenario go.

I managed to pass Norman's Ice Cream & Freezes without stopping, though I cranked my neck awkwardly to peek through the crowd at the window. Then all that stood between us and the wide, dark bay was Fisherman's Wharf.

We took a right turn on Embarcadero after the Chowder Hut. "I could seriously go for some halibut and chips. Or clam chowder," I said. Yeah, so I was highly suggestible. What else was new?

I checked my phone. "According to the blue dot, we're here."

"The vampire wants to meet us at ..." — Warner glanced up at the sign hanging above our heads, which depicted a mermaid riding a giant crab — "...the Franciscan Crab?"

"Can't you feel it, dragon?" Kett's cool voice emanated from the darkness at the top of the beige-and-black-tiled stairs that led to the second floor of the restaurant. I imagined the eatery boasted some of the best waterfront views in San Francisco.

"Can't I feel what?" Warner snapped into the darkness, not bothering to turn toward Kett. Probably because he couldn't sense the vampire's dark peppermint magic and it bothered him. I often forgot that he — or Kandy or Kett — couldn't taste magic like I could, and didn't think to mention when we were approaching a magical object or person.

"The magic," I murmured, reaching out with my dowser senses beyond the two of them. "Lots and lots of Adepts are near."

Kett stepped down the tiled stairs, his hands casually tucked in the front pockets of his designer jeans in a learned human gesture. Not a white-blond hair was out of place, despite the fact that the evening offered a cool breeze. He had nary a wrinkle on his gray cashmere crew-neck sweater either.

Warner grunted at Kett's appearance. Though the sentinel was particularly skilled at using shadows to his advantage, he hated when others had the ability to sneak up on him. But then, didn't we all?

"Well," I said, "that's enough of the 'standing around and staring at each other' portion of the evening, don't you think? You said something about dancing."

"Hunting is what he said," Warner corrected. Ah, so dragons did read other people's text messages.

"That's what vampires do." Kett's cool smile was meant to utterly infuriate.

"Am I tasting a bunch of Adepts nearby?" I asked to deflect the tension. "Or just a few of significant power?"

"A gathering," Kett said. Then he slipped off into the shadows to move farther up the quiet, mostly empty street.

"Are we just supposed to follow?" Warner asked through gritted teeth.

"Yeah. He deals out information in bits and pieces. It's part of the hunting instinct." I meant the last part as a joke, but judging by Warner's grunt and nod, he agreed with my assessment.

On the edge of the bay, San Francisco felt like a quieter, smaller city. A few cars drove by, but the sidewalk remained mostly empty. All the buildings and businesses that encompassed Fisherman's Wharf appeared closed — or closing soon — for the evening.

"So you don't actually know this amplifier?" I asked the darkness between me and the strip of grass that bordered the bay on my left. A mostly empty streetcar passed us on the right.

Kett didn't immediately answer.

"This isn't going to be the same thing that happened with the skinwalkers, is it?"

"Skinwalkers?" Warner asked.

"Adepts of First Nations ancestry. They have the ability to cloak themselves with the form of a spirit animal," I said. "They were thought to be extinct. Kett had me hunting for them without … you know, telling me that we were hunting rare Adepts." I glanced at Warner. He kept his gaze on the sidewalk ahead of us and his mouth shut. "It doesn't sound so good when I put it like that."

"No, it doesn't."

"This Adept is … shy." Kett fell into step beside me, placing me momentarily in a peppermint-and-black-forest-cake sandwich. It was less appetizing than I would have thought. Good to know …

"Shy, as in scared of you?" I asked.

"She doesn't know me … yet." Kett flashed a toothy grin.

Warner shook his head.

"She's a mercenary of sorts," Kett continued. "Just difficult to contact and hire on short notice."

"Amplifiers of any real power are exceedingly rare," Warner said. "Her freedom is probably her top priority."

"Witch magic?" I asked.

"A form of it," Kett said. "But she hasn't forged ties with the witches' Convocation or the sorcerers' League. Both would be options for her."

"Just another set of chains," Warner said.

"Indeed," Kett said.

The sentinel didn't seem pleased by the vampire's amiable agreement.

"Then she doesn't have any protection?" I asked.

"I didn't say that," Kett said. "Though I doubt it would be anything we three couldn't handle."

Warner grumbled something under his breath. Kett laughed quietly to himself.

Wow, this was going to be a fun evening.

"So the dancing?" I prompted.

"Time is tight," Kett said. "Too tight to wait to make contact through proper channels."

"So you propose to use the alchemist as bait." Warner's disdain was almost as impressive as it had been in the nexus with the treasure keeper.

"There's a lot of that going around today," I said.

"The alchemist is far from bait." Kett paused before a two-storey building complex, set before what appeared to be a number of huge piers jutting out into the bay. "More like the trap."

Bold white lettering on a turquoise and orange sign drew my attention. Across a narrow bank of grass and a pedestrian walkway, nestled between a bike rental place and a moored yacht, an oasis beckoned. I gripped Warner's arm in excitement and gestured toward one of the most beautiful buildings I'd ever seen. "Oh my God! He's taking us to Ben & Jerry's!"

Kett pivoted and darted completely in the wrong direction, across the tram tracks running up the side of the street to the opposite sidewalk. There, a four-storey concrete parking garage took up the entire city block. Stairs of blue steel and concrete wound up the exterior.

"No," I moaned. "He completely tricked me."

"I think the ice cream place is closed," Warner said helpfully.

"Don't take his side! He lured me with ice cream because he didn't want me to see the parking lot!"

"You have an issue with parking lots?"

"Yes. Yes, I do."

I watched Kett slip around the dark side of the lot. I sighed. Heavily. Warner was a silent but comforting presence at my side. Just a couple of blocks away from us the city was quiet … in that way that ever-present car engines, sirens, murmured conversations from balconies, door chimes from twenty-four-hour convenience stores, and wind through tall buildings can be quiet. So not quiet, but normal.

I trusted Kett. And I wanted the map back. That's all any of this came down to. So no matter where the vampire was leading me, I would go for those two reasons.

Pushing previously disastrous choices out of my head and remembering to look both ways, though there wasn't much traffic, I jogged across the street toward the open-air parking garage.

Floodlights jutted out over the top of the Pier 39 public parking lot, illuminating a mural of humpback whales sticking their noses out of a bright blue sea. Behind us, small shops and restaurants blocked most of the pier from sight, though I could see a white and blue boat — perhaps some sort of small ferry — moored off to one side. The entire vista reminded me of Granville Island and Fisherman's Wharf in Vancouver. Though the buildings were older here and more tightly packed together.

I found myself thinking about coming back by day and wandering down one of the piers or side wharves. I wondered if I could buy crab fresh off a boat. I used to love doing that. Crab … sweet spot prawns … You know, before my life became consumed by cupcakes, portals, and duty.

I could see a bus depot a block ahead and to the left of us, but halfway along the base of the parking garage, Kett veered off to the right. And apparently went down a set of stairs, since he disappeared from sight and didn't have the ability to walk through walls. Not that I knew, anyway. I probably would have missed the stairwell if I hadn't been following his peppermint magic.

Turning away from the piers was enough to remind me that I had no idea where we were anymore, or how to get back to Haoxin's apartment. Yeah, my sense of direction was terrible. I wasn't sure that was a skill I would ever be able to hone, actually. It would probably have been a good idea to note the freaking address of the apartment building before we left. Then I could have at least followed the blue dot on my map app back.

Would have, should have, could have. That was my life. Right?

"Why have us meet him at the restaurant in the first place?" Warner grumbled at my side as we neared the almost-hidden set of stairs.

"Maybe he was enjoying a glass of wine and the view," I said.

Warner snorted, then momentarily lagged behind as I cut right down the concrete stairs. I'd forgotten — again — that he couldn't track Kett like I could. No wonder being around the vampire bothered him so much.

I paused halfway down the stairs to let my eyes adjust to the darkness, and to assess the well of magic I could feel beneath and before me now.

"What does his magic taste like to you?" Warner asked from behind me, his tone hushed.

"That's a rather intimate question."

"I thought you wanted to be intimate," Warner teased.

"I do. Just not in the dark on a grubby set of concrete stairs."

Kett laughed from within the deep shadow that cloaked a nondescript steel door at the base of the stairs. Warner grumbled underneath his breath. Vampires had great hearing.

The door was either dark blue or black, but I couldn't distinguish the color in the low light emanating from the street behind me. Nor could I see a handle. But the aboveground parking garage obviously had a sublevel.

"Peppermint," I murmured, answering Warner's question. "And something else I haven't figured out yet."

Kett stepped out of the shadows and triggered a motion-sensitive light above the door.

"Blood?" Warner asked mockingly.

"No." I stepped down into the concrete vestibule at the base of the stairs. Kett was watching me with that slight head tilt he often seemed to get stuck in, but he hadn't fallen into one of his fugues. "I know the taste of blood."

Warner moved to occupy the space one step up behind me. He didn't comment further. Kett slowly turned his head to regard the sentinel with a look he usually reserved for interesting magical artifacts.

And, technically, that's what Warner was. A magical artifact. I stifled a smile. Kett noticed, lifting the corners of his mouth in response.

"Sixteenth century here is accustomed to working alone," I said.

Kett inclined his head half an inch. "As am I. Though only for the last few centuries. I had two companions throughout the sixteenth century."

This intimate detail was dropped before us as if we were simply friends and it wasn't actually a thinly veiled assertion of Kett's elder status.

"Yeah, we get that you're older and wiser, vampire," I groused.

"Older, maybe." Warner's tone was almost teasing, almost banter. But then he ruined it by gruffly adding, "The door and immediate area are warded."

"Only for sound … outside," Kett replied, even more coolly.

"There's no handle on the door," I said, stating the obvious to insert myself into the conversation.

"Not yet." Kett backed into the shadows so deeply that the motion-sensor light flicked out. The vampire wrapped himself so completely in darkness that he disappeared from sight, though I could still taste a tingle of his peppermint magic.

Warner grunted, impressed despite his ingrained prejudices.

"Yeah, Kett has mad hunting skills," I muttered. "I'm hoping it's a learned trait and not particular to every vampire, because there are a couple I already wouldn't want to meet in broad daylight." I still hadn't gotten over the encounter with Kett's maker in London, who dressed like Audrey Hepburn but could probably rend me limb from limb. And, as terrifying as she was, I shuddered every time I thought about coming face to face with his grandsire, the big bad who'd banned me from reentering the United Kingdom.

"I doubt they would enjoy such a rendezvous either, dowser," Kett said dryly. "But back to the matter at hand. I believe your magic will gain you entry."

"Because yours won't?" Warner asked, more interested than snarky.

Kett didn't answer as I stepped up to the door. "The vampire is magic," I said as I pressed my hand to the middle of the steel-plated entrance. "So he doesn't exude a residual signature or trace."

"Plus," Kett said, his tone still dry and lightly mocking. "My kind isn't welcomed here."

The door opened a crack. I could now feel, more than hear, a faint beat of music.

I laughed. "You did bring me dancing!"

I pressed the door open farther, feeling the sound-barrier spell tingle along my hand and arm as I did so, but seeing only deep darkness. By its taste, the spell was sorcerer magic. "An underground club for Adepts?" I was completely impressed — and completely ready to dive into the crowd I could feel just beyond the door but not yet see.

"Indeed." Kett touched my back lightly as he slipped alongside me, entering the curtain of black just inside the door. Riding my magical signature through the door in some way until we both stood in a sort of limbo of darkness.

"There's a bodyguard," he whispered against the skin of my neck. His breath was cool, and all about the peppermint.

"Of course there is."

"She and I aren't well matched."

Then the vampire was gone, peppermint magic and all. It was as if he'd been absorbed and diluted into the pulse of magic I could feel before me.

Delightful. I had no idea what he meant.

Chapter Seven

$\mathcal{W}$arner's black-forest-cake magic rose and fell behind me. The sentinel's clothing was just a manifestation of his dragon magic. Something inherited from Jiaotu, according to my best guess — similar to my knife and my father's sword — but I didn't know much about the guardian of Northern Europe. I glanced over my shoulder, completely prepared to ogle my new boyfriend in whatever he'd decided was more appropriate clothing for a night of dancing in an underground club.

Groan.

He was still standing in the door. The motion-sensor light an inch or so above his head created a halo effect around his golden-brown hair. He'd swapped out his T-shirt and leather jacket — an ensemble he favored due to Kandy's influence — for a jade-green silk shirt that fit tightly across his broad shoulders but slightly loose around his waist, tucked into low-rise dark blue jeans. He was even wearing a pair of freaking gorgeous Fluevog boots — brown, zippered 760 Turbo Svenskas with a manly square toe.

An utterly insuppressible grin spread across my face. Warner grinned back at me.

"It's difficult to look as good as you, Jade," he said. "But I figured I should try."

Oh, God. I had nothing to say to that. No witty comeback. In fact, I was rather parched all of a sudden. I continued to grin like an idiot as he stepped forward to place his hand on my lower back and escort me farther into the building.

"Do you know how to dance?" The curtain of black between us and the magic I could feel ahead swallowed my eyesight.

"I'm a quick learner." Warner's words were a whispered promise in the dark.

God, yes. He was a quick learner. And I relished watching him learn … every single minute of it.

We stepped fully through the barrier blocking sound and sight — the sorcerer magic letting us bypass it effortlessly — and were immediately assaulted with pounding music and glaring lights.

All the magic contained in the cavernous room crashed over me. I gasped, completely buzzed within seconds of stepping into the club — instantly high on the wild magic whirling in the air around us. Sorcerer magic. Witches and shapeshifters, and more I couldn't identify. Every single person before me was an Adept.

A year ago, this would have been too much for me to bear. Now, I reached out with my dowser senses and gathered it tightly around me. My limbs loosened and my spine limbered. I hadn't realized I was so tense.

"It's a buffet," I murmured. Warner didn't answer me, making me pretty sure he couldn't hear me over the din.

A guy — big and ugly enough that at first I thought he was a shapeshifter in his half-form — stepped up to greet me with a wide, lopsided smile.

"Payment?" he yelled. He held a flat steel disk out toward me, with a short, sharp spike protruding from its center.

I stared at it, blinking. "Am I supposed to slap my hand over that? You demand a ... blood sacrifice to enter?"

The guy laughed. "Nah," he said. "Just Adepts only, you know?" He was wearing some sort of earpiece. I couldn't get a taste of his magic, so I was guessing it wasn't terribly powerful or he was some sort of Adept I hadn't met before.

"I got through the door, didn't I?"

The guy lost the smile as he pushed the spiked disk toward me.

Warner flicked something that flashed gold as it landed onto the spike — a coin with a hole in its center. The guy flinched, as if he hadn't noticed Warner behind me.

"That's enough, I'm sure," Warner said, completely intimidating in a totally nonconfrontational way.

The guy nodded to Warner and swallowed nervously. The sentinel brushed his fingers against my hand, then stepped to the right, obviously heading to case the room. I let him go without following. With him and Kett prowling around, there was no reason I shouldn't make a beeline for the dance floor.

"Drink?" the guy asked as he lifted the gold coin off the spike and pocketed it. "We've got Bellini charms on special. They're potent but fun. The euphoria wears off in an hour or when you exit."

"Nah," I answered. "I'm just here to dance."

I stepped around him, heading straight toward the crowd.

The underground space was easily three thousand square feet. Its ten-foot-high walls were constructed from thick, undecorated concrete. Stage lights hung from steel girders overhead, all colored by different gels. A lighting sequence flashed as I crossed through the apparently random clusters of black-lacquered tables and red vinyl-topped stools between me and the floor. The seating areas were obviously moved about according to the whims of the club's patrons.

A bar ran the entire length of the wall to my left. Adepts were lined up three deep for drinks and what appeared to be — by their unnatural, vibrant color and the various flavors that tickled my senses as I passed — some sort of magical potions. Not everyone got as easily buzzed on magic as I did, except for maybe Kett. The vampire was as much a magical magpie as I was — just more reserved about it. As far as I could tell, there wasn't a single nonmagical person in the vicinity.

Last time I'd been in a club like this, it hadn't even been an eighth as full, and Sienna had been by my side. Now instead of hunting me, Kett was hunting someone else in the crowd. But I was still 'the trap.' Then, unbeknownst to me, I'd been set by Sienna, and now I was being put into play by the vampire.

Ha. Some things never changed. Except, of course, I was now one of the most powerful people in the club — some of the others there knew it, judging by how they stepped away as I passed. I knew I should learn to dampen my magic as Kett, Warner, and the guardian dragons did, but it wasn't at the top of my most-urgently-needed-skills list right now.

Questions shouted in friends' ears became whispers behind my back. "Who is that?" they asked in various phrasings and accents.

Give me a second. I'm going to show you.

It wasn't just frivolous, this urge to dance and show off. I had a necklace that needed topping up, and a willing crowd casting off magic as they simply breathed around me. It wasn't stealing if it was offered so freely

— even if unknowingly. It would take me years to collect what I could grab in five minutes in this single location.

The music was techno, which wasn't my thing. I didn't care.

I stepped into the center of the crowd, as best as I could judge. Then I slowly pivoted, looking over the heads of the bouncing and gyrating crowd until I laid eyes on the heavily tattooed DJ. He was a sorcerer, his blue-tinted magic dancing underneath his hands as he pawed his boards and records.

I laughed. I was quite possibly in heaven, though there wasn't enough chocolate nearby to make this a true paradise.

The crowd around me was large enough that I couldn't quite see the edges in the flashing multicolored light. "Every Adept in San Francisco must be here!" I yelled at a dark-haired guy with a thin beard next to me — a spellcaster, judging by his taste.

"At least half of us are out-of-towners," he answered. Then with an appreciative leer, he added, "But why do I get the feeling that the party just started?"

I laughed, turned my shoulder to him — politely shutting down the conversation — and began to dance.

I threw myself into the beat. This wasn't a slow build sort of music. This was all day, every day, hard, fast, and forever sort of music.

The crowd pressed against me, shoulders, fingers, and arms brushing. Magic crashed over me from all directions, so many tastes and scents and colors. I had no guidance, and no need for any. It was just me, the music, and the magic.

Peppermint tickled the back of my tongue. I opened my eyes, not realizing I'd closed them. The crowd was all around me, twisting and moving as the magic moved, but I couldn't see Kett or Warner.

I lifted my hands, stretching my arms back through the jumping and twirling crowd to gather all its wild magic to me. I pulled it … drop by drip, strand by thread … pulled it to me, through me, and into my necklace. I gathered the wild cast-off until the chain and wedding rings were heavy against my heart. A comforting barrier to all the aches that had resided there for so long, and all the worries that threatened to live there forever. A magical shield of golden links. Heart armor.

I threw my head back and laughed.

If I was an egotist, I would have referred to this as an offering, but it was a freely given gift. A gift the crowd didn't even know it had to give.

All this gathered, multicolored magic roiled around in my necklace. I coaxed it to settle, molding it with my alchemist power. Then, shielded from the crowd, I found some clarity on the dance floor. Some reminder of my duty, my hunt.

I wasn't sure who we were hunting. Who I was supposed to seek within the crowd.

An amplifier, Kett had said … who wasn't a witch or a sorcerer, but who could have sought allegiance among either. And a bodyguard who wasn't 'well-matched' to a vampire. What did that mean?

I'd gotten so wrapped up in the prospect of dancing — and honestly, of managing the tension between Kett and Warner — that I'd been forgetting to ask all the right questions. Again.

I drew from the protective magic of the necklace, then visualized it creating a thin, sparkling barrier between me and the onslaught of the Adept magic surrounding me. If I was going to see myself coated in magic, it might as well be sparkly, right?

My head cleared further, and I briefly mourned the lessening of the buzz. Being too drunk to think was freeing.

Refocused, I surfed the crowd with my dowser senses for magic I couldn't easily and immediately identify. The taste of sand, ashes, and some sort of spice — maybe sun-dried red pepper? — filled my mouth. For a split second, I thought I was somehow picking up my own magic, which might be possible if an amplifier was near. If that was what an amplifier did.

But it wasn't me. The taste was coming from an unknown Adept two dancers away. An Adept who appeared to have a diluted orange-red aura that screamed of possible demon ancestry. Which was freaky, because based on my minimal knowledge, demons ate Adepts for breakfast rather than buying them waffles with strawberries and whipped cream the morning after. Though maybe waffles the morning after was just my thing.

I focused on the spice of her magic, which I was pretty sure was paprika. I caught another glimpse of orange when the crowd before me shifted, then closed again.

She didn't appear to be a half-demon, as far as I could see. A woman a couple of years younger than me, her dyed blond hair chopped short — almost ragged, as if singed at the ends. She was swathed in different shades of orange, tangerine to deep sunset. Head to toe. T-shirt, jeans, and shoes. And magic.

But she wasn't the most interesting being on the dance floor.

Paprika's two dance partners were exceedingly intriguing. Number one — a completely nondescript guy who needed a haircut, and who should really try a T-shirt color other than white. And number two — a woman. She was cute with her slightly upturned nose, though her eyes were too widely set for her sweetheart-shaped face. But it was the gorgeous, scroll-etched tan leather bag that she wore slung across her body that really drew my attention.

The guy was interesting because he didn't taste like anything. Not one drop or color of any magic in him — yet he sure as hell wasn't wholly human.

And the second woman with the lust-worthy bag? She tasted of everyone else around her. She was still tasting of paprika, but every time she dropped her shoulder to the beat, twisted left, then curved back toward me, she bounced the grassy base of the group of witches right behind her directly at me. I wondered if she had any idea she did that.

So, yeah. Interesting trio.

I swiveled my hips to the beat, threw my hands up in the air, and sidled a step nearer to my prey … err, targets … err, soon-to-be friendly acquaintances.

Closer, I continued to dance as if with abandon, but I let my own dowsing magic leak out through the barrier the necklace maintained. I wasn't good at dampening like Warner and Kett, but I was good at attracting all the wrong types. Usually I did it without trying. This time, I was laying out a welcome mat.

Paprika reacted first, stumbling. Her singed blond bangs brushed across her cheek and ear as she whipped her head to look at me. Once I was in her sights, a slow grin loosened her pinched features.

I got that look a lot. Supposedly, my magic was tasty.

I twirled away from eye contact, dancing near them but not trying to force myself into their group. They followed — moving together almost as one — shifting until we were riding the beat side by side.

Then Warner was half-behind, half-beside me, slipping into my space without touching me or making me miss a beat. The girl with the wide-set eyes, who I thought might be the amplifier, missed a beat or two, though. The guy who tasted of nothing scowled at her, then turned his head to see what had her attention — and dropped his jaw at the sight of Warner.

The sentinel slid his hand across my hip and up my back, causing me to arch into him. My heart was racing from more than just physical exertion by the time his caress reached my shoulders, his fingers tangling in the damp curls at the base of my neck.

"I like modern dancing," Warner said, his unshaven jaw prickly against my left temple and cheek.

Jesus. Dancing had always been about sex for me. Better than sex actually — less commitment, fewer bodily fluids, and no aftermath hassle. But I'd never actually had sex on a dance floor. That would be crazy ... and illegal ... and embarrassing.

But I wasn't a hundred percent sure I could say no to anything Warner wanted right now. My newly constructed heart shield opened right up and let him in ... deeply in ... like I wanted him to be in ... Hey, maybe I should wear the necklace slung across my hips. A loin shield would be much more helpful right now.

"Peppermint," I shouted, vocalizing the instant I tasted Kett's magic. The vampire was near, and his cool peppermint always steadied me.

Warner glanced over my shoulder. I stepped fully in front of him, placing him at my back and the trio directly in front of me.

"Peppermint," I muttered. "Good safe word."

"Safe word?" Warner asked in my ear. Both his hands were on my hips now, as I attempted to focus on dancing.

"I'll explain later," I answered. Not adding that I'd like to do more than freaking explain later. I tamped down on my instinct to press my ass back into his groin as I laid a blistering smile on the wide-set-eyed woman before me. She was staring as if I was a porn star or something.

Sex with dragons. There was an unexplored niche market.

I laughed at my own joke. Warner threw his head back and laughed behind me. His power rippled through the room, then bounced back at me from the woman. That definitely seemed like the sort of power an amplifier would have.

My knees turned gooey at this utterly delicious, two-front magical assault, confirming that I had absolutely no shielding ability when it came to Warner.

The crowd shifted, pressing even closer. Tasting magic might be a fairly unique power, but every other Adept in the club could feel, see, or sense magic in some way ... even if they didn't know it.

The guy finally snapped his jaw shut, but a frown was firmly etched across his unremarkable face. Yeah, only scary people thought Warner was sexy ... like Kandy, Haoxin, and maybe even Kett. To everyone else, he was terrifying.

I wondered if that made me one of the scary people.

Kett was standing behind she-who-might-be-an-amplifier, having just appeared out of nowhere within the thrashing and gyrating crowd. His ice-blue gaze flicked up to meet mine. He was utter stillness brought to life. He was the antithesis of music, of beat, of breathing.

Speaking of scary people.

His eyes were blood red.

Shit.

I lunged forward. One second, I was dancing. The next, I was feeling the girl's soft, shiny hair slide across my fingertips as Kett grabbed her across her shoulders and spun her away from me.

Her guy friend shouted, but his words were lost in the music. He was a few seconds behind me as I spun to scan the crowd for peppermint magic and blood-red eyes.

Then something hit my shoulder. I turned my head to see that my sweater and hair were on fire.

Double shit.

The guy shoved by me and dove into the crowd.

I slammed my hand on my shoulder to smother the flames, spinning to come face to face with the orange-swathed girl whose magic tasted of paprika.

Half-demon. Not girl.

She swung at me, slow and clumsy. Warner caught her fist as if she might have been standing still. She needed to learn not to telegraph her punches.

Surprise spread across Paprika's face, then she smiled wickedly. Which would have been fun, except it was directed at my boyfriend. Her fist, still enveloped in Warner's hand, started to glow.

Yep, orange.

The half-demon controlled heat or fire.

Cool. Except —

"You ruined my sweater," I shouted. "And my freaking hair!"

Warner stepped into her, twisting her hand down as he did so. The dancers around us were still oblivious to our scuffle. Or maybe they were just accustomed to magic breaking out on the dance floor.

Paprika lost the smile.

I stepped closer so she could hear me, still completely pissed about my new sweater. "You don't use fire against a dragon, stupid!"

Suddenly, the crowd wasn't pressing us anymore, though people weren't abandoning the dance floor quite yet. I didn't blame them, on either count.

I turned to scan the dancers for Kett, but came face to face with the ordinary guy.

"Nice moves, buddy," I said. "No one sneaks up on me."

Ordinary guy really had no sense of humor, because he glared at me — the furious scowl looking seriously toddleresque — and grabbed my shoulder. My scorched sweater crumbled underneath his grip, and I barely stopped myself from ripping his head off over it. Instead, I opened my mouth to give him a tongue-lashing about grabbing unknown Adepts — which is when he grabbed my magic … or took my magic … or stopped the flow of my magic.

It hurt.

My shoulder, my arm, and the side of my neck went instantly numb.

That terrible emptiness was creeping up the side of my face, and I reacted … badly.

I rewarded this rare and damn impressive talent by slamming my hand into ordinary guy's chest and stopping his heart.

I told myself he should have known to not play with powerful people who didn't know their own strength, because they were always the weakest in the room … well, in rooms full of dragons, at least.

I caught him before he hit the floor. So I wasn't a complete asshole.

Then some sort of foam retardant fell out of the ceiling and blanketed the club.

Well, that was really going to ruin my hair.

The crowd scattered, slipping and slinging foam as they all attempted to vacate the space at once. Naturally, they all instantly bottlenecked at the entrance and stairwell. The cloaking spell that had obscured the exit apparently dissipated when the foam was triggered. A safety-conscious underground club. Nice.

The foam was laced with some kind of spell — fire retardant spelled into a magical suppressant.

I spat the icky stuff out of my mouth as I lowered the guy to the floor, holding his head above the foam layer even as I knelt in it myself.

The suppressant spell stung me, like little mosquito bites attempting to quell my magic. It was annoying, though easily countered with an extra tug on my necklace's topped-up reserves. Not that a personal ward could do anything about my ruined outfit.

Feet — loud enough that they sounded as if they were shod in hundred-pound cement boots — thundered around us. As I pressed my ear to now-Not-So-Ordinary's chest and confirmed that his heart wasn't beating, I saw five huge bouncers form a circle around the four of us. Nope — the six of us. Kett and the wide-set-eyed woman were still in the mix. I couldn't tell if the amplifier had been bitten or not — but then, I was rather more concerned about the guy I'd just killed.

Warner's magic rolled up and around him. And then — voila — he didn't have a speck of foam on him.

Paprika stumbled away from the sentinel like he was the second coming and she was a dreadful sinner. Too bad for me — and the guy whose heart I'd just stopped — he wasn't.

"He's not breathing," I cried, wishing for the hundredth time that I had some healing magic at my fingertips.

"Hit him again," Warner growled as he stepped closer to me, placing Paprika between him and the bouncers.

"Step away from the man," one of the club's enforcers intoned. They were wearing riot gear. I hoped for their sakes that it was magically enhanced.

"Warner! I'm not hitting him again!"

Warner lifted up his foot, then deliberately slammed it back down. The concrete floor cracked. The layer of foam coating the floor lifted about a foot in the air all around us. Paprika and the bouncers lost their balance, tumbling every which way. I slammed my knees and the guy's back against the floor.

Dragon magic — smoky, black forest cake — flooded the room.

The guy jerked in my arms, gasped for breath, then scuttled away from me like an upside-down crab. So hitting him again might have actually worked.

The bouncers fled, following the last of the patrons out of the club and into the dark night beyond. I didn't blame them. We were way above their pay grade.

I gained my feet as Not-So-Ordinary blindly crashed into Paprika, knocking her back down just as she'd been trying to stand. They tumbled around in a tangle of limbs and foam.

"Don't let him touch you," I muttered to Warner. "He did something to my magic. Stopped it up. It hurt."

"Nullifier," Warner said. "Sorcerer. But opposite in wielding."

That was as freaking clear as freaking fudge.

"Hey!" I raised my hands palm forward in a sign of surrender, even as I watched Kett — who was still red-eyed, fangy, and far too close to the amplifier. She was either so freaked out that she couldn't move, or Kett had managed to bite her and drain every ounce of resistance she might have had. "We come in peace."

No one laughed.

The nullifier and Paprika finally sorted themselves out and stood.

Keeping what I hoped was an apologetic look on my face, I sang, "Eh! Oh! Where did all the good go," while raising my hands in the air for emphasis. "Come on. Marianas Trench? I can't be the only one who knows that song."

"There isn't going to be any more dancing," Paprika spat as she wiped foam off her face, neck, and arms. "You've managed to ruin that."

"I believe it was your fire spell that caused the problem, demon-spawn." Warner spoke with no hint of condemnation in his tone, but I winced nonetheless.

"Who are you calling a demon, asshole?" Paprika growled. "I'm an elemental."

"Such beings don't exist," the sentinel calmly informed her.

Her clenched fists glowed orange, and the spice of her magic intensified despite the foam suppressor. Management was really going to need to reassess that spell. "I'll show you existence."

"Yeah," I interrupted. "Name calling isn't exactly diplomatic, sixteenth century."

"I was simply stating the truth," Warner said. "But you don't bring a dragon and a vampire to a dance club and expect diplomacy either."

Kett laughed.

"Don't you get started," I snapped at him. He was still standing way too close to the girl I thought might be the amplifier. "Again."

He shrugged, but lifted only one shoulder in an attempt to ape that human gesture. Between him and

Warner, I was ready to swear they were going to drive me batty. I found myself wishing Kandy were there.

"There was too much magic in the room," Kett said. "Including yours, dowser."

"You knew that going in."

"Indeed. My control is not as it once was."

"Don't play the London card with me!"

"We're not going to stand here while you bicker, lady," the nullifier said. He was rubbing his chest. "You attacked us!"

"Lady? Who the hell are you calling a lady?" Next thing, he'd be calling me 'ma'am.' Then things were going to get nasty.

"Actually," Warner said, raising an arm to quell my desire to gouge the guy's eyes out, "you attacked first."

"After he grabbed Cicely!" the nullifier shouted and pointed toward the wide-set-eyed girl, who I was starting to think really wasn't okay because she hadn't spoken yet.

I sighed, loudly and deliberately. "You bring me to the best parties, vampire."

The trio froze. Prey-in-the-headlights stock-still. Even the guy's arm remained suspended in the air, hanging there as if he was afraid of putting it down.

"What?" I asked, still attempting to defuse the tension. Covered in foam and with nary a cupcake in sight, though, I was feeling completely off my game. "No one noticed the vampire?"

The amplifier — Cicely — flung her hands up over her head and somehow managed to clamp them on either side of Kett's face behind her.

Peppermint magic exploded all around them. Kett stumbled. Cicely twisted away from him, ran toward her friends, and pulled a gun out of her etched bag.

A gun.

She pressed back between Paprika and the nullifier, shaking almost uncontrollably as she alternated pointing the gun at Kett, Warner, and me. I couldn't tell if her tremor was from nerves or from the magical toll of whatever she'd just done to Kett.

The vampire shook his head. Then he shook it way harder. "Impressive," he murmured, closing the gap between us so Cicely didn't have to swing the gun so wide.

"What is that supposed to be?" Warner asked, not sounding the least bit concerned. Of course, it helped that he looked like a million bucks while the rest of us resembled foam-covered rats.

"A gun," I answered. "A human weapon. I don't know what kind. I've never seen one in person before."

"Canadian," the nullifier sneered. "That's the accent."

"The true north strong and free," I said agreeably. He didn't get the reference.

"It's a Smith & Wesson," Kett said. "An M&P Shield. A striker-fired, polymer 9 mm pistol. The safety is built into the trigger. Lightweight. A good choice to carry concealed, though I doubt she has the permit to do so."

I stared at Mr. Know-It-All. Cicely started to sneer some retort — probably about the permit — but then snapped her mouth shut on whatever she was going to say.

"How can an Adept not be aware that I can simply reach out and take her toy?" Warner asked, unintentionally — but still extremely — intimidating.

My boyfriend, the accidental badass. "It fires bullets," I said. "Bullets are fast."

Warner snorted.

Cicely pressed the trigger halfway. Paprika placed her right hand on the amplifier's shoulder, then her left hand actually burst into flames.

"Well, that confirmed you're the amplifier," I said.

"One step closer," Paprika hissed.

I waited a beat. "Oh, that's it? I thought you were going to say something witty or sarcastic." Where was Diplomats-R-Us when you needed them? Not here, obviously.

Cicely leveled the gun on me.

"Yes," Kett said. "Shooting the dowser is the best choice. The only choice."

"Kett!" I cried.

"The bullet won't slow me," Kett continued, nonplused.

"I will," Paprika snarled. Ashy magic filled my mouth and I resisted the urge to spit it out. Geez, I hated swallowing.

"The dragon's magic will likely cause a misfire," Kett coolly assessed.

The trio looked at Warner. Dragon either meant nothing to them, in which case he was a complete unknown. Or, he was a myth standing before them, and they were starting to wonder if the entire confrontation was all happening in their heads.

"Magic in this concentration," I said, practically grinding my teeth as I gestured around us, "will cause the gun to explode in her hand. That's the most likely outcome."

Kett smiled and inclined his head, as if he was ceding the point to me.

I glared at him, then spoke to Cicely. "You can feel the magic in the room, can't you?"

Cicely slowly nodded.

"And what if I were to tell you that the vampire and the dragon are experts at dampening their magical signatures. And that I wear a personal shield to help contain my own?"

"Except on the dance floor," Kett added.

"Well, that was the point!"

Cicely bit her lip. "What do you want?" she asked, her voice was less childish than her appearance. Under the full fluorescent lights of the club, they were all older than I'd thought them. My age, at least.

"You, of course," Kett said.

Cicely didn't lower the gun — and neither would I, if a vampire said that to me.

"Kett, don't tease." Except I wasn't entirely sure he was teasing.

Warner reached into the pocket of his jeans and flipped something into the air over the trio. It flashed gold as it spun up, then down, reflecting the overhead light.

A gold coin.

At the last possible second, Paprika snatched it out of the air. She turned it in her fingers, showing her companions. I realized at once how green, untested, and ignorant the three of them were. First, stupid enough to touch me. Then, silly enough to grab an unknown item out of the air. Even I hadn't been that dumb when first confronted by a vampire. Well …

"You're for hire, aren't you?" Warner asked as he flipped two more coins toward the trio.

The nullifier caught one. Paprika caught the second.

"What is this?" the nullifier sneered. "Some joke? Gold coins from a guy who calls himself a dragon?"

Kett laughed, completely involuntarily.

I joined him. "That's pretty funny, sixteenth century," I said. "You know, because dragons hoard gold."

"More practical than funny," Warner said huffily. Then he turned to lay a blazing smile on me. My knees turned to goo, but I refused to acknowledge this with a gun trained on me.

"Even if it's gold," the nullifier continued, "what the hell are we supposed to do with it? It's not American dollars."

We all stared at the moron. He stared back, mouth still open as if he was jeering us while he waited for an answer.

Cicely cleared her throat apologetically. Paprika elbowed nullifier-guy in the ribs.

"What?" he asked.

"We exchange it, idiot," his orange-swathed friend hissed.

Warner reached out and took the gun. A second later, Cicely reacted to the loss of her weapon with a shriek.

The sentinel turned the Smith & Wesson 9 mm around in his hands. Kett stepped over to peer at it as well. They completely ignored the trio, all of who turned too-large and way-scared eyes on me.

"Sorry about that," I said. "Immortals get bored quickly." With the situation vaguely defused, I attempted to rid my hair and outfit of as much foam as possible without a shower and a washing machine.

Something plastic snapped. Warner let out a disappointed huff. "I wanted to see the bullets."

"You broke my gun," Cicely said. "I didn't even see you move." Brave woman, finding her voice so quickly. I might have misjudged her earlier silence.

"I'm sure the gold will cover its replacement," Warner said, looking to me for confirmation.

"You broke my gun," Cicely repeated.

"You've broken the amplifier," I said to Warner, gesturing toward the wide-set-eyed woman as she visibly stopped herself from repeating the bit about her gun a third time. I also narrowed my eyes to express my disappointment with Kett.

"She didn't return my phone call," Kett said. He'd taken the gun from Warner and was trying to fit the broken pieces back together.

"I was taking a sick day," Cicely said.

"Plus, there's like a three-month waiting list," Paprika said. "That's if we decide to take you on as a client."

"Well," Kett said, "if the dowser wasn't here, I could have simply snatched the amplifier and killed the two of you. That would have been much smoother. And more satisfying."

"Less boring," Warner said agreeably.

Oh, God. I didn't need those two in cahoots with each other.

Paprika opened her mouth, but I interrupted her before she could speak. "Please don't say, 'Why don't you try it?' I'm covered in foam and getting hungry. And I'm the nice one."

She snapped her mouth closed.

Now we were getting somewhere.

Chapter Eight

The trio, fronted by Cicely, led us along empty sidewalks and through quiet industrial streets to a derelict warehouse about three blocks away from the underground club. They whispered between them for the entire walk, hastily dissecting the events that had transpired at the club and cobbling together a plan on how to deal with us now.

Apparently, they were unaware that the dragon and vampire behind them could hear every word. I didn't bother to try to listen in, beyond the few words that filtered through.

The warehouse appeared to be empty from the outside and wasn't magically warded. Even the soft moonlight that now filtered through the skyscraper-filled backdrop couldn't prettify the peeling paint and boarded windows. I would have thought a hunk of real estate this close to the waterfront in San Francisco would have been way too pricey to sit half-abandoned.

The interior of the warehouse was littered with broken pallets, piles of blackened rope, and worn-out buoys. Three derelict fishing boats occupied the large main room. A lofted second floor ran the length of the back of the warehouse.

After unlocking an exterior side door, Cicely cut immediately right to a narrow set of wooden stairs. We climbed up to the loft, from where we could look down and see the fishing boats.

We passed a bathroom at the top of the stairs that scared me into not needing to pee, even by the muted moonlight filtering through its cracked window.

"Which one of you?" Cicely asked, rather abruptly, as she unlocked a paint-challenged, grimy glass-windowed door and led us into what appeared to be a makeshift office.

Again, I couldn't taste any magic, not one single ward on the door, windows, or building.

"I don't even know what sort of magic he wields," the amplifier continued, eyeing Warner distrustfully. "And I'm guessing you're a witch of some sort. Dowser, they called you. You need help finding something?"

"All expenses paid," Paprika said as she threw herself onto a faded couch against the wall to the right of the door. Even in the low light of the single shoddily wired fixture in the center of the ceiling, I could see a cloud of dust rise up around her. "Hotel. Travel. For all three of us."

An electrical cord ran through the rafters from the light to an outlet on the far left wall. The desk was actually propped up at one corner by a column of ancient phonebooks. Three mismatched chairs that looked as though they'd been salvaged from the dump completed the dingy decor.

"Three-month waiting list," I muttered as I glanced around. "Right." I caught Kett's gaze.

"A lifetime of education is direly needed here," he said. "About magic and etiquette."

"Not our circus," I said. "Not our monkeys."

Kett nodded. Well, he tipped his chin about a millimeter, so I took that as agreement. The trio was going to have to find their own way in the world of the Adept. And make plenty of mistakes while doing so. Just like we all did … well, just like I did.

Warner snorted as he cased the room, then followed the smell of burnt coffee through a door to the back and right of the desk. I hazarded a guess that this led to a break room of some sort, and shuddered to think of seeing it in the daylight.

"I'm the client," Kett said. His cool tone cut through the shabby atmosphere just by being completely at odds with it.

This really wasn't what Cicely wanted to hear.

"How could we help a vampire?" the nullifier sneered.

"Sorry, what's your name?" I asked before fangs were dropped and knives were pulled. "And you?" I looked at the orange-swathed fire wielder, who was so moronically confident she was lounging on a couch. Oblivious to — or in spite of — the two predators and an unknown 'witch' standing in her office. "It's silly to enter into verbal contracts with people you don't even know."

They all exchanged glances.

I stifled a sigh. Kett was right, maybe we should school them … maybe just a tiny teachable moment … like about the wisdom of leaving the hall door hanging open behind three Adepts of unknown power, who — as soon as Warner took two more steps — occupied the entire center of the room. We were unencumbered by furniture or other bodies. They had no perimeter or defensive positioning.

Yeah. I thought about things like that now.

"Smells like fish in here," Warner said, curling his lip as he returned from the break room.

"You like sushi," I said placatingly. Then I let the teachable moment dissipate from my mind and attitude. "Look, I'm Jade. This is Warner and Kett. I caught Cicely's name. I can just keep calling you Not-So-Ordinary and Paprika if you want to be babies about it."

Paprika sneered and opened her mouth as if she was intent on continuing her stupid streak, but Cicely interrupted.

"Ash is on the couch," the amplifier said.

Of course the fire wielder had a cute nickname.

"I'm Dave," the guy said. So Not-So-Ordinary guy had a completely ordinary name. Not surprising.

"I gather this is a new venture for you?" I gestured around the office. Warner wandered off a second time to case the windows, then walked the perimeter of the front office again as I spoke. The floor creaked under his weight.

"Not that new," Ash snapped.

"But you don't know power when you feel it," Kett answered.

"Yeah, you here to school us, vamp?" Dave said.

"I believe the dowser has already taught you a valuable lesson," Kett answered coolly. "One you've obviously blocked, because you're intellectually incapable of understanding that you just died and were revived by the grace of the most powerful being you will ever meet."

Dave's gaze flicked between Warner and me as he tried to decide which one of us was most 'graceful.'

Kett looked at me and shook his head. Just a single head shake, but he was as exasperated as I'd ever seen him. Which was saying a lot, because he was still mentoring me.

"You brought us here," I said.

"Perhaps my ... intel was incorrect," he said.

Wow, 'intel'? And the vampire admitting to a possible mistake in judgement? I stopped myself from looking outside to see if pigs were flying.

"Listen, you wanted to hire us," Ash said, backpedaling.

"No," Kett corrected. "I wanted the amplifier. The dragon offered to hire you. I would have dealt with you two ..." — he looked pointedly at Dave and Ash — "... quite differently." Then he looked at me. "I've never had to repeat myself so much in a single evening ... or year ... before."

"And you thought I was bad," I said.

"You were raised well," Kett said. "Justifiably sheltered."

"You should mention that next time you chat with Gran," I said with a grin. Kett and Gran didn't speak. Like, not ever. I'd seen them spend hours together and still manage to not even make eye contact.

"How are we supposed to help you?" Cicely asked, attempting to be somewhat professional. "I can't ... I won't amplify vampire ... powers."

"The other two will step into the hall."

"No way," Ash said.

"Screw that." Dave's vehement assertion overlapped that of the fire wielder's.

"Now." Kett's voice resonated around the makeshift office, heavy on drama and magic alike.

I felt the vampire's command brush by me. Ash and Dave stiffened. Then Ash stood up from the couch awkwardly and they both crossed to the door. Dave had some trouble opening it.

"Interesting," Kett said. "He's fighting the compulsion. I wonder if that's an aspect of the nullifier power."

Cicely gripped the edge of the desk, staring helplessly after her friends as they managed to open the door and exit into the hall.

Warner followed them, raising an eyebrow at me as he passed. Yeah, I didn't like the compulsion trick either, but I was damn surprised that Kett had been this patient already.

"You're scary, you know," I muttered.

"Not to you." Kett pulled one of the guest chairs farther away from the desk and turned it ninety degrees. Then he patted its back.

I sat in the offered chair, not disputing his assertion.

But Kett had changed after London. The power that ran through his veins — literally — wasn't entirely his own. I wasn't sure, especially after the display in the club, that he was wholly in control of that power yet. I wondered how long that took for a vampire. How long did it take to absorb the magic that reanimated them? I'd never met a fledgling vampire, but all the deep, dark rumors — all the whispered stories that even humans told about sunlight, wooden stakes, and feeding frenzies … well, I was fairly certain those were based in some sort of reality.

So was Kett a different type of uber-powerful fledgling now? Would the Conclave have made him an elder in that case? I knew that the witches' Convocation had ancient ways of sharing magic, and when filling their thirteen seats, they typically only selected members from the most powerful and influential covens. Perhaps the Conclave was the same and Kett's inclusion was power-based only. Or maybe it was a way to rein their suddenly unpredictable executioner in.

Kett pulled out a second chair, turned it to face me, and sat down. He looked at Cicely expectantly.

She looked at us, utterly scared and completely perplexed.

"She's going to need some words," I said to Kett. "Some explanation. Most of us don't own manuals on what to do when powerful Adepts show up at your window and demand your participation."

"You will amplify my telepathic abilities," Kett coolly informed Cicely.

Her mouth dropped open. Yeah, vampires were terrifying. I'd gathered that — similar to witches or even dragons — they didn't all come with a specific set of abilities beyond their immortality, strength, and invulnerability. I was fairly certain all vampires could use some form of compulsion — that was part of the whole hunter/prey aspect of their magic — but that not all of them were telepathic.

In fact, before he'd mentioned it yesterday, I hadn't been a hundred percent sure it was an ability Kett wielded. The vampire was a lot of smoke and mirrors, right up to the moment he wasn't.

Kett tilted his head, still looking at Cicely. "Does she require more words?" he asked.

Cicely shook her head and stood. Her legs looked shaky. I felt sorry for her ... well, as sorry as I could feel for someone who'd given serious thought to shooting me.

The amplifier crossed around the desk to stand behind Kett. He reached forward, grabbed the arms of my chair, and tugged me and it closer until our knees were sandwiched together.

"I've ... I've never done a vampire before." Cicely caught my gaze over Kett's head and bit her lip.

"If it doesn't work, no worries," I said.

"But the dowser will know," Kett said.

I sighed. "I'm trying to calm her."

"I'm trying to keep moving."

I looked back at Cicely. "I already know what your magic does … what it tastes like … namely, the Adept you're amplifying. So I'll know if you don't at least try."

She nodded and reached to touch Kett's temples from behind. He, in turn, pressed his icy fingertips to my temples.

Peppermint magic tickled my taste buds. Ah, this was going to be rather intimate. Maybe even uncomfortably so. I thought about closing my eyes instead of staring directly into Kett's ice-blue orbs, but didn't want to appear intimidated. For Cicely's sake, not my own. Kett seemed to be walking a narrow line of self-control, and acting at all like prey might tip him to the wrong side of that balance.

"It might be more helpful if you removed the necklace," Kett murmured, his voice low.

"And let you get your grubby paws on it?" I teased. "No way."

"I am neither grubby, nor do I have paws." A smile flickered over the vampire's face.

I glanced up at Cicely, who did have her eyes closed in concentration. "Leaving it on would be better." Removing my necklace around unknown magic was a terrible idea, though I might be forced to do so if it blocked Cicely's amplifier power.

Kett tipped his chin in a nod. "You've worked with a telepath before?" he asked Cicely.

"Sort of," she murmured.

"Well then, you know where to focus."

Cicely's magic rose underneath her fingertips, glowing a pale tint of blue that was a couple of shades darker than Kett's eyes. Now that I was closer — and not surrounded by so much other magic — I could taste the amplifier's own power ... a subtle hint of rosewater Turkish delight. But though her magic appeared as a shade of blue, it held no hint of the grassiness I associated with witches or the earthiness that usually accompanied sorcerers. I wondered if that aligned her more with oracles and readers — Adepts who worked with mind magic — than witches.

Cicely's rosewater magic was quickly overwhelmed by Kett's deep peppermint. The vampire's eyes glowed red, though his touch on my temples remained gentle and his gaze didn't shift from mine.

"No screwing around in my head, Kett," I muttered. "Or I'll gut you."

He laughed, low and husky. He was enjoying himself. But then, who didn't when given a legitimate reason to exercise their powers?

"Think of the map, dowser," he coaxed. "Relax. And don't call up the power of the necklace or the knife. I'll be in and out in a breath."

"I bet you say that to all the girls," I muttered.

Cicely snorted involuntarily and I smiled at her. Then I closed my eyes to focus.

"Open," Kett said. "Windows to the soul and all that."

"Except you aren't looking for my soul, vampire."

He smiled, revealing his very white, very straight, and thankfully not yet pointy teeth. The expression was completely at odds with his red eyes. "I'm looking for your heart, Jade," he murmured. "That's where you keep all your darkest fears. And you fear the map."

I swallowed. Then, refusing to dig meaning out of his words, I focused on the whirling shards of red ice I could see in his eyes.

I thought about the map. I thought about the centipede. That, I could see clearly in my mind because I'd felt its magic, and because I still had Rochelle's sketch stuffed in my satchel. I'd seen the centipede shift, moving across the tattoo. Then the map had shifted as well. Blue and green reformed into ... more green and blue.

"Hmmm," Kett said. His cool peppermint magic intensified against my temples, as if he were icing my skin underneath his careful touch. My jaw began to ache. Red shards of ice danced and danced and danced in Kett's eyes. Then I could feel the shards behind my own eyes, with more ice filling my sinuses and plugging my nose ... burning across my tongue, coating the back of my throat ... choking me. Slicing into my brain —

I pushed the peppermint magic away, shoving it all back toward Kett without stopping to think about it.

Cicely shrieked, stumbled back from Kett, and almost fell. She was holding her hands, with her fingertips curled as if she'd burnt them on something.

Kett grunted. He'd pulled his hands away from me, and quickly. "Not necessary, dowser." He sounded as unruffled as always, though he was rubbing the tips of his own fingers together.

Trying to not look too relieved, since I'd obviously hurt them both, I asked, "Did you see the map?"

Kett nodded, and I slid my chair back from his knees until I had enough clearance to stand. He mimicked my motions.

"Thank you," I said to Cicely. "If you're ever in Vancouver ... British Columbia, that is ... I run a bakery called Cake in a Cup."

Cicely nodded. She'd retreated behind the desk and was holding her arms crossed, with her hands tucked underneath them.

I stepped to the door. Kett got there before me to open it. Feeling insanely bad about running away from an Adept so clearly traumatized, I turned to look back at Cicely. She looked tiny and young behind the desk. I wondered if the evening would haunt her.

"Will you be okay?"

She bit her lip but nodded. I took her at her word as I stepped out into the hall. Kett followed.

Ash and Dave were leaning against the far wall, eyeing us as we exited. Kett snapped his fingers and both the Adepts jerked to life. Then they quickly cut a wide swathe around us to step back into the office. The conversation within turned quickly heated, but I tuned out the actual words. They'd been paid well for their troubles. Each one of those gold coins was worth hundreds of dollars — maybe a thousand or more — even if only sold to be melted down. A true collector, or an Adept who knew of guardians and dragons, might be willing to pay much, much more.

"You're mad at me," Kett said as we walked down the dimly lit, grimy-walled hall.

"That usually doesn't bother you," I answered.

"It always bothers me."

"I'm not mad. Just claustrophobic."

Kett nodded and stepped sideways into the shadows — still in the hall with me, always at my back, but not so present magically or in my mind.

Warner was waiting at the end of the hall. He looked at me, concerned. I shook my head.

"I was making the fledglings nervous," he said.

"Yeah," I said. "Not all of us can be centuries old and uber powerful."

Warner smirked at me. I managed to grin back at him, though my brain was still feeling peppermint-iced over.

"Where to, vampire?" the sentinel asked the shadowed hall behind me.

"South America," Kett answered. "Peru, specifically. It's been many years since I've visited, but the shape of the country's coastline is unmistakable even on a hand-drawn map."

"Great," I groused. "That's the territory of the healer, and we all know how much he likes me right now."

"Yes," Warner said agreeably. "Too much."

I'd been diligently doing my homework for the last three months or so, so I knew there was a grid point portal located in Peru somewhere. Over land, not water. Thankfully. But I knew little else about the region — so much so that I obviously couldn't identify it on a map.

"I guess the grid point portal is the place to start," I said as we stepped out of the warehouse and onto the night-shrouded city sidewalks, turning back toward Haoxin's apartment. At least, that's where I assumed Warner was leading us. I was still shaking off the residual feeling of having my brain frozen by peppermint ice.

"We'll need Qiuniu's permission to travel there," Warner said. "And perhaps some guidance if he is amenable."

We hadn't needed Haoxin's explicit permission when we'd used the portal to travel to Hope Town for the first instrument of assassination — nor had we gotten it to come to San Francisco, which in hindsight might not have been a great idea. Though technically, we weren't hunting down the next instrument here. Like I'd said, things had changed among the guardians since we returned with the braids, but maybe I just hadn't noticed that the nine weren't always in agreement before. They certainly hadn't been in agreement about me — so that, thankfully, my continued existence hadn't been put up to a vote. Not that I knew whether the guardians exercised real democracy ... it didn't seem likely. By the prevalent mood in the nexus, however, it was apparent that Baxia wasn't going to be the only guardian to close their territory to us and our mission.

"Text me," Kett said. Then he stepped off into the shadows and around the block before I'd taken another step or opened my mouth.

"Text you what?" I called after him.

The nearest airport to the portal. Kett's voice sounded suspiciously like a whisper in my mind.

My step faltered. "Did you hear him?" I asked Warner. "About the airport?"

Warner shook his head.

Damn it. Telepathy?

"A side effect, perhaps," Warner said.

"It'll wear off?"

"Hopefully."

I sighed. I liked Kett well enough, but I didn't want anyone in my head. Pulou could communicate with me like that, but only when we were both standing in the magic of the portals. And for some reason, it wasn't so disturbing then.

I'd started walking again, but hesitated when another thought occurred to me. "You don't think he ..." I glanced back over my shoulder toward the warehouse and the amplifier's offices, realizing midway into the question that I didn't want to vocalize less-than-fantastic thoughts about a friend. And especially not to Warner, who was genetically inclined to be prejudiced toward vampires.

"I think," Warner said, placing his hand on the small of my back and guiding me up the sidewalk past a closed pizza place, "that Kettil, the Executioner of the Conclave, collects more than he kills."

I tried to not squirm uncomfortably at Warner's vocalization of my thoughts.

"He's different," I said.

"And you feel responsible for that difference." Warner tapped his left thigh where he wore the sacrificial knife when he was dressed in his dragon leathers. The knife was still there, of course. The clothing simply an aspect of Warner's chameleon magic.

"Sometimes I think he'd prefer to be dead," I whispered. "True dead, full dead."

"The vampire values his immortality. But perhaps he also chafes at its restrictions."

"Yeah?"

"Yes."

Two more blocks and two more left-hand turns, and we'd somehow arrived back at Haoxin's steel-and-glass apartment building. Standing at its base, it felt like the skyscraper was towering over the city, though only because it sat two blocks from the water's edge. The streets were quiet here but not completely empty.

A cool breeze made me shiver, though it didn't stir my still-sticky-with-dissolved-foam hair. Warner brushed a kiss across my lips without warning.

"We'll find the map," he murmured.

I reached for him, for the strength of his arms, wrapping my fingers around his biceps as far as they'd go. I took a moment to breathe in the smooth, creamy-chocolate-and-sweet-cherry magic that he held so tightly coiled around him.

"We don't know she's in Peru," I said. "Or that she can even read the map."

"If she is who she claims to be, then she's the daughter of the former treasure keeper and can most likely unlock the map. If not, then whoever she is, she seeks an object of power and for you to unlock her magic. She'll follow us to Peru."

"What does 'to break with the guardians' mean, exactly?"

"If, as she appears to be, Shailaja is in league with the shadow leeches, then I would conclude that she believes in immortality."

"But dragons aren't immortal. Only long-lived and difficult to kill."

Warner shifted his shoulders uncomfortably, glancing around the street. "Is the vampire near?"

"Classified dragon secrets?" I asked, teasing but still somewhat serious.

Warner huffed out a laugh. Behind him, through the glassed entrance of the apartment building, a tired-looking businessman stepped out of the elevator with his pure white English bulldog. The dog made a beeline for the front doors, tugging his master after him.

Instead of reaching out for a taste of Kett's magic to answer Warner's question as to the vampire's proximity, I took the sentinel's hand and pulled him into the building before the door closed behind the man and his dog, who were now wandering up the sidewalk.

If we hadn't opened the shades earlier, the apartment would be pitch black, but the glow from the city below and around us lit the room just enough to distinguish the furniture. And Warner, of course. He was kind of hard to miss as he stepped into the living room. Not that I'd had a chance to test that in the dark yet.

Warner sighed and ran his hand through his hair, leaving it a mess. Something about the gesture made me pause. So much of him was cobbled together from the people he'd first come into contact with when he woke from stasis ... my accent, Kandy's ideas of clothing, Pulou's raised eyebrow. But right now, all I could see was Warner ... watching me as I watched him.

I wanted him to close the space between us, but he didn't. He wouldn't. I had a feeling that the level of intimacy I wanted, that I craved, was unusual for his time period. Not that he'd been a monk, but I think everything private took place behind closed doors in the last life he'd lived.

He certainly didn't kiss like a monk.

And the door was most definitely shut and locked right now.

I closed the space between us. Slowly, deliberately. A smile spread across his face, and he leaned back against the couch and stretched out his legs. I would have to walk between them to get as close as I planned to be.

Yeah, he definitely wasn't a monk.

"I like dancing in this age," he said.

"You're a quick study."

I stepped between his legs but left the last few inches open between us. He ran his hand up over my invisible knife, resting it on my right hip, but he didn't tug me closer.

"I was supposed to take you to dinner before the dancing." His face was deep in shadow, but I could see the glint of golden magic in his eyes.

"Supposed to?" I murmured. I reached up and tucked my fingers into the collar of his silk shirt to feel the warm, smooth skin where his neck met his shoulder. If there had been more light, I might have caught a glimpse of his tattoo, which I still hadn't seen beyond the thick black edge that curved over his collarbone.

"Drake indicated that our third date should be dinner and dancing."

"Drake is fourteen," I said with a laugh, then sobered quickly. "Wait, this can't be just our third date."

"Fourteen years spent living in your century," Warner said. "And having a fortress collapse on you, then almost drowning, might feel like a hell of a date, but it wasn't."

I leaned into him a little more, swaying forward to capture his lower lip in a kiss. Then I said, "Dragons aren't immortal."

Yeah, I was unfocused. I was slowly warming up from the imagined brain freeze of Kett sifting through my thoughts, and oh so ready to collapse into Warner's arms. Yet I was exceedingly aware that the map — and Warner — were compromised, and that the world was full of secrets I suddenly needed to know to move forward. Secrets I'd needed to know three months ago but hadn't been aware of — because no one, not even Pulou, had known of Warner's or Shailaja's existence. Even guardian dragons weren't infallible.

"But guardians could be immortal," Warner answered as he brushed a light kiss across my left cheek. "And some argument could be made for the children of guardians, I suppose."

That piece of information cut through the comfort of the kisses. "Sorry?"

"It's rare for a dragon to mate after taking on the mantle of a guardian. Often, the children of guardians become guardians themselves. As I believe is the case for Chi Wen, Baxia, and Haoxin."

"And guardians relinquish their power every thousand years."

"Give or take, but yes. Willingly."

"But they don't have to?"

"An argument could be made."

"What's the argument against?"

"The magic a guardian carries is taxing, even divided as it is between the nine. It can wear on the mind and physical body. And living that long is disorienting. Elder guardians tend to withdraw, like Baxia. And delegate their day-to-day responsibilities, as Chi Wen soon will with Drake. Haoxin and Qiuniu have already begun to walk the far seer's territory upon request."

"You think that Shailaja broke with the guardians because she believes in immortality."

"If she is Shailaja, then the company she keeps is telling."

"And the sacrifices made to create that company." The shadow leeches were most definitely a product of the blackest sort of magic, whether or not the sorcerers had been willing participants in their own 'evolution.' "She was attempting to collect one of the three ways to kill a guardian."

"Yes." Warner sounded grim, and I didn't much feel like hashing through it all again. I would rather have continued with the soft, intimate kisses. But I didn't.

"Does it bother you that I'm slow?" I asked, abruptly changing the subject. "You assimilate so quickly —"

"No," Warner interrupted. "You aren't slow, Jade. You're thoughtful … focused on what matters to you. Life is not so clearly defined for most of us."

"Life isn't so clear to me at all."

He laughed. "Well, you make it seem that way."

"You make it seem that way!"

"Another reason we are well matched," Warner murmured.

And just like that, I was exceedingly interested in renewing the kissing session. Just with more vigor.

"What was the first reason we're well matched?" I asked, flirting as I reached up to tease open the second button of his shirt.

The portal blew open behind us.

"Goddamn it all to hell," Warner muttered, more viciously than I'd ever heard him.

I threw my head back and laughed. Why not? I was terrible at delaying gratification. I might as well enjoy it while it was being forced upon me.

Haoxin, the guardian of North America, stepped through the golden magic of the portal and offered us a sunny smile. The petite blond was wearing a pretty pink-and-white, long-sleeved, form-fitting dress that showcased her every smooth curve.

"Just passing through," she said, giving Warner a saucy grin as he slowly stepped away from me to offer the guardian a low bow.

I mimicked the movement.

Haoxin waved away the formality of our greeting. "Did you find what you were looking for?"

"We have a lead, guardian," I answered. "Peru."

Haoxin snorted. "Qiuniu is going to love that." Then without further comment, she crossed through the living room toward the kitchen. "The far seer awaits you," she said as she glanced around. Then she added disappointedly, "You didn't bake?"

"No, guardian," I answered. "We've only been here —"

"Joking, warrior's daughter," Haoxin said as she pulled an expensive-looking espresso machine out from a lower cupboard. "The brownies are lovely, but they couldn't make a great triple-shot, extra-foam latte if my life depended on it. And some mornings, it does."

Warner winced, probably at the afore-forbidden dissing of brownies. Then he said, "Thank you for your hospitality, guardian," as he turned toward the still-open portal.

I wasn't in such a rush to see the far seer, but I also couldn't just hang around Haoxin's living room …

Sigh.

A shower would have been nice, too … with Warner washing my back. If by 'back,' you understand I meant everywhere, all over, upside and down. Yes, in the shower.

Double sigh.

"My employee Todd is a wizard with espresso. He makes a mean shot," I said over my shoulder to Haoxin as I stepped into the magic of the portal. "Or so I'm told."

"I shall hold you to this proclaimed wizardry, Jade Godfrey," the pretty guardian called after me with a laugh. "And consider it an open invitation to visit you at your bakery."

The thought of Haoxin — or any guardian — in the bakery gave me heart palpitations. I really, really had to work on connecting my brain to my mouth. Like, before I opened my mouth. I got into more tight spots just by being polite than doing any other thing … except for crossing paths with the far seer.

Chapter Nine

'The far seer awaits you,' was pretty much the worst thing anyone could ever say to me. Ever.

Just to make that statement even more soul-crushingly terrifying, I walked through the portal to find the far seer — as expected — waiting in the nexus, and decked out in his usual gold-trimmed white robes. He glanced at Warner, eyed me up and down, and said, 'Ah. Not today." Then he wandered off toward the dragon residences.

I looked at Warner, who shrugged.

"A shrug is not an appropriate response in this situation," I said, then instantly regretted my tone. "I'm sorry ..."

"Walking under the gaze of the far seer must be unsettling," Warner said.

He didn't step closer to me, though I couldn't blame him. My father might walk in on us at any moment, and I wasn't sure how the warrior of the guardians felt about his newly found mortal daughter dating the sentinel of the instruments of assassination. God, my blood ran cold every time I thought of my dad and the instruments at the same time.

What the hell was I doing standing around?

I turned toward the door that led to the territory of South America, looking at it closely to make sure it was the correct one. It was constructed out of a smooth deep-red wood — bloodwood, I thought — and intricately carved like all the other doors of the nexus. I wasn't sure of the nature of the design, though. Incan? Or Mayan? I knew those were cultures from South America's history, but I wasn't sure of the differences between the two.

The only good thing about walking through the portal into the nexus was that it somehow seared off all the dissolved foam that had dried on me, so I didn't feel so sticky anymore. Though I steadfastly refused to acknowledge the crisply burnt shoulder of my pretty new sweater.

I reached for the door, pausing when I realized there was no visible handle. That was different … I hadn't realized that certain territories could be closed. Or maybe I was reading too much into it and all it needed was a solid push —

"We should ask permission." Warner's tone was measured and slightly cautious, as if he thought I might explode for absolutely no reason. "And get supplies."

"Supplies?" I said testily. I hated that walking-on-eggshells tone, especially from men, even if I was just imagining it now. I also hated being questioned as I was about to charge into battle. "You need supplies?"

"No," he answered. "You need supplies."

I turned on him. "Yeah? Like a bathing suit?"

"No," he answered calmly. "A bathing suit would be unwise at the top of the Andes in January … well, at any time of the year."

I snapped my mouth shut to chew on that piece of information. I actually wasn't too sure what the Andes were … mountains, from the sound of it.

"I'd hate to see you ruin that pretty dress further …"

"It's a sweater," I said petulantly, though I was amenable to him cajoling me out of my temper before it got out of hand.

"Sweater," Warner corrected himself with a smile.

"You think my outfit was pretty?"

"No, but I think you look beautiful in it."

Jesus, I wasn't sure I'd ever been involved in a mating dance that took this long to seal the deal. It was screwing with my focus.

"We should just get it over with," I blurted, instantly regretting my words even as I waited for Warner to respond.

He frowned. "This is not the Bahamas. And getting on the wrong side of the healer would be … well, unhealthy."

"No," I said, glancing around while I gestured between him and me. "Us. Together."

Warner tilted his head, still not completely sure what I was talking about. "You wish to seal our bond, now? So quickly, and without your father's blessing? Parents …" — he amended — "… without your parents' approval?"

"Okay, let's call it that, but skip the creepy part about my parents. And, yes. We can be slow the second time."

"Slow the second time," Warner repeated. Then a light went on somewhere in that quick mind of his. "Ah …" He shifted his shoulders. "Yes, I understand that … mating is different in this century."

Jesus. He was going to say no. I could tell from the way he'd angled his body away from me. God, I didn't think I'd ever had anyone say no to me before. Not that it was a question I asked often.

"I would prefer —"

"Forget it." I interrupted him by doing a one-eighty toward the door that led to North America. "So I'll need a ski jacket and hiking boots."

"Jade," Warner said.

"No," I answered, yanking open the door. The magic of the portal whipped around me, and I desperately wanted it to instantly sweep me away. "You find the healer. I'm tired of dancing around the freaking instruments and the asshole map." I stepped into the magic, hoping its golden light covered the shame I could feel spreading through my body. Then I remembered that Warner didn't see magic in color anyway. No matter. If I couldn't hide, I'd run away.

"I'll find the healer," Warner said behind me.

Wrapped tight in rejection, and in my anger at all the things I'd done wrong today, and yesterday, I stepped through into the bakery basement without looking back.

If Warner wanted arm's-length, I could do arm's-length. Jesus, he was the one who'd broken into my apartment to make me freaking pancakes!

He was also the one from the sixteenth century …

I tamped down on my need to counter my own irrational behavior, then slammed the portal shut behind me.

Well, I imagined slamming it closed. Because it didn't actually work like an actual door.

Never freaking mind.

Where the hell were my hiking boots?

Before I crossed back to the nexus, I slipped into the bakery to find it tidy and looking freshly renovated. The floor had been sanded and varnished. The windows sparkled. And, though they had been getting slightly worn around the edges, the bistro tables now shined. The bakery had been completely healed — maybe looking even better than it had before Shailaja knocked on my window.

The only evidence that remained of the rabid koala's assault were the five broken trinkets that Blossom had placed on the desk in my office. And I could fix those myself.

Feeling blessed — and, though I was loath to admit it, thankful for Warner's intervention — I pulled some day-old cupcakes out of the fridge and arranged them in a heart shape on the stainless steel workstation in the bakery. The daycare we usually donated them to hadn't been open yesterday. I hoped that Blossom popped in to collect my thank you, but I vowed to leave a heart shaped in cupcakes behind every night until I knew she'd seen it.

Warner wasn't in the nexus when I returned, swathed head to toe in a water-repellent, fleece-lined ski jacket and various pieces of knitwear. Yeah, not a great look. I'd owned the hiking boots for over seven years and maybe used them three times.

Still feeling childish, I went through the door to South America without waiting or looking around for the healer or the sentinel. I figured that the gold-carved handle that had appeared on the door, where there had been none before, was invitation enough. I'd never walked through this portal before, so I didn't actually know where I was going, but I'd learned that the door of a particular territory led naturally to that territory's main grid point. If there was more than one in any given territory, the door was usually only actively connected to one grid point at a time.

Just in case I was wrong, which certainly wouldn't be a rare event, I thought about the North Shore Mountains as I stepped through the portal. The mountains that I viewed every day from my apartment were my clearest frame of reference when it came to ranges. I assumed that the portal's magic could sort out that I meant the Andes instead. So yeah, deep down I was still an idiot. Now I was just an asshole as well.

Warner and Qiuniu were waiting on the other side.

A wave of dizziness hit me the instant I stepped through the portal. And the lightheadedness wasn't from the spectacular view — of the mountains, because I flat-out refused to ogle the men waiting for me. Yeah, I was that pissy. Nor was it from the way the natural magic of the area sparkled from every rock and patch of moss.

A massive body of water spread before Warner and Qiuniu, who had turned from their conversation to watch me appear. I would have assumed it was an ocean — a really still ocean — except I was fairly certain we were seriously high up. Way, way high. Like, fourteen thousand feet high, according to the quick googling I'd tried to do in between pulling on wool socks.

I inhaled deeply, not allowing myself to panic about the air being so thin up here. The dizziness I'd felt cleared enough that I was pretty sure I wasn't going to faint from instant oxygen deprivation.

A second breath steadied me further, so that I remembered I should be glaring at Warner … and at the healer, because why not? He'd started it, after all. They were still staring at me.

"You were planning on skiing?" Qiuniu asked, his tone somewhere between mocking and flirting.

"It's cold here, guardian," Warner said, before I could take a bite out of the healer myself.

"Of course," Qiuniu said. "I forget the warrior's daughter is not wholly dragon."

Well, that was the politest way anyone had ever called me a half-breed before.

"Even I, the son of Jiaotu, can feel this cold."

Qiuniu inclined his head. Yeah, I wasn't sure this conversation was about a ski jacket anymore.

Warner's magic rolled around him, and I tried to ignore its insane deliciousness. Dark chocolate with a hint of smoke, alongside sweet cherry topped with whipped cream was a lot to ignore, but I persevered. As I watched, his clothing transformed to a toned-down male version of mine. He was missing a scarf, probably because mine was tucked into my zipped-up collar, which was so tight it compressed my chin uncomfortably into my neck. Since we didn't appear to be in the middle of a blizzard, I could probably afford to unzip it an inch or two.

I tugged the extra scarf I'd brought — a navy, gray, and green-striped cashmere number knit by Gran — out of my bulging satchel as I crossed to join Warner and Qiuniu at the edge of the lake.

I wrapped the scarf around Warner's neck, and he obligingly unzipped his navy-blue ski jacket to allow me to loop-knot it. I kept my eyes on my task — pulling the well-worn cashmere through my hands and gently tugging it to a snug-but-not-too-tight knot — but I could still see Warner's slight smile without looking up.

"Where are we, then?" I asked as I zipped Warner's jacket up against the scarf.

"The Coastal Highlands of Peru," Qiuniu answered proudly. "At the shores of Lago Puarun."

"Big lake," I said.

"Very," Qiuniu answered agreeably.

"I assume there isn't an airport or a private airfield nearby?"

Qiuniu frowned at this question but didn't ask me to elaborate. "Huanuco will be the closest. Follow the road and you will arrive at Cerro de Pasco at the tip of the Andes first. They are known for silver, not luxury accommodations."

He had gestured into the sun so that I couldn't see which road he referred to, and the 'luxury accommodations' comment chafed. Kandy had nearly died on our last treasure hunt — a fact well known to the healer, who'd practically refused to help her.

"The healer has a vehicle parked nearby," Warner said, interrupting the biting retort I was formulating.

"It bothers me, warrior's daughter," Qiuniu said. "Not only that this task falls to you … and the sentinel. But also that it brings you to my territory."

I nodded. I knew now what it felt like to have your home invaded, or even to house a potentially lethal weapon under your roof.

"It bothers me more that I cannot accompany you," the healer continued. "I'm considering defying the treasure keeper's … assessment of the situation."

Warner's shoulders tightened, then he forced himself to relax. "You have felt the magic of an instrument, guardian," he said.

Qiuniu turned his gaze from me to Warner. In this setting, he looked almost human. I guess he fit here. Or perhaps, surrounded by the magic of the grid point, his demigod status was lessened somehow.

"I have, sentinel," Qiuniu said. "I don't see you fearing the possibility of feeling such again."

"It's my duty."

"It's my territory."

I glanced back and forth between Warner and the healer. "Geez, guys. We don't even know for sure it's here. Or, rather, where it is in Peru."

"Yes. It also bothers me that this ... dragon could be in my territory without my permission ... or sensing." The healer closed his eyes and lifted his chin up as if listening intently.

"Guardians can sense magic in their territories? Not just demon summonings?" I asked Warner, momentarily forgetting I was being pissy with him. "Like how Suanmi found us in London? She felt Sienna's triple demon summoning."

"Only great amounts," Warner answered. "Massive summonings or incursions. The child is not so powerful, healer. She walks unhindered because we hesitated to harm her and she resisted our offers of aid."

"She's not big on the idea of returning to the nexus," I added.

Qiuniu opened his melted-milk-chocolate eyes and smiled at me. It wasn't a pleasant smile — so that when my heart skipped a beat, it came with a wash of fear, not any sort of attraction. "You have my permission to return her as you see fit, Jade Godfrey."

Magic, called forth from his words, hung in the air between us. Reminding me of the life debt I'd offered to the healer and he hadn't accepted ... yet.

I nodded. His 'permission' settled over my shoulders, and I automatically absorbed the magic into my necklace.

Well, that was new.

"I leave reluctantly," the healer said, brushing by me before I could speak. He touched my shoulder lightly as he passed, leaving a kiss of his magic there — though I wasn't sure he'd done so deliberately.

The portal opened and the healer walked through, taking the comforting, buoyant, and warm portal magic with him.

I turned back to find Warner squinting at me. His body language and expression were at the edge of pissed off, but not full-on glaring.

I flashed him a blinding smile.

"Don't fake smile at me, Jade Godfrey," he said. Then he marched off in the direction Qiuniu had indicated.

Behind his back, my smile tempered into something heartfelt. The sentinel was jealous of Qiuniu. So though I might be having trouble getting him there, he did want to be in my bed.

"So," I said to Warner's broad shoulders, "what was that? A 'get out of jail free' card?"

"I'm not sure what a 'jail free card' is. But yes, I believe the sentiment is apt."

"Monopoly," I said. "A human board game."

"A game you play while you're bored?"

"Yeah," I answered with a laugh. "I guess so."

Warner didn't ask any more questions, so I glanced around. It wasn't as crazy cold as I'd expected it would be, based on Warner's caution. But I wasn't going to be unzipping my coat anytime soon. Sunshine reflected off the huge, clear, light-blue lake. With only patches of snow on their craggy peaks, the mountains didn't look at all like the North Shore Mountains. But I had a feeling that was because we were standing in the middle of the range, as opposed to looking up at the mountains from below. The view was breathtaking but barren.

"So you think Qiuniu has a house here?" I asked.

"Most likely nearby." As Warner glanced over his shoulder, I caught sight of a couple of single-storey buildings at the edge of the lake in front of him.

"What is that? A farm?"

Warner shook his head. "I'm not sure what you could farm at this altitude."

"Llamas, maybe."

Warner laughed but didn't comment further. I'd slowly been figuring out that the sentinel wasn't actually all that much more worldly than I was. He knew a ton about dragons, magic, and duty. I'd even seen him get the better of the sword master in training — once. But other things were completely new to him. He just figured everything out a hell of a lot quicker than me.

Now that we were closer, the simply constructed but well-maintained buildings appeared to be two-car garages. Their siding was painted a light blue that almost matched the lake, while their roofs were unpainted aluminum without a speck of rust. Both were also protected by a ward of some kind, and based on the residual coffee taste of its magic, it had been constructed by Qiuniu.

"Warner," I said.

"I feel it." The sentinel wrapped his fingers around the plain steel handle of the nearest double garage door, then waited.

The taste of the coffee magic intensified, then abated. The door clicked open.

"Keyless entry," I said. "Handy magic. Though I'm not sure how the healer knew to key it to you specifically."

"He didn't. Any dragon who walked here would need to access it."

The garage was protected by a different spell than we'd seen in Haoxin's apartment. But that was a place we'd already gained entry to by way of a portal, so we simply had to remind the wards we were allowed to return. I had something similar on the alley door that led to the bakery, but Gran, Scarlett, Kandy, and I were the only ones who could use it.

Warner swung open the double doors to reveal a silver Mercedes SUV. Yeah, after driving around London with Kett, I now recognized the logo enough to know that much. It had been used recently enough that it was still splattered in dried mud. It was also coated in layers of magic — more wards constructed by the healer.

Warner grinned at me as he crossed to the driver's-side door.

"Wait," I said. "You can't even drive."

He shrugged. "It's a long trip with empty roads. Sounds like a good time to learn."

"Seriously? Now?"

"What could go wrong?"

"I don't know. Did you notice the huge lake? The cliffs?"

Warner laughed and opened the driver's door.

I crossed my arms. "You're supposed to open my door first."

He paused, surprised. Then he grinned as he crossed around the vehicle to open the other door.

Completely haughty, I squeezed by him. But as I turned to step up into the seat, he blocked me with his hip. Then he laid a fierce kiss on me that started on my lips and exploded in my nether regions.

I clenched the sleeves of his jacket, holding myself firmly away from collapsing into him, when all I wanted was to wrap my arms around his neck. With one hand curled around my waist and one at the back of my neck, he held me so firmly that I might not have been able to break away if I'd tried. And, yeah, that thrilled the part of me that wanted to be … wanted. My heart rate skyrocketed, and every pissy thought drained out of my pretty little head.

The possessiveness of the lip lock eased, then turned teasing. Warner brushed his thumb lightly against my neck, pulling back until we were barely touching.

"Always?" he whispered against my swollen, suddenly empty lips.

"Always what?"

"Do I always open doors for you? All doors or just cars?"

"If you're going to be old-fashioned about it."

He regarded me for a moment. Then he nodded and released the back of my head, stepping back to allow me entry to the vehicle.

I almost moaned at being released, but I managed to control myself. Though my legs were rubbery, I climbed into the passenger seat without making too much more a fool of myself.

The sentinel packed a lot into a single kiss.

We headed in the direction Qiuniu had indicated, finding the road easily. The SUV came fully equipped with heated seats, a GPS, and a charging station for an iPhone. Though I opted against blasting music while Warner was learning to drive.

All the technology was heavily warded against magic, and interestingly enough, by Qiuniu. I'd tasted similar, though less powerful wards, on the SUV Kett had stolen from Blackwell while we were hunting Sienna in Scotland. Magic and technology wore against each other. Gran went so far as to suggest that technology and human industry were destroying magic. As the earth died, so magic withered. But the guardian of South America obviously had a healing touch with more than just magical beings. As did Jasmine, the reconstructionist's cousin, who'd laid the wards on Gran's computer. So maybe everything wasn't quite as dire as Gran thought.

After figuring out that the gas pedal was seriously sensitive, Warner drove like he'd been doing so his entire life. Honestly, if he wasn't so sexy — and judging by that last kiss, so into me — I might have hated him for his endless adaptability … just a little.

I pulled out my cellphone and checked it for a signal every few minutes. The plan was starting to feel flawed. I knew I should trust my elders, but I wasn't sure how being vaguely near the location of the instrument was going to draw Shailaja to me.

Except if she figured out she couldn't read the map, then she'd 'demand my aid' again.

"Did you check on the bakery?" Warner asked.

"It looked brand new," I said. "Better than before. Hopefully, an overnight facelift doesn't call too much attention to itself. Or didn't call too much attention already, seeing as how a day supposedly passed between Vancouver and San Francisco."

"Blossom was just claiming her dominion. Perhaps putting it back to what she perceived as its original state."

"She left the broken trinkets, though."

"She can't replicate your magic," Warner said, sounding proud.

"Thank you for introducing us," I said, feeling oddly shy and overwhelmed.

"Anything, Jade," Warner said. "Anything you need that I can supply is yours."

I nodded, threading my fingers through the wedding rings of my necklace. I placed my left hand on top of his where it rested on the center console, but I didn't speak.

The comfortable silence between us was better than any words I could have come up with anyway.

We stopped at a gas station in Cerro de Pasco, even though after what felt like most of the day — but was probably only a couple of hours — the SUV still had a full tank of gas.

We'd climbed farther up into the mountains to get here. The handy computer system in the SUV informed us we were now at 4330 meters. As Qiuniu had already said, this settlement at the very top of the Andes Mountains was known for silver ... and for not much else.

As we'd driven in, all the tiny houses and businesses appeared to be falling into a mining vortex. According to a quick Google search, the entire city of seventy thousand people was built around a gigantic pit.

The Google search also unearthed some not-so-nice opinion articles and blogs about the area. Something about an environmental disaster in the making ... or maybe it was already occurring. I wondered if Qiuniu worried about it, notwithstanding that he couldn't interfere. Not even a guardian dragon had any power here. Their guardianship — aka 'saving the world' — only revolved around the use of magic, specifically magical disasters or demonic incursions. Environmental issues or other catastrophes created by humans weren't under the guardians' purview or control.

As we climbed out of the vehicle at the gas station, the only magic I could feel for miles around was the power I brought with me ... Warner and the SUV. That was exceedingly odd. Whether or not there were Adepts nearby, I should at least feel some sort of natural magic.

I tried to dowse farther as we walked toward the convenience store situated behind the pumps, but I couldn't taste a trace of magic in the area.

After a few steps, Warner paused and shifted his shoulders oddly as if he was suddenly uncomfortable. "You feel that?"

I shook my head. "I don't feel ... or taste anything."

Warner made a noncommittal noise, then continued into the well-stocked store. I paid twenty American dollars for three one-liter bottles of water — knowing I was getting ripped off, but needing to hydrate in the extreme altitude.

Warner asked for directions, but those pretty much consisted of 'follow this road until you get to Huanuco.' But, you know, in Spanish, which neither of us spoke.

Warner might have learned English in a matter of minutes when he'd woken up in my bakery, but he'd had me all demanding and feisty in his face then, plus way more time than we wanted to take with this pit stop.

Thankfully, we had a translator app and spotty cellphone reception. So we muddled through a conversation and I texted Kett to let him know we were heading for the airport in Huanuco.

We drove out of town only a dozen or so minutes after we entered.

My phone pinged with a text from Kett as Cerro de Pasco was dwindling in our rearview mirror.

>*On my way.*

"The vampire?" Warner asked.

I nodded, but didn't answer out loud. I hadn't completely absorbed what I'd just seen and felt at the top of the Andes Mountains. I knew I'd been sheltered my entire childhood from magic. But I hadn't completely realized how sheltered from the wider world I was as a Canadian, and a Vancouverite especially.

"I've never seen anything like that … place," I said.

"Silver is exceedingly valuable to human society."

"But not so good for magic." Something about silver made it almost antimagic. Most alchemists used gold or platinum and gems to build objects of power. And the whole werewolves-being-allergic-to-silver mythology was pure truth.

The only Adept I'd ever known who could work with silver was Hoyt, the slimy spellcurser. He used silver ball bearings to hold his curses. When those curses triggered or exploded near another Adept, the silver added to their damage, even though it wasn't conducive to magic in general. I'd be interested to know how Hoyt had figured out how to contain a curse in a ball bearing, but I wasn't even remotely interested in having an actual conversation with the spellcurser. Unless maybe it involved breaking his collarbone, then dragging him around Stanley Park by horse-drawn carriage.

Yeah, I'd thought about that scenario enough to refine it down to one particular daydream.

"Did you notice the way the very earth rejected our presence there?" Warner asked.

"Ah, no," I answered. "I noticed a complete lack of magic, but you felt rejected? Just walking around?"

He nodded, obviously perturbed.

"Where dragons dare not tread," I muttered, quoting the text that appeared whenever any dragon touched the map. "You think the silver in these mountains is a natural repellent?"

"Not necessarily just to guardians or dragons," Warner said. "But I've never felt so unwelcomed by a physical place before."

"But I didn't feel it."

"You hold your magic differently. You collect it as you pass by, but because you also store it, perhaps you don't need to."

"And dragons?"

"Have evolved to walk the earth. To be anchored to stone and gem … to the magic that fuels creation."

Okay, suddenly it felt like we were on the edge of a spiritual conversation, and I felt uninformed. Or, rather, too uninformed to have settled on my opinion. "Instead of the skies, you mean?" I teased, wanting to continue but not quite so seriously. "With tooth and claw?"

Warner glanced over at me, deadly serious. "We no longer take that form."

"Excuse me? Dragons could be … dragons? I mean I've been reading up on dragon lore, but I … you know … didn't totally believe it."

"Only one guardian is capable of such now … if she can even recall the form. The power of shapeshifting is entrusted to her alone."

"Right, Bixi. But you don't think she's ever turned into a dragon-dragon?"

"Not that I know of. I understand it's a last resort sort of thing. A massive use of her magic. The guardians are not gods."

"But?" I could hear something left unsaid, hanging behind Warner's words.

He didn't continue.

"But …" I repeated, before supplying my own observation. "But we know at least one dragon who is an immortality seeker."

"Yes."

"And with age comes power? Like with vampires?"

"I'm not certain that is due to age only. Especially not in Kettil's case."

"He was ... created already powerful?"

"Perhaps. But I think he's earned the power he has ... or sought even greater power."

"Which is why he's called the executioner."

"The vampires keep their secrets close. I'm not sure what an execution entails. Does Kettil drain those condemned by the Conclave? Does he add their power to his own? I have no idea. In any case, he fulfills a similar role to your father."

"Who dragons call the warrior, rather than the executioner."

"The vampires selected their own titles. It's not our prejudice that named them."

"Fine. Back to the dragons."

"The power of the guardians doesn't grow with age. Their potential is there from the moment a dragon assumes the mantle of one of the nine. They must learn to control and access that potential, but its extent doesn't change. And no one guardian is more powerful than another."

"I bet the fire breather would disagree."

Warner laughed. "Outward appearances and manifestations are useless when it comes to guardians. Baxia's magic counters that of Suanmi's, for instance. The rain bringer and the fire breather. If Chi Wen had chosen to stop aging earlier, you would have no idea he was nearing the end of his ascension."

"You mentioned before that Chi Wen rarely leaves the nexus now. But he goes to see Rochelle."

"Which indicates how important he feels the oracle is."

Yeah, that idea didn't make me extra lightheaded and anxious at all. I reached for the second bottle of water and twisted off the cap.

"I know it scares you," Warner said. "What the far seer sees."

"According to Pulou, what he doesn't see should be a bigger concern."

Warner made a noncommittal noise, but he didn't try to talk me out of not worrying.

His support was appreciated. But I wouldn't mind living in denial a little longer.

I hadn't realized I'd drifted off to sleep until I said, "The dragonfly was silver." Vocalizing the words woke me from a dream I couldn't remember.

"What dragonfly?" Warner asked.

As I opened my eyes, both they and my ears were overwhelmed by a torrential rainfall. It appeared to be attacking the vehicle as Warner drove far too quickly down the face of a mountain ... literally. The steep gravel-edged road cut along a deep ravine to our right, appearing so narrow that I doubted an oncoming car could pass us — if the driver could even see us in the storm.

"Headlights," I muttered as I reached for the last swig of water. I desperately needed to rinse out my mouth — and, unfortunately, to pee. It was great that I wasn't dehydrated, but the timing for a pit stop was awful. I couldn't see much through the thwacking windshield wipers that were barely keeping up with the deluge, but it was full-on dusk outside.

"I can see," Warner said.

"Others need to see you."

He obligingly started looking around for the head-lights — which, rather disconcertingly, took his attention off the road. The sentinel might be able to survive a fiery car crash into the depths of a ravine in the middle of the Andes, but I was a hundred percent sure I wouldn't.

"Wait." I shucked off the heavy layer of sleep that often accompanied impromptu naps, then did the same with the chest strap of the seat belt and my ski jacket. I was way too hot now.

I ducked underneath Warner's arms and leaned across his lap to hunt around for the headlight switch on the left side of the steering column.

"Found it." I turned the lights on.

"Thanks," Warner said. "You could stay there."

"Slung across your lap?"

"Looks more comfortable than sleeping upright."

I laughed and straightened up. "Oh, yeah? And here I thought you were angling for a blow job."

Warner frowned like he did whenever his genetically built-in translator failed him. He didn't understand the reference, or had no context for it. Same with asking for directions in Spanish at the gas station. Give him a few more minutes and he'd be speaking like a native, but there would still be cultural or social expressions he wouldn't get at first.

Oh, God. Mortification flushed my already overheated face. I wasn't going to explain that one.

Warner opened his mouth and I cut him off.

"Three dates."

"Excuse me?"

"Nothing. Just the thing you said about us having only been on three dates."

"Shall we discuss that now?"

"No."

Silence fell, but I felt oddly settled. As if something had clicked for me, and I understood what point we were at in our mating dance. If having to explain what a blow job was mortified me, then I certainly wasn't ready to be giving any.

"You should sleep more, Jade," Warner said. "Listen to the rain. The city is just below us. I saw it right before the weather shifted. We're perhaps thirty minutes away."

"We need to stop at the next gas station, for a bathroom."

Warner nodded.

I shifted the seat until it was fully reclined, listening to him for once rather than insisting that I was fine. "I'll explain later."

"The 'blow job' ?"

"Yes."

"After more than three dates?"

"Yes."

"I understand."

"You always do." I closed my eyes.

"Not always," he whispered.

I smiled but didn't respond. Then I remembered the dream. "The dragonfly in the library was silver," I said, my eyes still closed. "A treasure of Pulou's. It was following Drake around."

"Metallurgy?"

"So Drake said. And I've been wondering about my pen. The one that writes runes." I was murmuring, drifting off as quickly as I'd woken. I couldn't remember the last time I'd slept, and the car was so warm … so cozy … with Warner driving.

"A metallurgist who worked with silver," Warner said.

I was too deep into the drift of sleep to answer, though I tried. I dreamed of books, of silver wings, and of there never being enough cupcakes.

I swore I'd only been asleep for five minutes when Warner hauled me out of the comfy, heated passenger seat to practically carry me to a gas station bathroom. Happily, I was too drowsy to freak out about my reflection in the mirror when I washed my hands and splashed water on my face. I did shriek a little over the lack of hot water, though.

I was still so tired that I probably wouldn't have been able to find the vehicle if Warner hadn't been waiting outside the bathroom for me. I wanted to immediately curl up back to sleep, but he practically forced me to drink another bottle of water and eat a few handfuls of trail mix. He kept blathering on about me needing the salt. I liked the sound of his voice, but I would have preferred to hear it lulling me back to dreamland.

I wouldn't have forgiven him for the force-feeding, except there were candied-coated Smarties in the mix — probably some generic brand, but still tasty. He was right about the salt too, but I didn't tell him so.

"You'll make a good dad," I said to him.

He laughed, then murmured something softly that I wished I could have heard. I was already back in the dream library, though … moving the pieces of the centipede on the map to match Rochelle's drawing, and wondering what I was missing.

I was always missing something that I always ended up discovering too late.

Chapter Ten

When I woke again, the night sky was clear and full of an impossible number of stars. I was alone in the SUV, which was sitting directly underneath a large floodlight in a fairly empty airport parking lot. Long-term parking, I guessed. I peered sleepily out the passenger-side window, thinking I could maybe make out the runway behind a chain-link fence and what appeared to be smaller, private hangars. The well-lit main terminal building was farther off to the left. I couldn't really see it from my low vantage point, but it appeared to be smaller than the Vancouver airport.

A brand new, still-chilled bottle of water was sitting in the cup holder beside me, along with a snack pack of dry roasted peanuts and a note scrawled on the back of a receipt. So Warner must have gone, come back, and left again quickly. God, if I hadn't already been crushing on him to the point of losing all dignity, I would have been doing so now.

I straightened my seat and downed half the bottle of water as I read the note.

I have gone to collect the vampire.
Stay in the vehicle.
Please.
With a cherry and chocolate on top.

It was signed with a scrawl that looked vaguely like a W.

I snorted a laugh and reached for the peanuts. Then I looked up to see the teenage Shailaja standing ten feet in front of the SUV.

The tableau of the teen with the chain-link fence and the lights of the airport behind her actually made me flinch violently enough that I spilled water across my necklace and chest. I couldn't taste a drop of her magic, meaning the SUV must be magically sealed within and without.

Shailaja smiled — like she enjoyed seeing my surprise. Then she said something I couldn't hear, nor could I read her lips.

I glared at her, all the anger that had been born in the bakery boiling up in an instant. Thrown by my own vicious reaction, I tamped down on my fury while undoing my seat belt as surreptitiously as I could.

The rabid koala had thankfully replaced the stretched-way-too-small yellow sundress. She was now wearing a quilted down jacket and skinny jeans tucked into knee-high, supple leather boots that I utterly refused to salivate over. A bright blue backpack dangled from her left hand.

Damn freaking dragons and their freaking endless ability to adapt.

I opened the door, not taking my eyes off the teen for a second as I stepped out from the SUV. A confrontation was coming. I preferred to be on my own two feet and not stuck in a tin can when it hit. Even despite Warner's request for me to stay in the heavily warded SUV. Shailaja had already ripped through the substantial bakery wards while in her child form. Though her magic wasn't fully unlocked, she'd definitely be even stronger and faster as a teenager.

The night was balmy, which was good, because I was wearing just my dark-green turtleneck merino wool sweater and jeans. I'd left my hat, scarf, and jacket in the backseat.

The moment I cracked the door, the taste of her magic — carrot cake with a dash of cinnamon and nutmeg — came to me. Burnt carrot cake, and not a lick of icing. So her magic had resolved into more than simply the sweet sootiness I'd picked up in the bakery. I was thankful for how the burnt taste helped with keeping my hate-on, because I really loved moist carrot cake. Especially with cream cheese icing ... and a half a cup of cocoa mixed in the batter.

Yeah, I was hungry. A girl can exist on water and a handful of trail mix only for a couple of hours.

Carefully closing the car door so that it wouldn't get between me and the teen when all hell broke loose, I glanced around for Shailaja's shadow leech pals, but didn't see any. Though they cast large pools of light directly beneath them, the parking lot floodlights were spaced far enough apart to create numerous deep pockets of darkness for the shadows to hide within.

"You made it difficult to track you, alchemist," Shailaja said. She was now standing immediately before the front bumper of the SUV.

I tried not to flinch at her sudden nearness but failed.

"I thought it was the portals," she continued. "But I see now it was this vehicle. Ingenious." She patted the SUV's hood like it was a puppy.

"It took you three months before," I said, having no idea why I was engaging in any conversation with the teenage dragon. Maybe I just always held out hope that kindness would prevail.

"Did it?" she asked. "My sense of time and self is less scattered than before. But I'm still not whole. I believe it was the necklace that kept me at a distance before." Her gaze fell to my chest. "I see you've begun to replenish it, but it won't be enough."

"Enough for what?" I snapped. It was a stupid question, since I knew what she wanted, but keeping her chatting seemed like a good idea while I figured out what to do next.

The teen reached into her backpack and pulled out the dragonskin map. She unfolded the tattoo across the hood of the SUV, not caring that the vehicle was still speckled with rain.

As she smoothed her fingers over the bottom edge of the tattoo, ornate runic calligraphy appeared along the top edge. The same calligraphy that had appeared when Warner touched the map.

"Where dragons dare not tread," Shailaja said. Then she laughed. She was better at hiding her crazy edge now than she'd been as a toddler, but I could still hear it in her amusement. "We know that isn't the complete truth. Not that I would expect anything more from the treasure keeper."

"We know you were stopped."

"But I made it all the way," she said, completely unrepentant. "You will collect this artifact for me."

"I really won't."

The sheen of gold that rolled across Shailaja's eyes was the only warning I got before she lunged for me. I called my knife into my hand even as I was thrusting it forward to meet her attack. Miss Cupcakes and Trinkets had taken a nap and woken up ready to rumble.

A step before I gutted her, the rabid koala was knocked sideways by Warner, who was moving so quickly that I hadn't even tasted his magic before he was slamming Shailaja down on the roof of a car parked ten spaces away.

I cringed as the roof caved, blowing out the car's windows. The owners of the super-cute old-style Mini were going to be seriously pissed when they got back from whatever trip they were on. Ironically, four parking spots on either side of the Mini were open.

"Sentinel!" Shailaja cried out as if she was greeting an old friend, rather than presently being throttled by an angry dragon. "I didn't recognize you before."

"I don't know you," Warner spat.

Tasting peppermint magic somewhere to my left, I whirled to the right to meet the shadow leeches as they unfurled from the pools of darkness between the parking lot lights. Ignoring me, the shadows swarmed Shailaja and Warner. Then Kett was beside me, his fingers morphing into long claws as I dove forward to slash the leeches with my jade knife. The vampire hissed and fell back as the leeches latched onto him.

I pulled up an extra layer of protection from my necklace and pressed forward, but my blade met no resistance.

The shadow leeches and Shailaja were gone.

Warner was standing as if still pinning the teenage dragon to the roof of the crushed Mini. Slowly, he straightened and scanned the parking lot.

"That's an intriguing mode of transport," Kett said. His cool voice drew my attention away from the sentinel, and I turned back as the vampire bent over to retrieve Shailaja's backpack. He had red sores all over his face and hands, but even as I stepped toward him in concern, I saw them heal.

Warner still hadn't moved from the crumpled car.

"She's gone," I called out as I crossed to see what Kett had uncovered. "I can't taste her magic anymore."

Kett dug through the backpack but didn't find anything that seemed to interest him.

"She left the map," I said, turning to take a closer look at the dragonskin tattoo where it was still spread out across the hood of the SUV. It appeared undamaged and unaltered, but I wouldn't have been surprised if Shailaja had used it as a napkin and corrupted it with black magic. She was just that arrogant. Which, for some reason, reminded me that I had yet to see her wield any sort of weapon. Shailaja armed with a sword or a knife was a sobering thought. I'd bet all the chocolate in my pantry that she'd trained as much as Warner had, which was easily fifty years more than I had so far labored under the sword master's tutelage.

Kett leaned in next to me to look at the map. He'd only seen a picture of it before.

"Words that look like runes appear at the top when dragons touch it," I said. I placed my fingers along the edge of the first block, coaxing the smoky magic out of the tattoo so I could shift it and begin to build the centipede. Then I realized I still hadn't seen or heard anything from Warner.

I looked over to see him standing over the crushed Mini as before, his hands still outstretched.

"She left the map," I repeated.

"It was her," he said. "She's alive." His tone — a mixture of surprise, anger and … grief — twisted my gut.

Kett laughed quietly. I looked at him, appalled and hurt by his insensitivity. He smiled tightly. "The almost-immortal have long lives, Jade," he said. "And the histories to go with them."

Then he turned his attention back to the map.

Damn, damn, triple damn.

And now I was jealous about more than just a psychotic teenage dragon's boots.

Ah, Warner.

I realigned the centipede on the map while Kett watched me intently … or rather, while he watched the magic. Warner and I talking about immortality and long lives reminded me that it was probably exceedingly rare for the vampire to experience new magic. I often suspected that the rarity of my own magic was the only reason we'd become friends in the first place.

Warner sorted himself out and joined us as the map shifted to reveal the location of the second instrument of assassination. Or at least to point us in the right direction.

"So in order to have tattooed this on his back, and to appoint Warner as sentinel of the instruments of assassination, the former treasure keeper must have tracked down all the instruments." Even as the thought was making its way out of my mouth, I knew that everyone else had already deduced that months ago. Not to be daunted by my own insecurities, I forged ahead with the train of thought. "So why not collect them then? And his daughter might say she wants this one in order to harvest the magic from it, but then why did she go after the first one?"

I looked pointedly at Warner. "You said she broke from the guardians because she believed in immortality." I carefully kept any hint of accusation from my tone … well, as best as I could without also screaming, 'You said you weren't an item!'

Warner nodded. His eyes were fixed to the map but unfocused, as if he was thinking.

"But dragons aren't immortal."

"No."

"She wanted to become a guardian, then."

Warner ran his hand across his face, then through his hair. "She should have been in the line of succession."

"But she wasn't?"

"No." Warner sighed — a heavy, lonely sound that actually hurt me to hear it. I was plainly misunderstanding his reaction to Shailaja …

"You were sure she was dead," I said. "Because you thought she'd done something for which she deserved to die."

"I never thought she was the reason for the treasure keeper's secrets. But yes. I assumed by Pulou's behavior that she'd met with the edge of the warrior's blade."

"The teenager with the shadow leeches is an immortality seeker?" Kett asked.

Warner nodded. I ran my fingers along the edges of the centipede on the tattoo. The dragon magic tingled underneath my fingertips.

"Do you think Pulou knew she was trapped in the fortress of the braids?" I asked. "Which is why you weren't summoned to her incursion there?"

Warner shook his head. "The timeline doesn't match. I was appointed sentinel of the instruments before she disappeared."

"Was your position common knowledge?"

"I assumed so."

"But you reported to Pulou alone?"

"Yes."

"Who never expected you to be in stasis for four hundred and fifty years."

Warner lifted his gaze from the map to lock eyes with me. "No, because he expected an incursion. Possibly multiple incursions."

"And there was one. By his daughter, Shailaja."

"To which I wasn't called."

"She knows about the map," I said. "But not how to unlock it."

I left the rest of the unvoiced questions and observations hanging between us to study the map further.

"Based on this gradation," Kett said, "we should head for the highest peak." He indicated a specific section of the green mass the map had revealed as it reformed — which, of course, looked like all the other green masses to me.

"Back toward the silver mines," I said. "Where magic doesn't flow properly. With a crazed teenage dragon tracking me. A friend of yours ..." — I looked at Warner, and this time couldn't keep the accusation from lacing my words — "... whose father went to great lengths to protect the instruments. Maybe from his immortality-seeking daughter? Maybe because she wanted to kill him and assume the mantle of the treasure keeper? Also, for the cherry on top, she apparently knows how to counter the magic that binds you to the location and protection of the instruments."

Warner nodded stiffly. "Those are ... strong possibilities." Then he crossed to the driver's-side door of the SUV without another word.

Kett ran his fingers along the edges of the centipede tattoo just as I had done, but he quickly withdrew them.

"Stings?" I asked.

He nodded. Well, he fractionally dropped his chin.

"And the leeches?"

"Were not pleasant, but also not a concern." He lifted his ice-blue gaze to mine. "I'm looking forward to the next hunt. Our prey is intriguing, and the prize worthy of my time."

I laughed, though I wasn't happy or amused. "Let's hope she knows she's the prey and not the predator."

"She will."

"I don't think she's that perceptive." I folded the map and placed it in my satchel.

"Not all magic is dampened by silver," Kett said as we circled around to climb into the SUV with Warner.

"Metallurgy," I said.

Kett grinned at me like I was his star pupil as he settled into the seat behind mine.

"Yeah, yeah, vampire," I groused. "I do learn, you know."

"Metallurgy," he said. "A branch of magic that the sorcerers of Ayar Cachi were particularly skilled at."

"Ayar Cachi?" I echoed, completely bungling the pronunciation.

"A god of the Inca. Reputably hot-tempered and prone to creating earthquakes."

"I'm not so into the earthquake idea," I muttered as I fastened my seat belt. "Been there, done that."

"Or perhaps the ancient worshipers of Illappa could be involved. A goddess of lightning and thunder. Or a god, depending on what history you subscribe to."

"How is that any better?" I asked, trying for a teasing tone despite the pit of dread growing in my belly.

"You know this from experience?" Warner asked, a sneer creeping back into his tone as he started the SUV.

"Not directly, dragon," Kett answered. "But not all elders hide their knowledge."

We circled the classic Mini that Warner had body-slammed Shailaja into. I knew I was trying to deny the tension building in the vehicle as I said, "I feel bad for the owner, maybe coming back from vacation and finding their car like that."

"The human police will take care of it," Warner said, not unkindly.

"I'll make a call," Kett said.

Warner snapped his teeth on whatever comment he was about to make. His eyes were riveted to the road as we pulled out of the parking lot and sped away from the airport.

Kett murmured something into his phone, a whisper that sounded like Spanish.

I laughed. I couldn't help it. The vampire was stiff competition in every category, and some part of me was pleased I wasn't the only one irked by feeling inferior.

Warner glanced at me. A begrudging smile curled the edges of his lips and eyes.

"A valuable asset," he murmured.

"Yeah," I answered. "Thank God he feels the same way about us."

The main road to and from the airport bypassed the city, so that I could only see a wash of distant lights as we drove away.

The map led us back the way we'd come and then off-road for a couple more hours. The vehicle was completely suited for the ride — just as I was completely not. Warner kept insisting we were still on a road, but in the absence of pavement, gravel, or noticeably packed dirt, it didn't seem like any sort of road to me. The pitch dark of the night didn't help either.

I screamed when we nearly went off a cliff. Warner slammed on the brakes and the SUV barely slid. He kindly didn't laugh at me.

With our supposed 'road' now completely obstructed by a deep ravine, we tumbled out of the vehicle and peered into the darkness that dropped off before us. I couldn't see a bloody thing, of course, but Warner and Kett appeared to be looking at various somethings. Landmarks, I guessed.

"We walk from here," Warner said.

"Well, you're carrying me, then," I said.

"Anytime." Warner flashed a smile full of white teeth at me, which I only caught because the SUV headlights were still on.

"Dawn is about an hour and forty-five minutes away," Kett said as he crossed back to the SUV.

"Will that be a problem for you, vampire?" Warner asked.

Kett didn't answer right away, so I paid attention. A long pause often meant that the vampire was about to offer up some information that he considered important, or even secret. He might think his elders didn't keep as many secrets as guardians did, but he was crazily closed-lipped himself.

Of course, he might not answer at all. That happened about 75 percent of the time.

Kett looked back at us, a backlit silhouette in the now too-bright headlights, his face in shadow. "I will persevere, dragon." He shifted his shoulders as if still thinking, then stepped to block the headlight that was currently blinding me the most. "I was reborn to a vampire who was reborn at the dawn of Christianity, but in a part of the world that the religion had yet to touch. Her sire is older still."

"The big bad of London," I said.

Kett nodded. "Some myths and legends tie the creation of vampires to the death of Judas Iscariot. Hence the suggestion that dawn, when Christ rose from the grave, is a time that all vampires fear."

"Some myths tie the creation of vampires to that of Lilith," Warner said.

"Indeed they do. But then, you'd also have to believe in Lilith."

"This is going over my head," I said. "Vampires are sensitive to sunlight, yes?"

Kett nodded. "Only fledglings, as a rule. And those who were turned when Christianity reigned also avoid churches, crosses, holy water, silver, and dawn."

"But you don't believe those things can harm you."

"I don't believe that many things can harm me, Jade Godfrey." Kett removed his lightweight ski jacket and began to roll up a sleeve of his thick, cozy-looking cashmere sweater. "I'm occasionally proven wrong. May I have your knife?"

That was an odd segue. "Sorry? What for?"

"I'll leave a few drops of blood under the bumper, and you'll absorb what you collect on the knife into the blade. Even if it rains, you should be able to dowse for my magic to get back here."

"Sorry?" I asked for the second time. "Are you planning on deserting me?"

Kett just looked at me steadily with his bare, pale arm extended. I looked at Warner. He nodded.

"The SUV is bloody magic," I said. "I'll dowse for that if I need to."

"You are more familiar with the vampire's magic," Warner said. He deliberately shifted his feet. "We're walking where magic isn't found in abundance. Kett is right to offer this precaution."

I pulled out my jade knife with a growl that came out more whiny than pissed off. I stepped toward Kett, flipping the knife in my hand so I was holding the blade and extending it hilt first to the vampire.

He accepted the offering with reverence.

I wasn't going to be the one to lay the sharp edge against his skin and slice open a vein, or whatever he intended to do. I tried to stomp away as he slit his forearm and left his blood behind for me … just in case I was the only one left standing …

Kett's peppermint magic filled my mouth. I wasn't able to stomp far enough in the darkness to avoid it — not without risking breaking my neck.

Warner crossed back to the SUV and turned off the headlights, leaving me in what felt like complete darkness. Then the sentinel crossed to me and gently pressed the ignition key into my hand. I snatched it from him, but he ignored my pissiness to run his fingers down my back soothingly.

"We are difficult to kill," he said.

"But not impossible," I said.

"You and I are both stronger than we were in London." Kett stepped up beside me and offered me my knife back. "It is an honor, dowser, to wield your blade. An honor to hunt by your side."

He slipped off into the darkness along the edge of the ravine before I could figure out how to respond. I could taste his dark peppermint magic coating the blade of the knife. I reached out with my alchemist power and absorbed the drops of blood into the jade stone, as I'd once done with my own blood and with Warner's. As it combined with all the other magic that sharpened and fortified the knife, that peppermint magic faded. But I knew I could call it up anytime I wanted to now.

Warner hunkered with his back to me. I could barely see him in the dark.

"You're not going to piggyback me like a freaking child!" I exclaimed. My voice was loud in the vast darkness. Kett laughed somewhere ahead of us.

"It would be my preference to have you where I can feel you, warrior's daughter," Warner said. "Not limping and ... pissy."

Hmm, 'feel' me? Well, who says no to that? Not me.

I climbed onto Warner's back. He wrapped his arms around my thighs, stood, and immediately stepped into the darkness to follow Kett.

I slung my arms around the sentinel's shoulders, making sure to press my breasts fully against his back — which would have been more effective had I not been wearing a bulky ski jacket. Then murmured in his ear, "I like you."

He growled something that could have been pained, but which sounded closer to pleasure. German words, I thought, satisfied with the tone and the notion that I'd forced him back to his native language. Even if I didn't completely understand the sentiment.

Our pace was erratic enough that I was actually happy I couldn't see in the dark. At times Warner would climb for what felt like hours, sometimes in crevices so narrow that the rock on either side brushed against his shoulders. Then we would plunge so swiftly it felt like he was surfing the craggy edge of a canyon.

We stopped three times for Kett to reorient himself and to consult the map. I'd started carrying a compact Maglite in my satchel after the fortress escapade. So I wasn't entirely useless for this stretch of our hunt.

I should have just allowed Warner to carry me the entire way, spreading the map out on his shoulders when I needed to read it. Except, of course, the map wouldn't work when touched by a dragon. So, at the first hint of light, I had to be Miss Independent and demanded to be put on my own two feet.

By the time the sun rose, we'd reached a relatively flat plateau but found ourselves stymied and staring at an exceedingly wide mountain peak erupting before us. A mountain peak that appeared impassible — even though, according to the map, we were meant to go through it, not around.

"I can't climb that," I said. I was sitting cross-legged on the ground, attempting for a fourth time to decipher the dragonskin tattoo spread across the rock before me. "You didn't mention mountain climbing when you mentioned supplies, sentinel."

Warner didn't answer. He and Kett were hunched over me, staring down at the map, then up at the sheer granite cliff face before us.

The patches of snow on the bare stone had increased the more we'd climbed, but not as much as I would have thought. Moss and some type of low bush still appeared to be attempting to grow, but I hadn't seen a tree for miles. The chill cut uncomfortably through my jeans, and sitting on the ground was no picnic for my ass either. I would have bought a longer ski jacket, but anything that puffy and my hips really didn't go great together.

"This one is hidden way better than the first," I said.

"No tourist brochures," Warner agreed.

"No wolf," Kett said.

Yeah, I missed Kandy too. Kett and Warner weren't exactly chatty or chummy while walking through the darkness of the Andes. Kandy knew how to mix serious business with fun.

"We could go around," Warner said. "The entrance might be on the other side."

Kett shook his head. "Not necessary. I believe we are here. Dowser?" He gestured toward the craggy rock wall before us.

"You think the mountain peak is the fortress?" I asked as I tucked the map into my satchel and stood. "I can't feel any magic here. Nothing like the doorway into the pocket of time that hid the first instrument."

"This won't be the same," Warner said. "Each instrument was created, or collected, or contained by different Adepts. The magic will be different."

Warner and Kett stepped away from me, winging out to the left and right of my back to give my dowser senses space.

I shivered despite my fleece and cashmere knitwear. Then I realized it wasn't the cold air or the chilled stone I was feeling, but the lack of magic underneath my feet. I'd been surrounded by peppermint and chocolate and cherries, so I hadn't registered what was missing.

Reaching out with my dowser senses, I stepped toward the rock face before me, but I still couldn't taste any other magic.

I pressed my palm to the cold granite. It was so icy I was fairly certain I'd lose some skin if I lifted my hand away before my body heat could warm it.

"Nothing," I called back over my shoulder. "I got nothing."

Then the pile of boulders to my left tried to bite my head off.

Fortunately, I noticed.

I ducked and twisted away from the attack. Steely magic flooded my senses, leaving a nasty metallic taste in my mouth as it swirled around the pile of rocks that were animating before me. The massive boulders, each easily three or four feet in diameter, reformed into something with arms and a head, but no neck.

I rolled underneath the boulder creature's second swipe, coming to a stop only inches from Warner's boot-clad feet as he stepped over me.

I gained my feet, calling my knife into my hand as I pivoted. Kett tucked next to my left shoulder as Warner effortlessly sprung up and punched the now easily eight-foot-tall mass of rock in its head.

Not rock. Metal.

Or at least silver-infused granite. The morning light sparked back at me from everywhere it touched the creature.

Warner's fist made contact. The sentinel grunted and something snapped.

Rock didn't break like that. But bones did.

The boulder creature stumbled back, hitting the cliff face I'd just been touching. Then it hunkered down like a hockey goalie waiting when a fight breaks out during a game — completely ready and willing to take a swipe at anyone who skates too near the net.

Yeah, if that was the first image that came to mind when a rock creature attempted to maul me, I really had been hanging out with Kandy too much.

Anyway, the move appeared to be a retreat, but was actually a protective offensive position.

Warner landed at the exact spot from which he'd leaped, but he was cradling his right hand as he eyed the rock creature. The sentinel stretched his arm to the side, then let out a muffled groan as whatever had broken snapped back into place.

"Has that ever happened before?" Kett asked. "Is it an old injury?"

"No," Warner answered, blunt and pissed in equal measure.

"Silver in the rock," I said.

"I see," Kett said. "Primitive construction, but effective. It should be oxidized, but perhaps the metallurgy maintains the polish."

"Silver isn't a problem for you, though," I said, recalling the bits of information I'd gleaned from our earlier conversation. "Because you don't believe in it, right?"

"I doubt it's usually a problem for dragons," Kett answered dryly.

"It's a naturally occurring magical repellent," I said. "A dragon holds a lot of magic."

"Yes." Warner stretched his arm over his head, then behind his back. "But I'm adaptable."

Kett laughed.

The hunt was on.

I stepped forward and around to Warner's right as Kett stepped to the left. We fanned out to block the boulder creature in, but stayed far enough apart that we wouldn't hinder each other's movements.

"I can't get a read on its magic," I said. "Definitely not sorcerer, which is what I expected."

"Witch?" Kett asked. "Earth based?"

"No. It's all metal, metal, metal. No earth, no chocolate, no fruit. Nothing."

The boulder creature swiveled its head as if it was looking at each of us, then it folded its arms tighter around itself.

"Does it even have eyes?" I muttered.

"It doesn't need eyes," Warner answered.

"Better question," Kett said. "What is it guarding? A door? Do we have to vanquish the creature for it to open?"

"And is it the only one?" I added, eyeing a second set of boulders to the right. "I triggered it when I touched the cliff face."

"So it sees or feels magic," Warner said. He glanced over at Kett, who nodded.

Both of them pulled all their tasty magic tightly inside themselves. Dampening it as much as they could. It was a technique they both excelled at. They couldn't completely hide from me — I knew their magic too well — but I still felt suddenly alone, left with only a metallic stain on my tongue. I took it to be the taste of metallurgy, though neither the dragonfly nor the pen had tasted so nasty.

"Don't let it hit you," Warner growled at me.

"Yeah, figured that out already, sixteenth century," I said with a smile.

Warner huffed. Then he and Kett stepped in separate directions into the shadows of the cliff face that the morning sun had yet to illuminate.

So, yeah. Leaving me alone under the gaze of the boulder creature. If I was going to be bait — again — I might as well own it.

I pumped my alchemist magic into my knife as I twirled it in my hand. Boulder guy's head shifted. If I wasn't accustomed to hanging out with a vampire who appeared to be carved out of ice, I probably wouldn't have noticed the subtle movement.

So Warner was right about it sensing magic.

I threaded my fingers through my necklace and called up all the different magic I'd recently stored in it. Even diminished, I was hoping it would create quite a glow.

The boulder creature shifted its shoulders and stepped toward me — almost involuntarily, it seemed. This placed it slightly away from the cliff at its back, in a more accessible position.

Kett dropped down from the shadows of the cliff face where he must have scaled quickly upward. He slammed his feet into the boulder creature's left shoulder, though I think the vampire had been aiming for its head.

The resulting boom from the two-footed slam-kick hurt my ears. The creature dipped to one side as a crack formed across its shoulder.

Warner took advantage of the creature being off-balance, pushing out from the cliff on its right to slam both his feet into the side of its head.

It stumbled closer to Kett, who'd been trying to get a grip on its head. Failing that, the vampire had wrapped himself around the creature's cracked arm instead.

I reached for its magic again and again as it struggled, trying to figure out what fueled it and how it had been created. However, I couldn't grab at anything beyond the creature's metallic taste. I briefly thought about darting into the fray and stabbing it with my knife, but I was worried about all that silver breaking the jade blade like it had broken Warner's arm.

Kett and Warner continued to wrestle and pummel the stone creature. More hairline fractures formed in its boulders, but the attacks barely managed to shift the creature more than a few feet away from the sheer rock wall behind it. Then the boulder creature abruptly spun to slam Kett back against the cliff face. This stunned the vampire enough that he fell limply to the ground.

The creature swiveled the lower section of its body and raised a thick stone leg over Kett's head — completely ignoring Warner's attempt to rip off its arm. The sentinel had twisted the granite limb up over the creature's shoulder while perched on its back.

I darted around Warner, who reacted to my proximity with a vicious rolling growl filled with what sounded like German curses. Then I attempted to drag Kett out from underneath the creature. Problem was, I didn't exactly have any place to move to quickly.

I got my hands underneath Kett's shoulders and shifted him a couple of feet out of the way. But now we were both trapped between the cliff face and the creature.

It slammed its foot down where Kett's head had just been, and the resulting earthquake knocked me on my ass.

Warner bellowed, then ripped its arm off.

Kett closed his hand around my wrist, dragging me underneath the opening created when the creature stumbled. We sprinted by Warner as he twisted to throw the creature's arm away as if it were a Frisbee.

The sentinel stumbled back to join Kett and me a few feet away. As we watched, panting — or in Kett's case, just shaking his head to clear it — the creature stepped back. Two steps was all it took to close the gap behind it, and it was hunkered down like a one-armed hockey goalie in net again.

"Jesus," I said.

Warner let loose with another long string of vicious-sounding German. I assumed he was swearing, but all German tended to sound a bit brutal to my ear. He could have been saying anything, but just really fiercely.

Kett nodded and said something back in German, then switched to English. "We will eventually tear it to pieces."

"This is silly," I said. "It's magic. There must be a magical means to disable it."

"Magic none of us wields," Kett said, his cool tone as close to testy as it ever got. I wasn't the only one who didn't like being called silly, or feeling stupid, or unskilled.

I looked over to Warner. He was battered around the edges — ruffled hair, a red bruise on his cheek that was slowly fading, torn jacket and jeans — and sexier for it. He smiled at me in response to my ogling him, but then shook his head sternly. "No, Jade," he said. "It punches like a fucking mountain."

My smile widened at his impassioned profanity, in English this time.

"What is your suggestion, dowser?" Kett asked, calling me back to the present predicament.

"We could try to find a silversmith. You said way back that you thought Hoyt or Blackwell must employ one to get Hoyt's curse in his silver ball bearings. But I doubt a silversmith's magic would hold much sway here, and I loathe the idea of going to an evil sorcerer for help. A second time, I mean."

"I doubt such sorcery would work here," Warner said. "Unless the silversmith was exceptionally talented. Skilled enough to pull every bit of metal from the creature."

"Enchanted metal," I murmured. Something clicked in my mind suddenly. "I spell metal."

"You combine vessels already containing magic together to make a new whole," Kett said, reprimanding me lightly but pointedly.

Ignoring him, I took a step toward the boulder creature, which shifted its head to track me. Warner reached out as if to stop me, but when the creature didn't move farther, he let me kneel on the ground.

"Some space?" I asked, probably far too snarkily for someone attempting to do something she wasn't actually capable of doing.

Warner and Kett backed off to either side of me and dampened their magic again.

I crossed my legs, which forced my satchel to sling across my lap. Denying the cold that began to immediately seep through my jeans, I closed my eyes and let my dowser senses reach out for magic. Again, the metallic taste flooded my mouth, but I couldn't grab or channel it. I was a witch and a dragon. Witches pulled their magic from the earth. I was sitting on an entire freaking mountain and getting nothing. Dragons were magic personified, but based on Warner's earlier observation about feeling rejected by the earth, that must be the ultimate source of their power as well. At least in part. Guardians had something else going on — a secret rite of passage, an ascension of some sort — but that didn't matter right now.

I opened my eyes to stare at the boulder creature, then scanned the rock all around it.

"No hidden marks," I said. "No runes or keyholes."

"No," Kett said. "I see nothing like that."

How did magical beings who weren't witches or dragons access magic? Well, runes were important for sorcerers. They had to physically create spells to call magic, but I couldn't write runes …

"Jesus Christ on a cupcake!" I cried, thrusting my hand into my satchel. I didn't have to look back to feel Warner glance at Kett behind me, or the vampire shrug in response.

From the satchel, I pulled the pen that Pulou had given back to me. The pen I'd collected in Tel Aviv months ago. The pen I had assumed was simply a sorcerer-charmed gold Cartier ballpoint. But now — based on its ability to annoy the treasure keeper — I thought it might be something more. Perhaps even a form of metallurgy.

The pen that wrote runes.

Of course, I didn't have any paper.

I uncrossed my legs and scrubbed my feet against the moss and dirt that covered the somewhat flat granite in front of me, digging up and clearing it all away until I had a fairly smooth surface about a foot and a half square.

Kneeling before this cleared space, I placed the pen in the center and pulled out my knife.

Now ... what were the magic words?

"Open sesame," I said.

Kett snorted behind me, but his disbelief didn't shake my conviction.

Magic was about intention.

I ran the fingers of my left hand down the pen and whispered to it again. "Open sesame."

The pen perked up. I pushed my magic and my intention toward it.

It started to write. Its ink didn't make a terribly strong impression on the granite, but that was okay — because I just needed to see and copy its strokes.

It drew a line. I slashed a line after it with my knife. It drew a curve. So I slashed a curve.

It drew and I carved until five runes, each three inches tall and a quarter inch deep, were scribed in front of me.

The pen paused, waiting for more instructions.

"Thank you," I said as I slipped it back into my satchel. Then I placed my hands over the runes, calling up the metallic taste of a magic I couldn't actually manipulate. "Open sesame."

"Thrice said," Warner murmured behind me.

"Thrice meant," Kett added.

"So heeded," Warner said.

I'd never heard that invocation before — if that was what it was — but I could feel the power behind the words as Warner and Kett uttered them.

My magic filled the runes in a way I could feel rather than see. Then liquid silver rose out of the stone to smooth out all the gouges I'd carved.

The stone creature shifted to the side, then once more became a pile of benign boulders.

More silver runes appeared at the bottom edge of the cliff face, then those symbols slowly began to glow and spread upward to form an archway. The stone wall in the middle of this arch faded away to reveal an opening in the side of the mountain.

Kett and Warner stepped up beside me.

"Impressive, dowser," the vampire said. Then he moved forward, immediately crushing my sense of accomplishment by adding, "Keep the pen handy."

Warner laughed. When I glared up at him — more than a little hurt — he shook his head and nodded toward Kett's retreating back. "The cold bastard is amusing. I thought you were brilliant."

I snorted, pretending to reject the compliment even as it thrilled me.

Quickly sobering, I nodded toward the open doorway. "The rabid koala will follow."

"Let her come," Warner growled. "I'm tired of Shailaja's games. We'll draw her out, collect the instrument as the treasure keeper demands, then let the guardians sort it out. She alone is no match for us three."

"There will be other traps inside."

"Even then, she cannot possibly prevail."

I reached over and squeezed his warm hand. That was all I could do in the face of his simmering anger. He placed a kiss on my palm.

Then we followed Kett into the side of a mountain.

Chapter Eleven

Stairs carved out of the solid stone of the mountain led steeply down into the darkness. They seemed to widen as they did so. Heading downward was odd, because I would have expected to climb in the interior of a mountain.

Both Kett in front of me and Warner behind were dampening their magic like hot fudge smothered vanilla ice cream — though, sadly, the effect was nowhere near as tasty. So it was my first footfall that triggered tiny magical silver lights on either side of the third stair. Helpful, but not totally illuminating as we descended into the yawning, vast pit of darkness I could practically feel breathing beneath me.

Something dwelled deep in that darkness, but I couldn't taste, see, or feel it. Still, I knew it was there. Because that's how these sorts of things went, wasn't it?

When the first sliver of silver glowed about five feet away from me, I paused, waiting for another attack.

Nothing else moved.

The silver lights continued to trigger one by one, on every third stair as I passed.

"It would be more helpful if they lit up ahead of us instead of beside me," I muttered.

"You'll want to find your way out," Kett said, his voice disembodied in the dark. He was being helpful as always. Calming, even. Or not.

I stopped to examine the lights more closely. I hunched down to touch one. Warner hissed his disapproval behind me, even as the glowing light unfurled silver wings, which it flapped lazily as if just waking.

"It's a lightning bug," I said. "You know, a beetle. A firefly made of silver."

I brushed my fingers across the back of the insect's silver glow-bulb body. It appeared to be entirely constructed or cast out of silver. The design was simple — a beetle-shaped body that appeared to glow like molten silver, until I looked closer and could see actual liquid silver encased within it. Add a tiny head with tinier antenna, and gossamer strands of silver to form wings. Deceptively simple, but channeling complex, detailed magic. Or, more specifically, metallurgy.

The firefly took flight, hovering at my eye level as I straightened up. I lifted my palm to see if it wanted to land in my hand, but it flitted playfully away from me. I took a few more steps down, passing another stationary firefly that lit up as all the others had.

The first firefly moved closer, flitting up and around me. I laughed, delighted by its antics.

"Don't play with unknown magic, dowser," Kett said.

I stuck my tongue out in the general direction of his voice. Then I continued to descend, stone stair by stone stair, into the dark core of the mountain.

The stairs widened as we continued, the firefly lights spreading farther and farther away, until they eventually gave shape to high, rough-hewn cave walls.

I slammed into Kett, smashing my nose into the back of his head. He didn't move an inch.

"Some warning would have been nice," I growled, holding my nose. My nasal tone was annoying even to my ears.

Kett indicated ahead of himself with the barest of nods. I followed his gesture, and as if responding to me, the firefly flitted ahead, then cut right to illuminate a stone wall that stood about twenty-five feet ahead of us. It dipped up and down as it flew away, kissing or tickling each firefly light it flew over. Each of them glowed in turn, a line of silver lights forming along the edge of a walkway that appeared to branch off before us and run alongside the stone wall. The increased lighting slowly revealed the inverted dome of the massive cavern we'd descended into.

"Impressive," Warner said as he stepped up beside me. He'd unsheathed his knife, and I could taste the darkly tinged magic of the blade.

"Obviously a natural formation," Kett said, coolly dismissive of the grand scale of the cavern. "Simply and crudely adapted by its founders."

The vampire glanced down at Warner's knife. The sentinel noticed and sheathed the blade. I almost opened my mouth, then stifled my apology. Kett didn't constantly need to know how sorry I was for killing him. And hopefully it would be just that one time.

The firefly reappeared on our left, still triggering other stationary fireflies as it flew toward us. The lights now appeared to form a massive ring around the stone wall, which curved off to either side of us before disappearing into the darkness. The wall was maybe fifty feet tall, if what I could see was actually its top edge.

That was odd, wasn't it? A walled-off circular section deep within a cavern?

Wanting to get a closer look at the wall and perhaps spy a possible doorway, I started to step around

Kett only to slam into his outstretched arm. He'd held it up so quickly I hadn't registered it. It was like being punched in the gut, but with a steel pole. A thick, icy steel pole.

I exhaled every available molecule of oxygen available to me, then doubled over momentarily, unable to breathe back in.

"Really, vampire?" Warner asked.

"My apologies," Kett said. "I'm still growing accustomed to … myself."

"How long are you going to blame me for London?" I gasped.

"Would you prefer I let you walk off the cliff, dowser? I can't see the bottom, but it must end somewhere."

A wash of darkness that I assumed was just a deeply cast shadow sat between me and the wall. You know what happens when you assume, right? You look like a freaking idiot in front of your self-appointed mentor and new boyfriend.

The firefly zoomed back to me, illuminating enough of the walkway I was standing on that I could see the crevasse that began about a foot away. Reacting to my look, the firefly helpfully darted over the crevasse, but couldn't penetrate the darkness that fell away from the sharp edge.

"I imagine what we're looking for is on the other side of this wall," Warner said, glossing over my almost foolish misstep and keeping Kett and me on task, rather than bickering over who hurt who more and when.

Kett nodded curtly and cut right to follow the curve of lights along the edge of the walkway. The lights would have been much more helpful on the edge of the crevasse, but apparently whoever built the cavern hadn't been terribly safety conscious.

Warner pressed a hand to the small of my back and murmured into my curls, "Perhaps best to let the vampire lead? Since he can see in the darkness much better than you or I?"

I sighed. "Got it."

The firefly continued to beckon us forward, but I saw nothing other than stone, stone, and more stone as we traversed the edge of the dark fissure.

"Shouldn't there be more traps?" I asked.

"The door wasn't complicated enough for you?" Warner teased.

"There will be more," Kett said.

We rounded the wide curve, continuing to walk until we arrived at a narrow stone bridge. Or more of a ledge, really, which jutted out over the crevasse and led to a narrow set of stone stairs that cut straight into the wall on the other side.

The walkway continued onward, but I assumed it simply circled back around to the bottom of the main stairs. Plus, the firefly bobbed helpfully about halfway across the bridge. Or, from my perspective, the single-file stone ledge that ran across a crevasse with no safety rail and no perceivable bottom.

Fan-freaking-tastic.

"It isn't a wall, then," I said.

"The stairs lead upward. Perhaps to a wide platform?" Warner said. "Ringed by the fissure. We should circle it to be —"

Kett started across the ledge without a second thought.

"Don't look down," I called. I shook my head at Warner and moved to follow the vampire, who passed the firefly without bothering to answer me. Then he started to climb the stairs.

I really, really missed Kandy. The green-haired werewolf could always be counted on to laugh in the face of impending death.

Halfway along, the ledge was narrower and longer than it had appeared from the other — stable, thicker — side. I briefly wondered if it was a magical optical illusion.

Then the freaking firefly dive-bombed my head without warning. I instinctively threw my arms up to shield my face, but lost my balance on some inconveniently loose rock. Though perhaps the rock was convenient for the firefly, which had apparently been luring me to my death.

Damn my stupid fascination with shiny objects.

My ankle twisted and I went over sideways.

Warner snagged the back of my jacket.

I was suspended over the bottomless crevasse, hanging at an almost forty-five-degree angle out from the ledge.

"Holy fu —"

A light flared beneath me. Way, way too much silver light. I screamed as it seared through my eyes and into my brain, throwing my arms around my face a second time.

I was blinded. The silver light exploded through my mind as the metallic taste of the metallurgy flooded my mouth, plugged my nasal cavities, and choked off my scream.

"Bend your knees, Jade," Warner growled.

Clinging to the command in his tone for sanity's sake, I bent my knees. Even though I desperately wanted to claw the metallurgy out of my eyes and throat.

He hauled me back until I was crouched over my firmly planted feet.

I tried opening my eyes, but all I could see was silver, silver, and more silver. "I can't open my eyes," I cried.

"They're open," Warner murmured as he picked me up and — I could only guess — carried me the rest of the way across the bridge.

I twisted my fingers through my necklace instead of scratching at my eyes. "What the hell was that?" I was thankful I could talk, even though the silver felt like it had completely filled my throat. I tried to not cling to Warner as I attempted to rapidly blink away my apparent blindness.

"A river of molten silver." Kett's cool voice came from somewhere behind me.

Warner placed me carefully down on a step. I sat, desperately gripping at the edge of the stone rather than his leg.

"Impossible." Warner stepped away from me, perhaps to look at Kett's 'molten silver.' "It's just water spelled to appear silver."

"It's a crucible," Kett countered. "And we just stepped onto a platform at its center."

"But you can see?" I asked.

"Yes," Warner said. "As before, I can't feel any magic. But I assume the concentration of metallurgy is affecting your sensitive senses differently than mine or the vampire's."

Kett pressed his cool fingers to the back of my neck. "Shall we proceed?"

I still couldn't see a damn thing, nor could I grab or push away the magic that was affecting me, but I nodded.

"Give her a damn second," Warner said as I stood. I reached through the silver light toward his voice.

Still grumbling under his breath, he flipped me over his shoulder and followed Kett up the stairs. The taste of his black-forest-cake magic soothed me as I attempted to discern individual objects within the haze of silver that was all I could see. If I squinted madly, I was fairly certain I could see the line of the bridge behind us, but only because it was a slightly darker gray within the pervasive silver blur.

We made it to the top of the stone stairs without me seeing or doing another damn thing.

I heard — twice — some sort of kerfuffle ahead of us as Warner climbed. Some sort of smashing of what sounded like metal. I assumed Kett had confronted and overcome some sort of metallurgy, but the vampire didn't offer any verbal enlightenment.

Warner paused at the top of the narrow stairs, shifting me off his shoulder to set me on my feet in front of him. He kept his hand clenched into a fist at the back of my ski jacket, like I might wander off unexpectedly. But still silver-blind, I wasn't going anywhere.

"Kett is walking the perimeter of what appears to be a completely flat area, about three times the width of the nexus," Warner said. "The river of molten silver, if that's what it is, encircles us. As with the bridge, no barrier stands between us and a sheer fifty-foot drop into the silver lava."

"Magic?" I asked. "More traps? Doorways?"

"More of those silver lights have illuminated as you have passed, and I assume they will continue to do so. No traps or doorways that I can see, though a stone table set on a center pillar has been hewn out of the rock. It stands closer to the edge opposite to us than to the center."

God, I never had been great at visualizing things. I blinked a few more times, almost squealing in delight when I figured out I was seeing basic Kett and Warner shapes within the gray blur as the vampire crossed back toward us.

"Another altar, you mean?" I asked grimly.

"That would depend on the sect that created this site," Kett said. "But yes, most likely. I would assume that sacrifices were conducted here at some point. Tributes to whatever god they worshiped, from whom they believed their power over metal was a divine gift."

"Conjecture doesn't help us, vampire," Warner said. "Whether or not it was considered to be an altar doesn't help the alchemist get her eyesight back."

I sensed more than saw Kett shrug. "Is it always going to be altars?" I sighed.

"Would you prefer a treasure chest?" Kett asked.

"Yes," I answered, though I got that he was being sarcastic.

"There's one of those too," Warner said. "On the table." The word 'table' was delivered bitingly. Yeah, my boyfriend was in protective mode again. If I wasn't all freaked out and blind, I would have paused to swoon. I also would have questioned whether Kett had just tried to joke with me, except …

"Why is it getting darker again?" I asked.

The shadow leeches attacked.

Warner yanked me back and to the side, trying to shove me behind him, I think. I stumbled and fell instead. Standing over me, the sentinel pulled his knife. I could see and taste the sweep of the blade's magic, a blur of blue and gold.

Kett hissed in pain as he dove in next to me. "I'll need your knife, dowser. I doubt I can wield it as well —"

I pressed the blade into his hand, then he was gone.

Shailaja laughed. Shadows whirled around me, but the demons didn't bother testing the personal ward my necklace provided. So they learned, maybe. Did that make them sentient? Was that anything to be concerned about right now? No.

I could feel Warner and Kett moving around me. Seated on the cold stone, I wrapped my arms around my knees and pulled them into my chest to make myself as small as possible. Streaks of gold, blue, and red magic cut through the darkness as the sentinel and the vampire darted and spun to slash and stab at the shadow leeches.

Shailaja clapped one hand across my mouth and tightened the other to a fist in the back of my hair, whispering in her annoyingly uppity English accent. "Thanks for the way in, alchemist. Time to collect the prize."

Okay, maybe her accent wasn't the annoying thing. Maybe it was the fact she always had the upper hand — even though we'd been expecting her this time — that pissed me off.

Still holding me only by the head, she started hauling me toward the altar.

At least that's where I assumed she was taking me. Getting dragged by the head wasn't terribly comfortable. I was also exceedingly aware of how quickly, then insistently, my neck ached at this treatment, and how easily even a teenage dragon could snap my spine should she so desire. I'd already done the broken neck thing — twice — and I really didn't want to tempt fate for a third go. Even the healer had cautioned me about this vulnerability.

So I tried to bite her hand instead of digging in my heels or twisting away. Unfortunately, she held her palm firm but flat, clamped tightly across my lips and lower jaw. Actually, if her hand hadn't been covering my mouth, it might have appeared as if she was just hugging me from behind.

You know, if rabid koalas went around giving hugs. I gurgled a laugh at the ridiculous ways my mind kept me from going into shock or freezing up.

"Why are you being so lame?" the crazed koala whispered as she dragged me to my knees. "Tell me what you see before you, alchemist."

She lifted her palm partly away from my mouth, though she kept the side and heel of her hand clamped to my jaw and chin.

"I'm freaking half-blind, you stupid twit," I said.

"Jade?" Warner called through the dark … well, the grayish shadow. I wasn't sure he could see anything more than I could through the swarm of shadow leeches.

Shailaja giggled. "Over here, my sentinel."

Yeah, I really, really didn't like the 'my' part of that. If I'd had my knife, I would have jabbed it in her freaking eye. Instead, noting I could actually see the leeches roiling around us now, I reached up and wrapped my hands around each of her wrists.

She giggled again. "Shall we have a contest of strength, half-blood?"

"Nah," I said. "I get that you're stronger, but your nose ain't half as thick as my skull."

"I don't —"

I slammed my head back into her face. Something crunched, and Shailaja's hold loosened enough for me to pivot on my knees and knock her feet out from underneath her.

Unfortunately, she didn't let go, so we rolled together — scratching and fighting for a hold or a handful of hair — until we slammed against the stone altar. Me, forehead first, of course and always.

Starbursts exploded in my eyes. Had they not been accompanied by an instant migraine, they would have been a relief to the endless press of gray.

My limbs went rubbery, and for some reason, Shailaja let go of me. I rolled onto my back, lifted a shaky hand to my head, and felt warm liquid.

Lovely.

I just hoped my brains weren't leaking out. I really didn't have any to spare.

I could see Shailaja standing over me. Well, her general shape and golden-tinted magic. The region I assumed was her face was sparkling with gold, as was something else down lower. Blood on her face and hand, maybe.

I was seeing magic. The gray was the shadow leeches, and I could see flashes of gold and red among that gray. Warner and Kett.

Shailaja grabbed a handful of my curls, and I stood swiftly so as to not lose a good chunk of hair.

"Look," she hissed.

A silver treasure chest sat on the stone table. It was about one and a half feet square and deeply etched with runes that I couldn't have hoped to translate even if I wasn't still half-blind.

"Take the chest," Shailaja demanded.

"We've both played this game before, crazy koala," I said. "It would be seriously stupid to —"

All the shadow leeches left us so quickly that I was actually buffeted by the breeze of their passing.

Kett hissed in pain — a muted noise that pinched my heart.

I whirled around, dragging the ever-clingy Shailaja with me and wrenching my neck to do so. Warner was standing about ten feet away, his blade still extended in midslash though no leech was within his reach. Or at least I saw a gold-sparkling outline of him and his knife.

A vortex of gray shadows twisted and churned in a funnel around a red blur. Kett.

The vampire didn't make another sound.

"Stop it!" I shouted. "No one is fighting you, you freaking idiot. How many freaking times have we offered to help?"

"I don't like your terms," Shailaja said.

The Warner-shape pivoted to face us. He'd lowered the sacrificial knife to his side, but then he deliberately pointed it at the crazed teenage dragon.

"For me?" she asked. "A lovely gift, my friend. But not containing nearly enough of the power I seek."

"I don't know you," Warner said. His voice was low and deadly. Jesus, I never, ever wanted to hear him sound like that while speaking to me. It pained me to hear it directed at someone else.

"Warner!" Shailaja gasped mockingly. "We're equals. Unparalleled equals. Together, we could reign —"

"There is no together for us," Warner said as he advanced toward her. "You decided that for yourself without even consulting or considering me. And why? Because I was never a consideration for you, as you were never for me. I want no part of your grand delusion."

"Stop there, sentinel." Shailaja lost all sense of the sweetness she'd previously been attempting — and failing at. "Or my shadows will suck the vampire dry."

Warner shrugged. My eyesight was getting better, but my stomach bottomed out at the sight.

"The vampire is old, powerful," he said. "He wouldn't hesitate to sacrifice me."

My knife materialized in my invisible sheath. I moaned as I felt the weight of it against my thigh.

Kett must have dropped it in the vortex. He'd be defenseless against the leeches without it.

I called the knife into my hand and awkwardly slashed sideways at Shailaja. The teen saw me twist toward her and knocked my hand away, breaking my right wrist as she did so.

"Mother of freaking God!" I screamed, involuntarily dropping my knife and instinctively cradling my wrist as I spun away.

Unexpectedly, she didn't attack me again. I looked over to see Warner a few steps away, his arm outstretched. This stance placed him as far away from Shailaja as he could be while still having his knife pressed up underneath her chin.

She was up on her tippy toes, with her head tilted as far back as it could go. Even from this awkward position, she still managed to glare at me, not the sentinel.

A thin line of blood formed at her neck, seeping onto the blade.

"Sharp, isn't it?" I asked.

"How's the wrist?" Shailaja snarked back. Her words were muddled, but she could barely move her jaw to speak. Enunciation took a backseat to having your throat slit, presumably.

I brashly snapped my wrist back into place, trying not to scream while doing so and not quite pulling it off.

"Free the vampire," Warner said.

"Absolutely not," Shailaja answered. "The alchemist will retrieve the instrument and use its magic to restore me to my rightful shape and power." She shifted her gaze from me to Warner. "Then you will join me to hunt for the third instrument."

"Absolutely not." Warner threw the teenage dragon's own words back in her face, with no hint of the playful smile I'd grown to adore.

She shrugged one boney shoulder. "The alchemist is pretty enough. Not so beautiful to be threatening, and not powerful enough to be of any concern. I agree that her magic is valuable. We can keep her if you insist. But you will soon grow bored of her mortality. I would see you gain your rightful place, Warner, son of Jiaotu."

"Segue much, crazy?" I asked. "And, wow, that wasn't an icky image at all."

"I'm exactly where I'm meant to be," Warner said.

They glared fiercely at each other, with their dragon magic swirling all around them. The glare was sexy on Warner, and somewhat silly on Shailaja. No one takes a look like that from a teen seriously.

We were in the 'ignore Jade because more important things were being discussed and more powerful plays were being made' portion of the day. Which was fine by me, because peppermint rose to tickle my taste buds and focus my thoughts.

The vampire was still fighting.

I spun away from the Warner-and-Shailaja soap opera, circling the stone table while I looked for runes or hidden spells.

I was here to collect the second instrument of assassination, after all. Plus, I wanted Shailaja's attention on me, not on whatever Kett was doing in the swirling vortex of shadow leeches.

"Good girl," Shailaja said.

"Jade," Warner said tensely.

"Just get ready for the backlash," I said.

Warner widened his stance, his knife still pressed to Shailaja's throat. She spread her arms slightly, her fingers splayed as she grinned at me.

I reached for the lid of the heavily runed silver chest that sat in the middle of the stone table, but I couldn't lift it. I ran my hands around its edges and over its rune-carved top.

"No keyhole," I said.

"The runes?" Warner asked.

I nodded in acknowledgement, but continued to examine the remainder of the table first, just in case I was missing something. "No other magic here. Just the metallurgy."

"What did you expect?" Shailaja asked sneeringly. "Is she always this slow …?"

The teenaged dragon sucked in a pained breath that made me guess Warner had pressed his blade more firmly against her neck, but I didn't look up to confirm. I could actually feel the magic the leeches were siphoning off Kett, and was beginning to worry that was why I was tasting peppermint. The longer I took, the more they harmed him.

"Be helpful or shut up," Warner said.

"Oh, sentinel," Shailaja purred. Well, as much of a purr as anyone could manage with a crazy-sharp knife to their neck. "I like this forceful side of you."

"Oh, gag." I returned my attention to the silver-runed chest, very deliberately stopping myself from glancing over at the hot swirl of peppermint magic I could feel behind and to the left of Warner and Shailaja.

"You're a witch, aren't you?" Shailaja snapped. "That was your mother and grandmother, yes? Then do what a witch would do."

"Witch magic isn't going to work here," Warner said.

"And she's not only a witch," Shailaja countered unhelpfully.

I pulled the pen out of my satchel.

"A pen?" Shailaja snarled.

I looked over at Warner. "It can write runes," I said. "What are the chances it can read them?"

Shailaja snapped her mouth shut.

"I think it belongs to you," Warner answered. "And will attempt to do your bidding."

I placed the pen on top of the treasure chest and tried to just focus on it. Its magic was dampened in here, surrounded by silver, but its golden body stood out against the silver of the box.

I spoke to it out loud, though I probably didn't need to. "I need to open this chest. Some combination of the runes on this box mean open ... or something like open." I glanced up. "What's Spanish for 'open'?"

"*Abierto*," Shailaja said testily.

Great. I loved it when my rivals were more powerful and more accomplished than me.

"*Abierto*," I repeated, pressing my fingertips lightly along the pen. I used my left hand. My right wrist still ached like a son of a bitch.

The pen lifted underneath my hand, floating a few inches above the chest. Then it started moving, seemingly of its own accord. It was like using a Ouija board. If, you know, I'd been allowed to use such a thing when I was younger ...

The pen drew a trace of my magic from my hand ... maybe as if it was filling itself with ink? I didn't remember feeling it do so before, but maybe its magic was so dampened deep within the mountain that it needed the extra boost.

It wrote the first three runes it had drawn on the granite outside. Not that I would have remembered them without seeing them a second time.

The chest clicked open.

Something slammed against the side of the platform we were standing on. If a large stone area the size of a hockey rink surrounded by a river of molten silver lava could be referred to as a platform. Or was that a moat of molten silver? And no, I wasn't obsessed with hockey.

I stumbled, though of course neither Warner nor Shailaja moved.

"Hello, backlash," I muttered, tucking the pen into my satchel. "Always with the earthquakes. Well … second time, at least."

I lifted the lid off the chest, which was hinged along one side. Three silver centipedes were nestled inside three separate grooves carved in more silver. I was fairly certain now that the chest was actually carved as part of the stone table, with its bottom attached. Just as the stone table was carved directly out of the platform we were standing on. It was all one massive hunk of granite, with the interior of the chest simply polished to a silver sheen.

"I can't take just the box," I said, wanting to keep Warner up to date as to why I was now reaching inside the treasure chest. Everyone really hated it when I just grabbed magical objects. Well, maybe it was only those who loved me who worried about me screwing around with dangerous unknown magic.

The centipedes were identical, each about one inch wide by three inches long. They looked almost exactly like Rochelle's tattoo sketch, though not so smooth around the edges.

Yeah, the metal edges on these centipedes looked sharp. Like razor blades, actually.

I gingerly reached around one, brushing it with my fingers as I tried to lift it from underneath, rather than by its nasty edges.

It coiled up underneath my hand, then twisted around my forefinger. Ouch.

Something crashed into the other side of the platform, again forcing me to fight for my footing.

"That's not an earthquake," Shailaja hissed as a second centipede latched onto my middle finger just above the first knuckle. "You'll need to release me, sentinel. Otherwise we're not getting out of here alive."

The third centipede twisted around my ring finger as I was attempting to withdraw my hand from the chest. This triggered a third crash from yet another direction — this one violent enough to shake Warner and Shailaja.

Something was circling the platform. Something massive enough to make stone shake. Something powerful enough to exist in a river of molten silver ... or maybe it was the river.

Ah, damn.

The centipedes twisted around my fingers and up across my palm. It didn't exactly hurt, but the metal scraping against my skin was uncomfortable. More metallic magic flooded my mouth. If I had a better palate for metals, I might have been able to distinguish nuances in the magic. But it all tasted the same to me — terrible.

I stepped back from the table with my hand held out before me. The centipedes twined together, clicking end to end, then corkscrewed over the heel of my hand and wrist, heading for my forearm.

"Claim the magic, you nitwit!" Shailaja screamed as another boom sounded out, the impact coming approximately a quarter turn away from the last one.

Not a boom. A thing. A really, really big thing living in the lava. And circling us.

Another earthshaking crash — this one accompanied by an explosion of stone — threw me back against the granite table. I managed to not smack my head this time, but it felt like I might have cracked my back.

Warner and Shailaja stumbled closer to the edge of the platform. His knife was still at her neck.

I landed on my ass with my aching back resting against the pillar beneath the table, and my arm held as far away from my body as possible. The centipedes had wound their way around my bicep now. At a glance, they probably looked like a stylish upper-arm cuff, but there was nothing cute about their magic. I could almost feel the taste of metal boring into my brain …

Oh, God. Were they heading for my brain?

Freaking hell.

As the ground continued to rumble and roil, Warner and Shailaja were locked in some sort of awkward skirmish while fighting for their footing. Silver lava started splashing over the edges of the platform. I desperately tried to focus.

Jesus, I was wasting too much time. I needed to help Kett. The interconnected centipedes slipped up over my shoulder as I looked around for the vampire. He appeared to still be caught in the whirling vortex of shadow leeches. Beyond that, I caught a glimpse of what looked like gigantic silver antennae rising out of the river.

I squeezed my eyes shut.

Claim. Claim. Claim the magic.

The centipede was moving along my collarbone, almost at my neck. I instinctively reached out and coaxed an extra layer of shielding magic from my necklace.

The centipedes attached themselves to my necklace with a click.

Then nothing.

Even the ground stilled. Whatever creature I had awoken had settled back down into the silver river.

I opened my eyes. The centipede had separated into the original three artifacts, with each one threaded through a wedding ring on the right side of my necklace. They hung there like silver charms.

I reached up around my neck while double-checking the taste of the necklace's magic, which felt as neutral as it always did. Then I readjusted the loop so the centipedes hung at the bottom of the chain for balance.

"Hey!" I cried, grinning madly as I scrambled to my feet to look for Warner. "I did it."

Kett ripped his way out of the vortex of shadow leeches. Literally, rending his way through them with three-inch claws and fangs.

Holy Jesus.

Warner and Shailaja had been wrestling for control of the knife. The sentinel — being taller and stronger — had the upper hand, but his back to the edge of the platform meant he was distracted by his footing.

Kett — all bestial fangs and bloody red eyes — leaped for Shailaja. He landed on her back like an enraged monkey, then chomped down on her neck.

"No! Not her blood!" I shrieked, palming my knife and lunging for the trio poised on the edge of the river of silver lava … and the monster that lived within it.

Shailaja screamed and let go of the sacrificial knife, which off-balanced Warner.

One more step and I'd be right beside them.

I wasn't fast enough.

Even with Kett trying to drag her down, Shailaja managed to slam a kick to Warner's knee. Then, as the sentinel canted sideways — twisting to compensate for the fall, trying to catch the edge of the platform — she punched him in the chest and screamed.

"Your services are no longer required, sentinel!"

Magic exploded between them, the gold of it searing my still-sensitive eyes.

I blinked.

Warner was gone.

Shailaja fell to her knees. Kett, a pale demon perched on her back, followed her down.

A third step brought me to the cliff.

Too late. Too late.

I peered over the edge and saw nothing but silver, silver, silver. The sight of the molten river didn't blind me. Maybe I'd built up a resistance to the metallurgy. Or maybe it was a result of having the centipedes attached to my necklace.

But I wanted to be blinded.

Because if I was blind, I wouldn't know that I couldn't see Warner.

I couldn't even taste his magic.

Numbness flooded my limbs. I squeezed my eyes shut. The silver of the river's magic was imprinted on my eyelids, imprinted on my brain.

It had been difficult to taste Warner's magic before because of the interference from the silver ... so maybe ... I rationalized myself through the fear. I shut away the thought that I'd just lost Warner before ever really knowing him. I shut away thoughts of all the other people I'd lost and almost lost — Hudson, Sienna, and Kandy.

I spun to Shailaja and Kett. The vampire was still feeding from the rabid koala. She was — oddly — kneeling with her hands folded in her lap, as if waiting. Her eyes were closed, her face peaceful.

Kett stilled. His blood-red eyes snapped open. A wave of gold rolled across the red, then he fell back without a sound.

Shailaja's neck was a bloody open wound, all torn flesh, veins, and bone. Yet she still opened her eyes and smiled at me.

"Now it's just us," she whispered.

So I stabbed her in the gut.

Which was a bitch, because I'd been aiming for the little creep's heart. She deflected the blow with a downward strike of her palms at the last second, though.

My jade knife slipped smoothly through her dragon hide, stopping only when it reached the hilt.

This strike brought me to my knees and us face to face.

She blinked, her brown eyes surprised but surprisingly lucid.

"Let me properly introduce you to my knife," I growled. Yeah, that was trite and obvious of me, but I was really pissed off.

"Hello, knife," Shailaja whispered. A speck of blood appeared on her lower lip and she licked it off. "Are you done pouting? You have magic to perform."

Well, I had to give her points for style.

Her gaze dropped to the centipedes on my necklace and she smiled. Her teeth were slicked with blood. She'd underestimated my knife. I'd hurt her badly.

But not badly enough.

I withdrew the knife, aimed for her heart, and stabbed her a second time. Again, she deflected the blow, but by the hacking, bloody cough that followed, I was pretty sure I'd punctured one of her lungs.

Shailaja gripped the forearm of my knife hand, then wrapped her other hand around my head in a rough caress.

"Ouch," she said. Then she started laughing.

Bubbles of blood formed at the edges of her mouth, and still she hacked and laughed. My recently healed wrist screamed with pain as she attempted to twist my arm and the knife away.

"You've wounded me," she said between bloody bouts of laughter. Blood dripped from her mouth and down her chin.

I didn't take my eyes off her as I finally managed to pull my arm and knife from her grip. I drew it back to stab her a third time.

"Thrice said, thrice meant," I said, echoing Kett's and Warner's invocation just felt appropriate. But, as my alchemist magic rolled through the knife to absorb the dragon's blood into the blade, I twisted the saying with my own intention. "Thrice done is done."

Shailaja threw her head back and laughed.

"Stop laughing while I'm killing you," I cried.

"You aren't killing me, Jade," she said. Her use of my given name was sickeningly intimate. "Dragons don't kill dragons."

"I'm not that kind of dragon."

I grabbed her by the shoulder, leveling my blade in line with her heart. She wouldn't be laughing in a second.

A portal blew open behind me. Smokey, dark-chocolate magic blasted through the cavern, actually blowing my curls around my head and into my eyes. It was the kind of magic that made mere mortals quake with awestruck fear. I'd been wrong about thinking it was more terrifying when he laughed.

I didn't need to turn to see the warrior of the guardians step through the portal to find me with my knife poised over Shailaja's heart. His golden sword resonated behind me with a power I could actually feel. Guardian power. The blade's magic was a terrible song, similar to how I always heard music when Qiuniu used his healing magic.

The warrior had stepped where dragons dare not tread to rescue a daughter bent on becoming a murderer.

"Jade," he bellowed. "Enough."

Shailaja wrenched herself away from my grasp, scrambling to prostrate herself at my father's feet.

"Guardian," she cried.

Behind where she'd just been kneeling, Kett groaned and rolled away from the portal magic. I saw wisps of smoke rising off him and thought it might actually be burning him.

I didn't bother standing up. I simply turned my head and watched as my father, who was dressed head to toe in his samurai-inspired black armor, scooped Shailaja into his arms. His face was stern and unyielding.

"Gee, dad," I said. "Don't remember you ever holding me like that."

He frowned. Yeah, I'm not sure how I find the strength to wield scathing sarcasm when under stress. It's a gift. And maybe a curse.

"Come, child," Yazi said. "The treasure keeper can't hold the portal open for long."

I was pretty sure he wasn't talking to me, though he rested his green-eyed gaze on me for a brief moment. Then he turned to walk back through the portal with the sweet, bat-shit crazy koala cuddled in his fatherly arms.

Shailaja peeked over my father's shoulder as he carried her through the golden magic. She wiggled her fingers at me.

Good freaking riddance. Let the guardians deal with the crazed teenage dragon.

"I'd keep her away from the braids!" I yelled after them.

Jade. Amplified by the portal magic, my father's voice sounded out in my head. *I expect you to follow.*

I didn't follow.

I didn't feel like following, and I wasn't going to drag Kett through the portal or the magic of the nexus. I was a hundred percent sure he wouldn't survive.

"Go," Kett whispered. "Leave me."

"Yeah, right, asshole. That's so me."

Jade! My father roared through my head. *The treasure keeper can't —*

His voice cut off. The portal snapped shut.

"You're freaking welcome," I muttered. Then I crawled over to Kett. I could have stood. There was actually nothing wrong with me. But crawling seemed faster.

The vampire looked freaking terrible. I hunched over him to touch his shoulder and he flinched away from me with a hiss. He wasn't in full bestial form, but he hadn't retracted his fangs and his eyes were a dull red I'd never seen before. He looked withered. Even worse, I swore I could see the dragon magic he'd consumed writhing in his veins.

I sat back on my haunches and reached out with my dowser senses, but I still couldn't pick up any hint of Warner nearby.

Kett dragged himself into a half-propped position. "The sentinel?" His cool tone was marred by speaking through his fangs.

I shook my head.

"I'm sorry," he said, starting to shiver. "I thought to distract her, not him." He clasped his hands together as the shivering turned into violent shaking.

"You're going to need blood," I said, as pragmatically as I could suggest such a thing.

"Not yours."

"I get it. You should already be dead."

"Yes. I should."

Ballsy as ever — even though I was fairly certain he was dying — Kett grinned at me. Then he threw up a gusher of dragon blood. All over himself and me. "Damn," he choked. "Such a waste."

"Yeah, yummy." I wiped the vomit off my face, then dried my hands on my jeans. "Deadly and sweet."

"Just like you."

"Don't sweet-talk me, vampire. I already know I'm going to have to carry you."

Resigned, he nodded. "One of two things is going to happen next."

"Tell me."

"I'll lapse into a fugue state."

"Been there, done that."

Kett shook his head. "I will, for all appearances, be dead. I'll need you to take me to my maker."

Delightful. I really, really wanted to reenact the scene in London with Kett's maker. What had she said to me? If Kett died, she would suck the marrow from Kandy's bones and make me watch? Then if I set even one foot in London, she would take everything from me?

"Getting you through customs will be fun."

"You'll take the jet. There's a coffin among the cargo."

Wow, doubly delightful.

"No," Kett amended himself. "Take me to Vancouver. You're stronger there. Then you call her."

"You have her on automatic dial? Under what, Audrey Hepburn?"

Kett squeezed his eyes closed. "Under 'Master.' "

This was just getting better and better. "What's the second thing that might happen?"

"I'll try to rip your throat out."

"Well, that's always a possibility, isn't it?"

Kett huffed out a pained laugh. Except I hadn't really been joking.

"I'm not sure you would survive the assault, alchemist … Jade. I reiterate my plea for you to leave me."

"Yep, I hear you. But we both know that's not going to happen."

Kett sighed. "Quickly, then."

Chapter Twelve

The bridge was gone.

The silver lava river stood exposed between us and the entrance to the mountain cavern. The gap was far too wide for me to jump, even if I hadn't had Kett hanging off my shoulder.

"So …" I mused. "That worm thing that lives in the lava knocked out the bridge, eh?"

Kett's head was hanging to the side like a rag doll's. I could barely see him in my peripheral vision. This made me exceedingly aware that he might be in worse shape than he was letting on. Not that I needed to be even more anxious than I was already.

"Centipede," he corrected. "An impressive piece of metallurgy."

Right. I'd been joking with the worm comment, but trust Kett to correct me. You'd think he'd give up on the whole mentorship thing in the face of dying. Or maybe that was a good sign —

"Jump." The vampire dissolved the rising tide of my thinking positively about his potential survival with a single whispered command. Then he added, "You can make it."

"There is no way I can. Could you?" I laid on the snark to cover my mounting concern that he was going to try to force me across.

"Yes."

"We'll die in that molten silver ..." I faltered as an idea I'd been steadfastly ignoring rose unbidden in my mind. Namely, that I might have just watched Warner do that exact thing. This idea even came with interactive video — a completely imagined yet painfully vivid reenactment helpfully supplied by my jerk of a mind's eye.

I shoved the thought fiercely out of the way, tamping it deep down and pinning it there with the sharp need to get Kett out of the damn mountain alive. Well, as alive as he already was. 'Animated' might be a better word.

"At least it will be painless."

"Leave the comedy to the funny people, vampire."

"Dowser, I scouted. There are no other egresses. If you do not jump, you will die here. By my fangs or through starvation."

"I have chocolate." I jutted my chin out stubbornly.

"Jump, Jade," Kett whispered. "Or don't." His voice was so quiet on the 'or don't' that a tiny corner of my heart cracked.

So I jumped.

I dragged Kett up the stairs to the top of the platform and backed up to take a running start first, of course. I wasn't great at physics, but knew I wanted some lift. I figured it was better to jump from a higher point to a lower point, rather than across equal heights. But really, I had no idea. I was just doing my best.

Kett tried to help, pushing through his lethargy to run alongside me and jumping when I did, but I knew — microseconds after my back foot left the safety of the platform — that we weren't going to make it.

I flung my left hand forward, reaching toward the far side of the cavern in an attempt to add momentum, but to no avail.

We dropped short.

Then my right foot landed on something solid.

I didn't think. I sprung off this support to lunge the final six feet.

I hit the cliff edge on the other side of the river at chest height. Kett clawed his right hand into the stone, gouging troughs into it as we slid backward.

Then he hung there off one hand as I found footholds and hauled us up and over the edge.

I scrambled to my feet to peer over into the river. Two large antennae sank down into the liquid silver as I watched the centipede-creature swim away. Its segmented body looked even larger this close. Maybe it was just an optical illusion … things appearing larger in liquid. Yeah, I'd hold onto that thought, even though I was fairly certain I had it the wrong way around.

"Jesus," I muttered. "Was it trying to eat us or save us?"

"Or save the instrument of assassination." Kett was lying on his side by my feet, curled protectively around the hand he'd just clawed into the granite.

It pained me to see him so diminished. Then I chastised myself for that silly, little-girl reaction. "That's not a scary thought at all," I said.

"You think too much, dowser."

I barked out a harsh laugh. "That's rich coming from you, Mr. Fugue."

"That's meditation."

"You are so lying, old man."

Kett laughed, a quiet but warm sound. He turned his face to look up at me as I crouched down to pick him up. His eyes were still that dull, lifeless red.

"We get to save each other this time." He reached up to brush his withered fingers through my tangled, blood-and-vomit-speckled curls.

I didn't answer. I just got his arm over my shoulder and hauled him back to his feet.

But it occurred to me — just in the breath I took to lift him, which I quickly exhaled along with the thought — that Kettil, the executioner and elder of the Conclave, might be in love with me.

The asshole firefly dive-bombed us at least twenty times during the arduous climb up the stairs. Yes, desperate to focus on something other than my screaming shoulder and burning hamstrings, I counted. On the twentieth time, Kett snatched it out of the air and crushed it in his hand.

This display of ire was so out of the ordinary for Kett — who cherished all things magical — that it made me forget that my quads were ready to refuse to lift my legs up another stair. I dragged us, half-jogging, up the last dozen steps and got us out into the fresh air.

The day was bright and clear. Thankfully, my eyes had adjusted to the light as we'd approached the entrance. The sun was slightly higher in the sky, which was confusing. It had felt like days had passed, not just hours.

Kett pulled away from me, walking a few unsteady steps to rest a hand against the rocky outcrop that had transformed into the boulder creature.

I snapped my mouth closed on a warning. The vampire wasn't foolhardy ... if I ignored the fact that he'd just tried to drain a dragon, whose blood was purportedly poison to vampires. Either that was a myth debunked, or Kett was more powerful than any vampire who'd tried to feed from a dragon before ... or he was still dying.

I crossed to the runes I'd carved into the granite to open the entrance to the centipede's cavern. Then I slashed my knife across them so many times that they became nothing more than oddly crosshatched stone.

I glanced back to see that the door had sealed behind me, with no further evidence of the runes that had formed to create it. I tried not to think about Warner, maybe trapped inside. The door had to open from the inside, right?

"I had to close it." I spoke out loud to justify the action to myself. "The centipede thing ..."

"I understand," Kett whispered. His back was to me, his shoulders hunched. "I must leave you."

"What? Here?"

He straightened with effort. "Find the SUV. Go to the airport. Hangar 57. Take the plane. They're expecting you."

"No way! You're hurt, and Warner —"

Kett turned on me, his eyes blazing red and his fangs long and sharp. "You will go, Jade Godfrey. Vancouver is where you should be. I, and the sentinel if he survives, will find you there. There, I know you are safe."

I could still see the dragon magic he'd consumed writhing underneath his skin. He hadn't purged enough of it. I opened my mouth to protest further, but he was gone.

I stared through the barren landscape after him, tasting his tainted peppermint magic until it faded away.

Then I turned and tried to remember the way back to the SUV.

I stopped after what felt like an hour of slogging over rock and moss, around craggy outcrops, and over shallow fissures in which I could easily break a leg if I wasn't careful where I wandered. I tried to ignore that my mind was seriously attempting to convince me it wasn't getting enough oxygen, and that I was going to come out of this both mentally and emotionally devastated.

I drank the last of my water.

I checked my cellphone. As had been the case the last fifteen times, I had no signal.

I wasn't looking at the bottom of my hiking boot, though I knew I had to. For a while now, I'd been fighting the urge. My right boot had felt a bit off — the sole slightly thicker, slightly heavier somehow — the entire time I'd dragged Kett up the stairs. I'd assumed at the time it was because of his weight pressing on my shoulder. But I kept on feeling it — and ignoring it — for the trek through the Andes back to the SUV, because … Well, because because.

Yeah, I was all about logical thinking these days. If by logic, it was understood that I meant complete and utter denial of reality.

The bottom of my boot was covered in silver. I actually rapped my knuckles against it like a moron who doesn't believe her own eyes. Solid silver, at least a quarter-inch thick.

From when I'd jumped off the gigantic molten-silver-river-dwelling centipede's head.

Solid silver.

No one could survive being coated in solid silver ...

I abruptly stood up, reached out with my dowser senses, and caught a hint of Kett's peppermint magic — hopefully from the blood he'd left on the SUV. Then, my limbs responding jerkily as I fell into survival mode, I forced myself to continue walking.

No more thinking.

Kett was right. Thinking wasn't going to help me ... or Warner ... or the vampire. Thinking was the enemy.

I was going to count squares of chocolate instead.

I thrust my hand into my satchel and pulled out my emergency rations — a 100 gram bar of Lindt's 70 percent Madagascar. I had seven squares left.

If the chocolate was going to take me all the way back to the vehicle, I was going to have to run — even with one silver-heavy boot.

I weighed the benefits of just throwing the boots away. Then — realizing I was starting to think about reality again — I shoved two squares of chocolate in my mouth, seeking oblivion in trademark Lindt creaminess and heavy-handed vanilla.

Then I ran, following the trail of Kett's magic as fast as I could.

I made it back to the airport without completely melting down. Thank God for GPS, and being able to plug my iPhone into the stereo and crank the music so loud I couldn't think.

I wasn't sure any of the clocks were correct. The one in the SUV read 2:23 P.M., but guardians generally had no sense of time. My phone said it was 4:37 P.M., but I wondered if all the time spent surrounded by silver and metallurgy in the mountain could have messed up the phone's ability to automatically adjust, despite the fact I'd kept it in its lead-lined case.

That seemed like something I should know.

There were a lot of somethings I should know.

I parked the SUV in the airport long-term lot, noting that the crushed Mini had been towed away. I paid for a week of parking, having no idea who would retrieve the vehicle, or when. I left the key in the visor and locked the door manually.

Then, staring like a moron at the now-locked vehicle, I realized I probably could have found my way back to Qiuniu's garage and the portal using the GPS. But Kett had told me to go to the airport, so I went to the airport.

Admittedly, I really, really didn't feel like being anywhere near the nexus right now. A deep, blistering anger was boiling in my belly, and I was only remaining functional by denying it over and over and over again.

Rather than going through the hassle of checking in and passing through security in the main terminal, I scaled the chain-link fence and wandered out into the area where I thought the private hangars would be. I doubted Kett did any differently either.

The low buildings I'd seen the night before from the parking lot did, in fact, contain planes. Numbers hung directly under their gray metal eaves.

A few people were working in and around the hangars — mechanics and other private charter staff, maybe — but no one tried to talk to me. No one asked where I was going. I realized then that I was acting like I was on automatic pilot. It was as if Kett had somehow programmed me. Maybe that was an aspect of his magic.

Having once been inside my head, maybe he could plant suggestions and shit.

Or maybe I was just a cold asshole who'd watched her new boyfriend die and didn't even stop to shed a tear.

Pain lanced through my chest. I doubled over, pressing my hands fiercely against my heart, vaguely aware that I could suffer for only so long out in the open without drawing attention. I couldn't stop, couldn't talk to anyone right now. If I stopped, I might not keep going.

I straightened and forced my right leg forward in another step. The silver sole of my hiking boot clacked against the pavement. The sound drove tiny daggers into my heart, every single time my right foot hit the pavement.

I looked ahead, and only ahead.

They were waiting for me in hangar 57. Along with a white, sleek, almost-predatory jet.

A set of stairs near the front of the plane lowered as I approached. A dark-haired steward wearing a tailored navy suit and a white dress shirt — no name tag — escorted me inside the plane without a single blink at my disheveled, blood-and-vomit speckled appearance. My right foot clanged against the steel steps as I climbed. Again. And again.

The steward appeared to be human. I wasn't sure why I'd thought he'd be a vampire. He was about an inch shorter than me, and his dark hair was perfectly coiffed.

"Vancouver?" he asked. I couldn't place his lyrical accent.

I nodded as I looked around the white interior of the jet. Twelve double-wide white leather seats — six on each side — filled the passenger cabin. Luxurious seats, that looked as though they could swivel for conversation across the wide aisle.

Empty seats.

"Kettil has not returned?" I asked.

"No, Miss Godfrey," the steward answered. "But our standing orders are to take off immediately after you arrive, whether or not you came alone."

I nodded, and he headed up toward the front of the plane. I followed him just far enough to stand before the still-open door. He hadn't retracted the stairs yet. I looked out at the gray concrete beyond the gray aluminum siding of the hangar. I couldn't see the parking lot or the runway, but I didn't need to.

I couldn't taste a single drop of peppermint or black-forest-cake magic.

I didn't really want to think about the extent of my power, but if I was completely honest with myself, I knew I could dowse for miles.

"Excuse me," the steward said from behind me. "I'll have to close the doors. We're just waiting for the okay from the tower."

I nodded and crossed back into the passenger cabin. I threw myself into the third seat on the left side and stared out the window.

Then I chided myself for all the moping I was doing. And chided myself some more for all the other things I hadn't done, including all the easy things I had so much control over … like being smarter, quicker, and stronger.

The steward came back with a tray that clicked into the arm of my seat. It contained two glasses — one filled with water, one with ice — three lemon wedges, and five hot towels.

Yeah, five towels. Clearly, I looked even worse than I thought I did. No wonder no one had questioned me wandering around an international airport … or at least the private section of an international airport. I probably looked like the murderer I'd just attempted to be.

I opened my mouth to automatically say thank you. Then I saw the phone built into the arm just underneath the tray.

"Excuse me?" I called after the steward. "Do the phones work?"

"Of course," he answered, as if completely perturbed by the idea that they wouldn't.

"I mean while we're flying? Because I shouldn't use my cellphone, right? If I even have a signal at forty thousand feet."

He smiled kindly but was obviously eager to get back to his preflight tasks. "They work."

I called Kandy.

I hadn't realized until that moment that I knew her new cellphone number by heart. But I did.

"Dowser," she answered, gruff and gleeful at the same time. Though how she knew it was me without caller ID, I had no idea.

"I've lost Warner … and maybe Kett." I blurted the words like a blithering baby who couldn't even manage a polite hello.

"Lost, as in they wandered off in the mall?" she asked. "Or lost like you left their mangled bodies on the side of the street?"

I choked back tears and tried to formulate my thoughts.

"Or," Kandy continued, "third option. Lost, as in they were never yours to begin with? Because that last one would just suck."

I laughed. My nose was clogged with snot as I tried to suppress my tears, but I laughed. I squeezed my eyes shut and pressed my head back against the seat.

"Where are you?" Kandy asked, her tone serious now. "I'll come."

"Peru."

That gave her pause, but I knew it was only because she was probably formulating the quickest travel plans.

"I'm heading home," I continued. "I'm on Kett's jet." I had a hard time saying Kett's name. It came out with a thin squeak.

"I'll meet you there."

"Okay." God, I was a baby. Kandy was still healing, still needed to be near the pack, and I didn't even try to talk her out of coming.

"I doubt they're lost, Jade." The werewolf's gruff tone was soothing in my ear. "You know that disappearing is kind of the vampire's thing, and dragons aren't too reliable either."

The plane gave a lurch. Then we slowly began taxiing out of the hangar. I struggled to get my seat belt on one-handed, because there was absolutely no way I was putting down the phone. Then I decided the belt was a lost cause.

"Yeah … this didn't have anything to do with portals or the nexus or any time shifting. There was a river of molten silver involved."

"Silver? Geez, good thing I sat this one out."

Werewolves were allergic to silver. I wondered if that much silver would have made Kandy sick just by walking through the mountains.

"My boot is ruined," I said.

"Always good to keep some perspective."

"I liked these boots. They were ... sturdy. Sturdy is good sometimes."

"You like all your shoes. When Warner shows up, you can make him buy you a new pair for the heartache."

The airplane turned sharply, then slowed. I glanced out. We appeared to be waiting in line to take off, with two commercial airplanes in front of us.

"It's not like that," I muttered as I cranked my neck, then stood half hunched to peer out of the other side of the plane. I was still stupidly hoping to see broad shoulders or pale blond hair racing across the runway toward the jet. I saw neither. "Warner didn't ..."

I sat back down in my seat with a thump.

"Warner didn't what?" Kandy's question went in through my right ear but then just rattled about in my madly working brain.

"Your services are no longer required," I blurted.

"Losing me, dowser."

"The rabid koala. The crazy dragon kid."

"From the fortress? With the fucking shadow leeches?"

"Yeah."

Kandy muttered a string of colorful and inventive curses, but I didn't hear a single one. I felt like I was on the edge of working out what had happened in the cavern.

"She said 'your services are no longer required.' He was falling, yes, but then ... I thought she hit him with some sort of magic to push him over the edge ... but ... but ..."

The jet rolled forward as I squeezed my eyes shut to try to recall the scene on the platform. Warner and Shailaja wrestling for the knife, her punching him in the chest … the golden dragon magic that had hurt my sensitive eyes …

"But what?" Kandy prompted.

"But what if she … retired him?"

"Sounds like a bitchy thing to do."

"She said 'dragons don't kill dragons' while I was … you know, attempting to kill her."

"Jade, geez. How do you know this conversation isn't being recorded? And, you know, a bit unlike you, huh?"

"She'd just pushed Warner into a river of molten silver. And I thought Kett was dead."

"Okay, fine. But I think you should consider hanging out with the vampire a little less."

"She didn't kill him. She put him in stasis. I've got to go." I started to get up, but the jet suddenly rushed forward and threw me back in my seat.

I didn't know anything about planes, and honestly, I'd barely given this one a second glance. But damn, it was fast. The force of the takeoff pressed me back in my seat, and the plane lifted off after barely a few seconds hurtling down the tarmac.

"Trust the vampire to have some sort of top-of-the-line jet," I muttered into the phone.

Kandy snorted. "Why would you expect anything less from Mr. High, Mighty, and Toothy?"

As I watched the ground drop beneath us, I clung to my idea about Warner fiercely. I slipped my hand into my satchel to wrap my fingers around the map.

"You think you can call him back?" Kandy asked.

"I hope so."

"Better to do it in Vancouver, behind the bakery. Remember how he collapsed before. Plus, the magic worked there once. It might be imprinted on the area."

"When did you become wise and sage-like?"

Kandy laughed.

"Talk to me all the way home?"

"Am I still coming to you? I'll need to get on a plane eventually."

"How about ... I'll call ... if ... you know."

"Okay, then. Why the hell not? It's not like I'm doing anything important. And Audrey's driving me nuts with duties I should be performing and shit. She wants me to check up on the oracle, Rochelle. And her boyfriend, Beau."

"Yeah, I remember Beau. He's difficult to unremember."

"Lara calls him delectable."

"But you keep saying no to Audrey. Even though you're bored."

"It's the principle." Kandy paused. I could actually hear her thinking. I found myself growing anxious as the silence stretched, until all I could feel was empty air between us. The werewolf never spent this much time considering her choice of words.

I could hear some sort of static on the line. "You still there?" I asked.

"Yeah," Kandy answered. "I might go next time."

"Because the far seer paid you a visit?"

"He told you?"

"I saw Drake's T-shirt."

Kandy laughed huskily. "That's a good one. You see the banana —"

"Don't explain it to me!"

Kandy laughed harder. I could see her in my mind's eye — head thrown back, her green hair slightly longer and brushing the back of her neck. She gave herself over without question, without hesitation. She was fierce about life. I desperately missed that. I wanted to be that fierce, that vibrant.

The werewolf grew quiet at the other end of the line.

"Chi Wen?" I prompted. "Do you want to talk about it? I bet Desmond was pissed as hell when he showed up."

"He didn't come to the house. Drake found me at the gym, took me to a park. There were swings."

I waited, my heart aching for whatever Kandy was worried about. Whatever the far seer had said to shake her up.

"He asked why I wasn't wearing the cuffs. I told him the reason to wear them had already passed."

I groaned. Without the cuffs, which had originally been a gift from the far seer, Kandy wouldn't have been able to lift the slab of granite that had pinned me when the fortress had collapsed.

"You know, because he doesn't do great with time."

"Yeah, I know."

"He asked how I was healing."

"Really? He knew you'd been hurt?"

"Guess so ..." Kandy trailed off.

"Then he asked you to visit Beau and Rochelle?"

"He said the oracle was going to need me, but I wasn't going to like it. Then he laughed, and asked me to buy him Oreos because he never remembered to carry money."

I could see the scene. Chi Wen, an ancient Chinese man in his white robes, sitting on the swings next to a green-haired, slight, tough-as-nails woman who was probably wearing Lycra. Drake would have been wandering around in the background, testing all the playground equipment.

"So you're wearing the cuffs now?"

"Yeah. They don't really go, you know?"

I understood. The thick gold cuffs and their runes would be a poor match for any outfit … except maybe if pharaoh-chic became a thing.

"He didn't give me a timeline," Kandy continued. "So … I'll just go the next time Audrey asks."

"I'll come with you."

"No."

"No? Did the far seer say no?"

"I'm saying no."

"I … I don't think you've ever said no to me before."

"Get used to it, blondie," Kandy mock-growled. "You complicate things."

Did I ever.

The steward swapped out my tray for one that contained three Valrhona limited-edition chocolate bars, more hot towels, and — upon inspection — steamed milk in a silver teapot. I smiled at him and he wandered back up to the front of the jet.

"It's like they know me here," I whispered into the phone. "It's on the edge of creepy … except there's dark chocolate. Chocolate can't ever be creepy."

"Again, did you expect anything less from the vampire? He's such a show-off."

I laughed. Kett was kind of the complete opposite of a show-off, but Kandy loved to state the unobvious.

"So …" Kandy said. "Did you get the sentinel into bed yet?"

"God, no. He's taking it insanely slow."

"At least you have leverage now."

"Yeah, I totally want to guilt him into sleeping with me."

Kandy snorted. "Tell me about the new cupcakes you're testing for spring."

So I did.

I talked to Kandy all the way to Vancouver. The jet didn't even stop to refuel, which seemed crazy. But then, what did I know about these things? We both loaded up *Guardians of the Galaxy* on Netflix, which apparently came along with all the other luxuries on the jet, watching it together while I consumed the holy trinity of chocolate bars — aka Loma Sotavento from the Dominican Republic, Gran Couva from Trinidad, and El Pedregal from Venezuela.

I tasted the Loma first. I picked up hints of yellow plum and a touch of toasted almond, along with Valrhona's signature smooth chocolate. Overall, though, I found the bar on the too-sweet side — even though it was 64 percent cocoa — so I broke it up and stirred it into the steamed milk, savoring little sips long after it had cooled.

Gran Couva was sublime, with subtle hints of mint and fresh spices in the finish. A completely brilliant pairing — a smooth, creamy sweetness that recalled Kett's magic — though it was much lighter and more chocolaty.

I managed to stretch the final bar from Venezuela until the jet was circling the twinkling lights in the partially cloudy early morning over Vancouver. El Pedregal delivered a rich, deep cocoa scent that filled my nasal cavities and blocked out all my worries and concerns for the time that I inhaled it. The chocolate itself was well balanced, with a delightful hint of honey in the delicate, lingering aftertaste.

Very, very tasty chocolate.

Kett knew me well. He'd also known there was a strong possibility I'd be heading home alone, which made me almost unbearably sad.

The plane landed just after 3 A.M., and I climbed into the limo waiting for me outside the private hangar without blinking. I didn't set foot inside Vancouver International Airport. I didn't check in at customs or security, or collect two hundred dollars when I passed 'Go' …

Okay, I might have been unraveling a bit. The closer I got to the bakery, the closer I got to confirming if Warner was actually dead. I wasn't sure I wanted the confirmation. Denial might be a nice place to live for a while. I'd vacationed there heavily the year before through all the shit with Sienna — and screwing around with Desmond — and enjoyed the ignorance. Though coming back to reality had been a painful bitch.

Yeah, so, unraveling.

I had the limo drop me in the alley behind the bakery, then waited for it to pull away.

Then I waited some more.

And a bit longer.

Maybe I was the one locked in stasis …

Chapter Thirteen

The early morning air was cool and misty, which didn't happen often in Vancouver, where it usually poured rain rather than sprinkled it. A few lights, perhaps from TV or computer screens, were bleeding through the closed curtains of the apartments that faced onto the alley, but a quick glance up confirmed that my own apartment was dark.

I pulled the map out of my satchel and spread it in the middle of the alley, in the general area where Warner had appeared the first time he'd been called here. Not that it needed to be open for this to work. But I was pretty sure it needed to be away from any sort of magical warding, including me.

If this was going to work.

I was hanging a lot on that 'if.'

I'd gotten home on that 'if.'

I stepped away — one step, two steps, three big steps back — and pulled my knife. I wasn't sure the shadow leeches would make an appearance. They certainly wouldn't be in the nexus with Shailaja. If Shailaja was in the nexus ... but maybe she'd been whisked away to wherever Pulou kept the dragon prison. Maybe I'd jumped to conclusions, seeing my newly found father babying a crazed teen who I'd thought had killed Warner moments before.

Anyway … shadow leeches.

I just had to hope they'd be drawn to the map, whether I needed them in order to trigger the transportation spell that pulled the sentinel out of stasis or not. Warner was of the opinion that he'd been called to the alley — and me — by the presence of the map three months before, but a shadow leech had appeared right before he'd shown up.

God. Was that only three months ago?

Nothing was freaking happening. My neighbors were still slumbering, and even the cars a block away on West Fourth were few and far between. The predawn air around me felt devoid of life, empty of light and love and laughter. What if I'd miscalculated? What if Warner was locked inside the mountain with the centipede? What if I'd been meant to draw that thing out of the molten silver, slice its belly open, and free my boyfriend from its intestinal tract?

I took three more steps away from the map. Pulou had said I naturally shielded the magic of the map and the instruments …

The instruments of assassination.

I pulled off my necklace, stepping even farther back from the map as I did so. I didn't want to defend two objects, but if I had to choose, I'd sacrifice the map over the necklace with the centipedes. Especially if that was what it took to get Warner back. Especially because Shailaja hadn't needed the map to seriously screw with Warner anyway.

I laid the necklace on the dirty asphalt at my feet. My heart ached over treating it so badly, and I whispered a promise to it — so really, to myself — about adding the vampire wedding rings to the chain in the morning.

The silver of the centipedes caught in what little moonlight was filtering through the mist-filled clouds.

I stepped away, my knife held at the ready. The mist collected in a layer of moisture on my face and hair, mimicking the tears I should have released but couldn't.

I held my breath so long that I felt myself growing faint, but I refused to exhale. I wondered if I could asphyxiate myself through sheer willpower. I wondered when my body would take over to demand oxygen, to force me to move forward.

I was always moving forward, wasn't I?

Always forgiving, always resilient.

Maybe it was time to stop. Maybe it was too much.

I'd had these thoughts before and dismissed them … Warner. Warner had been in my kitchen … he had made me pancakes.

And I'd wanted that.

I had so, so wanted that life.

My lungs were going to explode. I was going to collapse in this alley. The garbage truck would probably run over me in the morning … no, Bryn would find me first when she came in for her baking shift.

I let my breath out with a gasp, then inhaled again, painfully filling my lungs and rebooting my brain.

A shadow streaked out from behind the bakery's green dumpster. It was heading for the necklace, not the map.

I lunged, thrusting my knife into that seething mass of evil incarnate, and taking wicked pleasure in slashing it apart.

I could feel other leeches gathering in the shadows around me. They hid in the crevices of apartment roofs. They hid between the slats of the fences that edged the alley, and underneath the car illegally parked two buildings away.

They watched me.

The first shadow leech tried to get away from me and my blade, but I held onto its magic. I sliced it to ribbons until it collapsed like the tangle of yarn in the bottom of Gran's knitting basket.

I let them all watch as I destroyed.

Warner was doubtful that we could kill the leeches. They'd sought eternal life. They had sacrificed their mortal forms and their magic to be reborn in this leech form, to serve Shailaja in her quest.

But I could rip and shred their magic. I could destroy the very thing that held them together.

And I would.

I would take on each and every one of them. If they fled, I would hunt them down.

Then I would walk into the nexus and wrap my bare hands around Shailaja's throat. The guardians would hesitate, just long enough for me to rip the magic out of her.

I'd done it before. I could do it again.

I was the avenger now.

I lifted my foot and its silver-bottomed hiking boot. I stomped the shredded shadow leech at my feet to crush the evil sorcery out of it. To destroy the black magic —

I remembered Sienna's eyes. And how dark they'd turned the deeper she'd delved into sacrificial magic.

I wondered if my own eyes would flood with black magic after I destroyed the shadow leech at my feet … after creating the sacrificial knife, the bakery wards, and draining Sienna's magic into my katana with blood magic … I wondered if this was what it felt like to be in the thrall of darkness.

I released my hold on the leech's magic.

It disappeared.

I stood, winded by my own viciousness.

I was alone.

Then light exploded in the alley, blinding my still-sensitive eyes so much that I had to shield my face with my arm. Magic hit me. I stumbled back, then leaned into it.

Golden transportation magic. Dragon magic.

The light winked out.

I stumbled again, forward this time, as I dropped my arm to look ... to see ... to taste.

Warner, once again wearing his training leathers, stood frowning at the map at his feet. The striped cashmere scarf I'd given him on the shores of Lago Puarun hung from his otherwise limp hand.

I stepped toward him and drew his attention.

His frown deepened. He looked me full in the face, but he didn't know me. My heart started beating madly in my chest, so hard and fast it instantly winded me.

He didn't remember me.

He slid one foot back and rested his hand on his knife ... the weapon I'd tailored for him by molding and honing the magic and blade of the sacrificial knife.

He was going to draw the blade and attack. I could see the instinct in his stance, in the way his shoulders shifted sideways. I would draw my own knife, then. I would defend myself.

He didn't remember the black forest pancakes ... the exchanged glances ... the kisses. The laughter.

He wrapped his fingers around the hilt of his blade.

I didn't reciprocate. Instead, I lifted my hands away from my body. I stood before him, arms lifted, hands empty, seemingly defenseless.

"Warner," I whispered.

His stern expression softened. His eyes widened with sadness, then clouded with anger.

I reached for him, and in two steps he'd crushed me in his arms.

I kissed him fiercely, high up on my tiptoes to grab fistfuls of his hair and press myself fully against him.

"Jade," he groaned.

"Warner," I whispered a second time. Then I disentangled myself and reached down to collect the map. Still holding onto Warner with one hand, I tugged him back with me to pick up the necklace and loop it loosely around my neck. Its rightful place.

Then I took my dragon to bed.

I should have immediately walked through the portal with the instrument of assassination. I should have sought out Pulou. I should have explained my actions to my father. They needed to know what Warner and I knew about Shailaja.

But I didn't.

I took Warner's hand and wordlessly led him through the wards of the bakery kitchen, then up the back stairs to my apartment. I didn't bother to turn on the lights or check to see if there was a note on the fridge from my absent mother.

I tugged him into the bathroom, closed the door behind us, and turned the shower on as hot as it would go. I wanted to take him directly into my room, but I just couldn't get over the fact that I had dried vampire vomit in my hair.

The tiny frosted window in the bathroom offered barely any light. I stripped off my clothing, throwing everything on the floor except my necklace. Then I stepped into the tub while Warner watched me. I left the shower curtain partly open, turning my back to the spray so I could wet my hair and take my turn to watch Warner undress in the near darkness.

The training leathers were actual clothing, not manifested by his magic. I could really only see his movements in the dark, but that was enough for right now, right here.

Warner stepped into the shower with me, and I traded places with him so he could enjoy the searing hot water while I washed my hair.

The pineapple scent of my shampoo mixed with the vanilla of my soap as we washed. We stood next to each other but didn't talk, nor did we touch other than a brush of fingers when I passed him the soap, or a moment's contact between our hips and shoulders as we traded places underneath the hot water.

As soon as we were marginally clean, I turned off the water. I offered Warner a fresh towel, and we dried off in the dark, steam-filled narrow bathroom. Warner was so wide at the shoulders that he had to angle his elbows so he didn't hit the walls when toweling his hair.

Still damp in various places I couldn't be bothered with, I dropped my towel on the floor and tugged Warner's out of his hand to treat it the same way.

Then I pulled him — naked — through the hall and into my bedroom.

This time, I locked the door behind us. I ignored the unmade bed and the messy pile of clean laundry in the chair, crossing over to light a chocolate-scented square pillar candle on the bedside table.

I had never lit this candle before, though I'd owned it for a couple of years. I'd purchased it from a gift shop on West Fourth Avenue as a tiny splurge, back when I hadn't had much money to spare while I was opening the bakery. I often smelled it, using it as a sensory treat before bedtime.

I turned, bathing in the soft glow of the candle as I looked back at Warner.

He stood with his back to the door, large enough that he filled the room before even really stepping into it.

I reached up and slowly pulled the necklace off over my head.

He groaned. The gold of his dragon magic rolled over his otherwise shadowed eyes.

Warmth melted through my lower belly at the unbidden noise.

Not taking my eyes off the length, breadth, and beauty of him by candlelight, I lowered the necklace onto the side table, letting it slowly coil in a pool of golden rings and silver centipedes.

I lifted my fingers away from the chain and sent my dowser senses out in search of his magic. Without the protective barrier of the necklace, his smoky-edged, creamy dark-chocolate-and-cherry magic flooded my senses so swiftly that my body jerked toward him involuntarily. I cried out.

Before I could feel embarrassed by this reaction, he was wrapping his arms around me, holding me fast and tight against his warm length.

"I'm here," he whispered into my wet hair.

I nodded.

"I'm here, Jade," he repeated.

I started to cry.

He kissed my tears. Then, cupping my face in his large hands, he wiped them away with his thumbs.

I inhaled, slowly and deeply, to calm myself, but the tears were only the beginning of the release of my grief.

"We'll go slowly next time," I said, my tone as firm as I could make it when I still felt as if my chest had been shattered into jagged puzzle pieces. Pieces that being physical with Warner might help to put back together.

I'd almost lost myself in the alley, and I wasn't a hundred percent sure I'd made it all the way back.

He nodded. "Only if you promise me a next time."

"There will be a next time." I ran my hands up his chest, catching the dark, short hair that bisected his expanse of skin in between my fingers. As I reached his breastbone, he pressed his hands against mine, pinning them there hard enough that I could feel his heart beating.

"Promise me," he said huskily. "Promise that we will —"

"I'm not the one who left," I said. "I'm here. I'm always here." Before I could regret the edge of accusation in my words, I pushed beyond my own issues and gave him the commitment I thought he was looking for. "I'll always call you back."

Warner nodded, seemingly satisfied by this. He reached across and brushed the hair away from my face. "I would never leave voluntarily."

I let the painful subject drop. I didn't want to talk.

I wanted to taste, to feel.

I knocked him playfully with my hip, turning him slightly so the candlelight fell across the tattoo I'd only caught glimpses of before. The image of a black dragon was wrapped over his right shoulder and partway across his collarbone. The edge blurred underneath his chest hair.

"On your back might have been a better choice," I teased.

"It wasn't an aesthetic decision."

I ran my fingers along the thick black lines etched across his shoulder. The tattoo was a simple line drawing, with just enough detail to identify it as a dragon — scales, long tail, teeth and claws. I could feel magic tingling underneath my fingertips, separate but entwined with Warner's. Something akin to the transportation spell that brought him back from stasis.

Warner nuzzled my neck and ran his hands across and down my shoulders, sides, and hips to cup my ass.

Yeah, I wasn't thinking about unknown magic anymore.

I nudged him back against the bed, hard enough to force him to sit down. He looked up at me with a smile, then tugged me closer by the hips to flick my nipple with his tongue. First the right nipple, then the left.

I groaned. My knees became gooey — which was okay, because Warner was more than willing to hold me upright.

He returned his attention back to my right breast, sucking this time, and for a moment, I forgot I was in a rush. I forgot I was initiating.

He slid his hand from my hip, splaying his fingers across my belly, and slipped his thumb down through the curls between my legs.

I cried out and pretty much collapsed against him. This involuntarily awkward movement briefly killed the moment. Which was fine, because I remembered I had an agenda.

I was done with the foreplay.

I pushed him down on the bed. He leaned back, willing and grinning. He was so freaking, insanely gorgeous lying there with the candlelight washing across him. Rough and ready. Really, really ready. Breathtakingly ready.

His grin widened.

"Yes, I'm ogling your manhood."

He laughed. "Stay there, Jade, standing over me all golden and pink, warm and ready. I'd have you there forever. I'd look at only you for the rest of my days."

"That would be a seriously long time, dragon."

"Indeed."

Grinning and definitely as ready as he thought I was, I bent over to fumble in my bedside table for a condom.

"What's this?" he asked as I pressed it into his hand.

Right. Sixteenth century.

"I'll show you. Birth control." I ripped the package open and pulled the condom out.

"We'd be so blessed," he murmured. But then he seemed to have trouble holding onto that thought as I showed him how to roll the condom on.

Getting that done as quickly as possible, I climbed on top of him.

He gripped my hips as I started to settle over him. I paused. "Wait," I said.

"Wait? Now?"

I laughed as I climbed over him to the other side of the bed. "I want you on top."

"Ah, good. I'm more versed that way."

My husky laugh was cut off as he slipped his finger between my legs, found his way, then settled his weight over me.

He slipped inside me with a groan.

I wrapped my arms around his neck and whispered in his ear as he took his first stroke. "Slow next time, okay?"

"I'm not sure I'll last more than a minute anyway."

He found his rhythm quickly and without further coaching. Which was good, because I was beyond any ability to form coherent sentences.

I wrapped my legs around him, tilting my pelvis up for deeper penetration. He groaned and buried his face in my neck.

Warmth spread through me, riding the taste of his creamy chocolate and sweet, sweet cherry magic. I let myself melt into the bed. I let myself be pinned by his comforting weight.

I gathered all his magic around me until all I could taste and feel was him. Him in my mouth, him on my taste buds, him in my head, tingling against my skin. Tiny shocks of pleasure rolled up and over me from where we were connected at our very cores.

Tight against each other … as close as two people could be.

He slipped his hand between us, lifting himself slightly away to do so, and I almost cried out at the change in total contact. But my cry turned into a moan as he pressed his thumb between us, between my legs.

The tiny shocks of pleasure turned hot and fierce.

He bucked, off rhythm. Then squeezed me too tightly as he came.

"Jade," Warner whispered, his thumb still rubbing me. I threw my head back, tensing every muscle in my body as the pleasure deepened and sharpened, radiating out from underneath his touch to flood across my belly and through my chest.

"Jade," he repeated as my orgasm washed over me and I shuddered underneath him.

I opened my eyes to find him smiling down at me. He was coated in the golden gleam of his own magic.

I ran my fingers up the back of his neck and he shivered with residual pleasure.

"That looked tasty," he whispered.

I laughed, completely content for this moment. "It was."

"Think how much better it will be next time."

I smiled. He lowered his head and kissed me softly … as if tasting me.

I sighed, then kissed him back.

Chapter Fourteen

My phone buzzed. Just a single buzz, but I heard it even though it was buried in my satchel in the bathroom and the bedroom door was closed.

I thought I'd been sleeping, but I guess I wasn't. Because when the phone buzzed, I realized I'd been staring at the darkness of my bedroom ceiling.

The candle had burnt out.

Warner was asleep next to me, pressing his naked shoulder and hip against me, but with his head turned away. His breath was deep, exhausted. I was lucky he hadn't collapsed immediately after the transportation spell. Lucky that being placed in stasis for only a few hours affected him much less than four hundred and fifty years had the first time.

The phone buzzed again. The interval told me I had a text message waiting for me.

I wanted to wake Warner, to shower and romp a second time, but I didn't.

I was sandwiched between him and the wall — my room wasn't big enough for the queen bed to fit without being pressed against the wall. But I sat up and climbed over him without waking him.

I retrieved a bra, T-shirt, underwear, and yoga pants from the clean pile of laundry on the chair in the corner. I padded barefoot out into the hall, then cut immediately left into the bathroom.

I retrieved my knife in its invisible sheath, tasting Gran's witch magic for just a moment before I strapped it on and my own magic neutralized hers.

The text message was from Kett.

>*I have survived.*

I stared at these three words for many minutes, trying to decide what to text back. Whether to make a joke, or tell him how terrified I'd been, or to thank him for the jet … and the chocolate.

Applying my thumbs to the phone, I simply typed: *I'm pleased.*

He'd like the simplicity of that. He knew all the other stuff anyway, but his cool vampire demeanor would get ruffled if I mentioned it. He'd know what to read into my message.

He didn't text back. I didn't expect him to, but I waited for a few minutes anyway.

Then I went to fulfill the duty I no longer wanted. To void an obligation I never should have taken on in the first place. An obligation currently attached to my necklace.

The obligation had been an adventure, once. But now it only filled me with unwanted anger. A fierce, fierce anger that the lovemaking had only reinforced.

Anger at having been given the almost impossible task of collecting artifacts that could kill guardians, who I'd thought to be indestructible. Anger that Shailaja had been allowed to run around for three months and trash my bakery. Anger that the guardians had lost track of her in the first place, over four hundred years ago.

Anger at the tone of reprimand in my father's voice.

And guilt. Guilt because I'd been fully prepared to kill Shailaja — assuming that was even in my power.

Guilt because I'd felt she needed to die. Who was I to judge such things?

Shailaja was dangerous. I knew that much, and I certainly didn't want her coming after the instrument of assassination currently sitting on my bedside table.

So no matter how torn I felt about it, and how much I just wanted to crawl back into bed — sleepless or not — I left Warner to return to the nexus.

The dirt of the bakery basement felt warm and welcoming underneath my bare feet. I didn't bother with the overhead light when I could open the portal with a mere thought. As always, its golden magic — even if just for the moment of crossing — filled all the dark places in my soul.

Chi Wen was waiting for me on the other side.

He was wearing his gold-trimmed white robes as usual. Nothing about the far seer ever changed. He actually blended so thoroughly in with the white marble floor and gilded columns of the nexus that for a brief second, I thought I'd dreamed him up. That my eyesight was more damaged than I thought.

But I wasn't so lucky.

I saw his eyes. They were full-blown white-gold. Terrifyingly bright orbs of gold.

I stumbled.

The portal shut behind me.

Instead of bowing, I fell to my knees before the far seer. For one beyond-petrified moment, I'd seen my future in his eyes. In his presence and his stoicism.

"Far seer," I cried, stopping myself from reaching for the edge of his tunic, stopping myself from begging for absolution. For what I didn't yet know, but I was terrified he was going to show me.

"Dragon slayer," he murmured as he touched the unruly curls on the top of my head. His guardian magic blew through me like a hurricane, electrifying my spine until it poured out of my fingers and feet.

But he didn't send me a vision.

He dropped his hand from my head. "I would see what you've collected."

"But is it safe? Shailaja ..."

"Is under the watchful gaze of the healer and the treasure keeper."

I reached down and unhooked the centipedes from my necklace. They came undone with the simple thought of undoing, lying dormant across my palm.

I raised my hand and the instruments of assassination to the far seer. He peered down at the artifacts, then he nodded.

"It's not every day you see your own death offered to you on the hand of a beautiful young woman."

I wrapped my fingers around the centipedes, holding them protectively against my chest. I suddenly wanted them as far away from the guardian of Asia as I could get them without running back through the portal.

God, I really, really wanted to run. But I was scared as hell that the far seer would give chase.

He chuckled.

"I ... you ... see your own death?" I managed to ask.

"No," he answered. "I cannot see my path, nor do I see the nine. Our destinies are hidden from me."

"But another sees," I murmured, remembering the far seer's words about Rochelle, the oracle, and the task he'd laid at Kandy's feet. Dread soured my stomach.

"Not yet, but soon. She has been resting. But now you have come, so she must wake."

"I don't understand."

He nodded, not unsympathetically. Then he held his hand out to me, as if he wanted me to give him the centipedes.

I shook my head so fiercely that the room blurred behind my own curls as they flapped around my face.

Chi Wen chuckled again as a silver box appeared in his hand. It was smaller than the box in the mountain cavern, and covered in raw diamonds, not runes. Dragon alchemy. And the metal was presumably platinum, not silver.

Still kneeling, I opened the box's hinged lid and placed the centipedes inside. They didn't wake as I snapped the lid shut.

Chi Wen raised the box to eye level and spoke directly to it. "To the treasure keeper."

The box disappeared, leaving me with the taste of lemon … Blossom's brownie magic.

The far seer turned and walked away. "Come. Come, dragon slayer."

I stood unsteadily, then followed him out through the arch that led to the dragon residences.

The far seer escorted me to an austere room that held a single bed, a paper-strewn desk, and a wooden stool. It was a room fit for a monk … or the eldest of the guardian dragons.

Though the desk was overly full, the room was tidy. The bed was made with a precision that spoke of ingrained ritual.

Every single inch of the walls was covered with Rochelle's charcoal sketches. Every inch.

I stepped forward — completely involuntarily, because I wanted nothing to do with Rochelle's visions. But they looked different somehow.

"Photocopies?" I asked.

"Ah, yes. Photocopies," Chi Wen said. "That is the word. I had no need of originals, and the collectors would not have parted with them easily."

"Blackwell," I spat. I found a sudden anger — sparked by the thought of the sorcerer — burning deep within my fear.

Chi Wen tilted his head questioningly.

I lifted my hand and pointed to a sketch that clearly showed Blackwell with the edge of his castle in the background. He was touching the amulet he always wore around his neck. A power source. One of many, I assumed.

Chi Wen waved his hand dismissively. "The figure in black is of no immediate consequence. It is you I see, Jade Godfrey. In here …" — he tapped the side of his head — "… and here." He swept his arm to include all the sketches.

Except for the solo image of Blackwell, which was attached to the wall at the lower left of the desk, every single one of the sketches included me … or some aspect of the last year and a half of my life.

I turned my back on the room, only to see sketches also attached above the door. I couldn't bear to look at the far seer either, so I twined my fingers through the wedding rings of my necklace and stared at my hands instead.

"This has all come to pass," I said.

"To study the past is to understand the future, dragon slayer," Chi Wen said.

"You keep calling me that. Dragon slayer." The words rushed out of my mouth without thought or edit. "And Pulou has me collecting … instruments … and you said … you said. The centipedes."

Chi Wen reached for me and I knelt before him again. I wasn't strong enough to stand in the face of the truth I was sure he was about to show me.

He laid his hand on my head. A gesture intended to be purely comforting. He didn't show me a vision, nor did he offer me enlightenment.

"That … this …" — I flung my hands out to the sides as I lifted my bowed head to look up at the far seer — "… please. It's too much." All the tears I'd tried not to shed since Peru now fell freely across my cheeks. "Please. This can't be my destiny. And yet …"

"And yet," Chi Wen murmured.

"And yet, you call me dragon slayer."

I was shaking now, terror and fear riding my adrenaline rush. The energy was forcing itself out through my limbs because I wasn't strong enough to hold the emotions within any longer. Give me something to fight, and I'd find my courage — along with a heavy dose of sarcasm. Give me something to conquer, and I'd find my way in, over, or through. But this … the future I could feel unfurling before me — the future I'd almost embraced in the cavern, and then again in the alley when I tore the shadow leech apart …

I couldn't do it. I couldn't bear it.

"The path might be set, but how you choose to walk it is your decision, Jade Godfrey." The far seer lifted his hand from my head. "I will see you soon."

He turned and walked out of the small bedroom, leaving me surrounded by Rochelle's prophetic sketches. Pictures pasted on every wall. Snapshots of the darkest moments I'd ever suffered.

I looked.

I couldn't move or fight any longer. So I knelt there and I looked.

I studied each stroke, every smudge and line.

The tears dried on my face. My knees started to ache.

I didn't know what I was looking for until I saw it. It wasn't what I expected. It wasn't one specific image. It wasn't a clue. It wasn't enlightenment. It wasn't good versus evil.

It was endurance.

I had endured.

I endured.

I will endure.

I got up and walked back through the nexus without seeing another soul. I crossed through the portal, back to the bakery. I climbed the stairs to my apartment, then climbed back into bed with Warner.

I would walk the path as I chose to walk it, with not another inch of it dictated by friend or foe.

Acknowledgements

With thanks to:

My story & line editor
Scott Fitzgerald Gray

My proofreader
Pauline Nolet

My beta readers
Leiah Cooper, Terry Daigle, Liz Dutcher, Angela
Flannery, Gael Fleming, Desi Hartzel, and Heather Lewis.

For their continual encouragement,
feedback, & general advice
Suzie O'Connell–for sharing her pictures
of San Francisco
Joanne Schwartz–fruit selection
Heather Faville–for letting Cicely borrow her gun
Heather Doidge-Sidhu–for double-checking (again)
The Retreat

For her Art
Elizabeth Mackey

ABOUT THE AUTHOR

Meghan Ciana Doidge is an award-winning writer based out of Vancouver, British Columbia, Canada. She has a penchant for bloody love stories, superheroes, and the supernatural. She also has a thing for chocolate, potatoes, and cashmere.

For recipes, giveaways, news, and glimpses of upcoming stories, please connect with Meghan via:

Newsletter, http://eepurl.com/AfFzz
Website, www.madebymeghan.ca
Email, info@madebymeghan.ca

Please also consider leaving an honest review at your preferred retailer.

ALSO BY MEGHAN CIANA DOIDGE

Instincts and Imposters (Amplifier 5)

Endings and Empathy (Amplifier 6)

Misplaced Souls (Misfits 1)

Awakening Infinity (Archivist 0)

Invoking Infinity (Archivist 1)

Compelling Infinity (Archivist 2)

Novellas/Shorts

Love Lies Bleeding

The Graveyard Kiss (Reconstructionist 0.5)

Dawn Bytes (Reconstructionist 1.5)

An Uncut Key (Reconstructionist 2.5)

Graveyards, Visions, and Other Things that Byte (Dowser 8.5)

The Amplifier Protocol (Amplifier 0)

Close to Home (Amplifier 0.5)

The Music Box (Amplifier 4.5)

Moments of the Adept Universe 1

Misson Recon: Bee (Amplifier 5.5)